# *Secret Lives of the Ton*

*What Society doesn't know…*

Meet Julian Carlisle, the Duke of Lyonsdale, Gabriel Pearce, the Duke of Winterbourne, and Phineas Attwood, the Earl of Hartwick.

In the eyes of the Ton, these three gentlemen are handsome, upstanding men who—mostly!—play by the rules. But what Society doesn't know is that behind closed doors these three men are living scandalous lives and hiding scandalous secrets!

Read Julian's story in
*An Unsuitable Duchess*
Already available

Read Gabriel's story in
*An Uncommon Duke*
Available now

And read Hart's story in
*The Unexpected Countess*
Coming soon!

## Author Note

The idea for this story came to me after I learned about a possible assassination attempt of the Prince Regent that occurred on January 28th 1817, when he was returning from the Opening of Parliament. Thinking about that event led me to imagine a second assassination attempt, taking place a year later, with other motives behind it. I know this isn't a very romantic thing to think about when you're beginning to write a romance novel, but that is where it all began.

Thank you for choosing to spend some time with *An Uncommon Duke*. I hope you enjoy Gabriel and Olivia's story. For more information about my next book in the Secret Lives of the Ton mini-series, which features the Earl of Hartwick, please visit my website at lauriebenson.net for details. While you're there, you can also find information about some of the other interesting historical titbits I uncovered while doing research for this book.

**Laurie Benson** is an award-winning historical romance author and Golden Heart® finalist. She began her writing career as an advertising copywriter, where she learned more than anyone could ever want to know about hot dogs and credit score reports. When she isn't at her laptop, avoiding laundry, Laurie can be found browsing in museums or taking ridiculously long hikes with her husband and two sons. You can visit her at lauriebenson.net.

### Books by Laurie Benson

### Mills & Boon Historical Romance

#### *Secret Lives of the Ton*

*An Unsuitable Duchess*
*An Uncommon Duke*

Visit the Author Profile page at millsandboon.co.uk.

Many thanks to my editor Kathryn Cheshire
for your insightful input and encouraging words.
And to Linda Fildew, Nic Caws, Krista Oliver
and the rest of the Mills & Boon Historical team,
thanks for all you've done to help
bring Gabriel and Olivia's story into the world.

To my agent, Courtney Miller-Callihan with
Handspun Literary Agency, your generous spirit is
a gift. Some day both of us will sleep past six in the
morning. In the meantime, I toast you with my coffee.

Jen, Mia, Lori and Lisa,
thank you for being such wonderful critique partners,
beta readers and friends. For Marnee,
Terry and Gareth, thanks for being there on those days
when chocolate and coffee were of no help.

To my family, I'm sorry to say there are no unicorns,
aliens or vampires in this book. Some day I'll write
a story about an alien vampire unicorn just for
the three of you. In the meantime, know that
your love and support mean the world to me.

For the kind people who helped me with my research,
thanks for taking the time to answer my questions.
And to those of you who shared unusual Regency era
titbits and antiques with me because you thought I'd
find them interesting, thank you. I hope you have fun
seeing how I used those items in this story.

# Chapter One

*London, England—1818*

Being shot at always left Gabriel Pearce, Duke of Winterbourne, in a foul mood. It didn't matter that this time he wasn't the intended target. It didn't matter that he had saved the Prince Regent by tackling him to the floor of his coach. And, it didn't matter that the shot had narrowly missed Gabriel. Being shot at was a nuisance that meant his orderly life would be thrown into chaos for the unforeseeable future.

Three hours after his coach had sped down the rutted country road, whisking the Prince Regent to the safety of Carlton House, Gabriel stood in his dressing room attempting to tie his cravat into a perfect *Trône d'Amour*. He had performed the task countless times. One would think he could do it in his sleep. Apparently, with the events of today playing out in his mind, one would be wrong.

Peering closer at his reflection in the mirror, he tore the linen from his neck. *Bloody hell! There should be no ripples in the knot, only one dent!* Hodges, his valet, immediately handed him another freshly starched neckcloth.

'Just tie it into a waterfall and be done with it,' his brother Andrew called out, walking into the room and dropping into the wingback chair beside the mirror.

'Too plebeian,' Gabriel bit out, his attention fixed on the task at hand.

'That's how I tie my cravats.'

Raking a critical gaze over Andrew's brown tailcoat and the unimpressive shine to his shoes, Gabriel arched a brow.

'Ho, I see now,' Andrew said with a smirk. 'Some day I will shock you and wear something you deem acceptable.'

'If you would finally allow me to find you an acceptable valet, that might happen sooner rather than later.'

'I'm quite content with the one I have, thank you. How many neckcloths have you handed my brother, Hodges?'

'Six, my lord.'

Andrew sighed and studied the coffered ceiling. 'Shall I wait in your study? If you continue on this path to perfection it might take some time and I could be enjoying your fine brandy while I wait.'

'I'll be but a moment. There is brandy by the window.' Gabriel closed his eyes and managed to push all thoughts of gunshots, shattered glass and a frightened Prince Regent from his mind. Concentrating on each specific turn of the cloth, he finally tied a perfect knot.

Now he could attend to more important matters.

He nodded to Hodges, and the elderly man quietly left the brothers alone behind closed doors.

'Please tell me we caught the blackguard,' Gabriel said, accepting a glass of brandy.

Andrew dropped back into the chair and stretched out his long legs. 'Spence jumped from his tiger's perch the moment the shots were fired and caught the man. He was taken to the Tower— however, he refuses to talk.'

Gabriel took his first sip of brandy since returning home. The heat sliding down his throat did nothing to relieve the tight tension in his muscles. 'We need to know if he was working alone. I don't care what it takes. Make him talk.'

Andrew pulled a scrap of paper from his pocket and held it out. 'My thought is he had assistance. We found this on him. I don't believe our gunman had access to Prinny's plans. Someone had to have given him this information.'

Scrawled in pencil were the date, the name of the road and town they had travelled to, as well as a sketch of Gabriel's coat of arms. Apparently whoever had supplied the information to the gunman knew Prinny would be travelling with Gabriel today and knew where they'd be going. But how was that possible when Prinny had only approached Gabriel last evening about taking him to purchase the painting?

Bringing the paper to his nose, Gabriel sniffed the unfamiliar pungent oily scent mixed with tobacco. The letter 'm' had an interesting swirl to it, but other than that there was no way to identify the author. 'There's no cipher, so it appears we are dealing with an inexperienced lot.'

As he took another sip, he organised the information before him. He was the man ultimately responsible for protecting the Crown. Unrest was rampant throughout the country. If his people failed to protect King George and the Prince Regent, there was no telling what anarchy might occur.

'How is Prinny faring?' Andrew asked, interrupting his thoughts.

'He is shaken but unharmed.'

'And you?'

'I have this scratch on my forehead from shattering glass and my right shoulder is a bit bruised. As you know, I've survived worse.' He handed the paper back to Andrew. 'Show this to Hart. He may be able to identify the smell. Then remain at the Tower and notify me when the gunman is broken. I need to know who else wants Prinny dead.'

Andrew stood and placed his glass on a nearby table. 'Please give my regrets to Olivia and Nicholas. I'm sure you'll devise a plausible excuse as to why I had to miss his breeching ceremony.'

Demmit! Nicholas would be devastated his favourite uncle wasn't there for such a momentous occasion, but Andrew was the only person Gabriel trusted completely. He needed answers and Andrew would make certain he got them. He shook off the guilt trying to settle in his gut. 'Make an appearance, but slip away shortly after the ceremony begins.'

'Very well, I will send word when we know more.'

'And watch your back.'

'I always do.'

Glancing at the ormolu clock on the mantel, Gabriel let out a curse. He was late. Now he would have to endure the customary icy demeanour of his wife. Tonight they might even be forced to actually hold a conversation. He took another sip of brandy, bracing himself for an encounter with the woman he had married.

Olivia, Duchess of Winterbourne, bounced her nephew on her knee and stole another glance at the longcase clock beside the drawing room door. The breeching ceremony should have begun twenty minutes ago. Her son was eager to take this first step towards manhood. How much longer would Gabriel keep them waiting?

She shifted her attention to her mother-in-law, who sat nearby talking with Olivia's mother. When their eyes met, the Dowager gave her a slight sympathetic smile.

The sofa Olivia was sitting on dipped as her sister, Victoria, leaned closer. 'Do you think he forgot?'

'What man forgets his own son's breeching?' Olivia rubbed her forehead and prayed her husband was not such a man. 'Mr James is a reliable secretary. I'm certain he reminded Gabriel of the occasion.'

'Perhaps Mr James was unclear of the time.'

Olivia had reminded him of the time during their daily meeting that morning. This delay fell directly on Gabriel's shoulders. She would give him five more minutes. Then she would ring for Bennett to locate him. It should be of no surprise to her that he was late. She had learned long ago Gabriel only thought of himself. 'I'm certain Mr James relayed the correct time.'

'Do you truly not speak at all now?'

'Being in his presence is still a constant reminder of what he did. It's best if I avoid him.'

'Mother taught us to expect nothing from the

men we marry. She always said that to them we are simply means to an heir. You should have listened to her,' Victoria said gently.

Their mother knew first-hand how true those statements were and Olivia had never expected more. Their father married their mother to create a political alliance with Olivia's grandfather, the Duke of Strathmore. He had never shown any interest in his wife as a person and their brother had followed suit with his wife. When he'd sought the Marquess of Haverstraw for Victoria, it was because the man had lands bordering their family's Wiltshire estate. And he could not have been more pleased when the Duke of Winterbourne, a favourite of the Prince Regent, had shown an interest in Olivia. His pleasure had nothing to do with his daughter's feelings on the matter. Not once had he discussed Gabriel with her before or after he consented to the marriage.

But Gabriel had taken her by surprise. This was a man who listened to her—really listened to her opinions and interests. To have the complete attention of a man who was that handsome and powerful had been intoxicating.

After having courted her for a month, he gave her the consideration of asking her for her hand before approaching her father. Foolishly she fell in love with him and believed some day he would grow to love her in return. But he never did.

'You cannot direct your heart's actions,' she said to Victoria. If she could, Olivia would have saved herself many tearful nights.

'I never understood why your heart became so engaged. The two of you fought quite regularly.'

'We did not. When did you ever witness such behaviour?'

'Usually during dinner.'

'A discussion of contrasting opinions is not an argument.'

'I would find such interaction with Haverstraw tiresome.' She held her arms out towards her son. 'I can take Michael from you. I fear he has become rather heavy.'

Olivia bounced Michael higher, pleased she was able to make him giggle. 'Nonsense, he is a feather. I remember when I could pick Nicholas up this easily. Now he will have his ringlets cut and leave behind his gowns to don skeleton suits.'

As she rubbed her nose against Michael's fuzzy blond head, he grasped a tendril of hair resting along her neck. 'How I miss the smell of a baby.'

'Should you hold him after he's eaten, you might change your opinion.'

Olivia grinned in understanding.

Then, she felt it.

Even though she had tried to ignore the sensation, somehow she always knew when Gabriel entered a room. It was as if a ribbon was tied from one end of him directly to her.

His tall, broad frame obstructed the view beyond the doorway and his unruffled demeanour told her he was unaware he delayed the ceremony—or, perhaps, he didn't care.

As if he felt the invisible connection as well, his unreadable hazel eyes found her and he nodded politely. He surveyed the room, his square jaw and carved features remaining impassive, until he spied Nicholas looking out the window with Gabriel's brother, Monty. Only then did his lips curve into a smile that made the corners of his eyes crinkle.

She forced herself to look away. Years ago, that smile was given only to her, and it would always make her heart swell. Now, whenever she witnessed it, her heart would squeeze painfully.

Gabriel paid his respects to their mothers before advancing across the room to where Olivia sat. His eyes softened briefly when they settled on Michael, who was shoving his entire chubby fist into his own small mouth.

'Duchess, Lady Haverstraw, I hope you're both well.'

The brandy on his breath told Olivia how he had been occupying himself while their families waited patiently for his arrival. 'Thank you, we are. I dare say I thought you might have been feeling poorly since you arrived so late, but I see you were relaxing with some brandy while we were debating on how long we could occupy the children before they began climbing the curtains,' she said in the sweetest tone she could muster.

'Forgive me. Urgent business kept me occupied until now. Had I been able to disengage myself and join you here, I would have.'

As he turned his head and watched Andrew approach Nicholas, Olivia noticed a thin red line over his left brow.

'Did you injure yourself getting dressed today?'

He began spinning the gold intaglio ring on his pinkie. 'I rode into a low-hanging branch in the park this morning.'

The only other time she'd witnessed him fidget with that ring was when he'd stood at the side of her bed after Nicholas was born—before she threw him out of her room. 'I imagine you would like to say a few words before the ceremony begins.'

He stared blankly at her for a fleeting moment. 'Of course.'

'Very well, while you collect your thoughts, I'll inform Nicholas we are finally able to begin.' She placed her nephew in Victoria's arms. As she stood, another whiff of brandy filled her nose. He was making it very difficult for her to resist the urge to step on his foot as she sauntered past him.

\* \* \*

Once the carriages of her last few guests had departed down the drive, Olivia returned to the Green Drawing Room to find her mother-in-law seated on a sofa watching Gabriel and Nicholas build a house of cards across the room. Gabriel's muscular form was stretched out across the Aubusson rug, while he supported himself on his elbow. She recalled the last time she had seen him reclining in such a casual pose. It was six years ago on a rug in her bedchamber. Squeezing her eyelids shut, she tried to force the image from her mind.

She needed wine. Unfortunately there was only tea. Heading to the table with the cups, Olivia looked at Gabriel's mother. 'Would you care for more tea, Catherine?'

'If you are having another cup... I recall how trying it was to prepare for this occasion. Tea will be just the thing.'

Olivia handed Catherine a cup and poured another for herself, resisting the urge to steal another glance at Gabriel. It would be close to impossible to endure his presence much longer. Resentment rippled through her and tea would never relieve it.

'Your sister's youngest is beautiful,' Catherine said, shifting so Olivia could sit next to her. 'Watching you with him reminded me of how you would play with Nicholas when he was an infant.

Now look at him. In those clothes and with his hair cut, he looks like a small version of his father and his uncles.' She studied Olivia over the rim of her cup. 'Soon he will be able to attend Eton.'

Olivia's heart stopped. Gabriel wouldn't do that to her. Would he? 'Has your son mentioned something to you about sending him away to school?'

'You're the mother of his heir. Haven't the two of you discussed plans for his education yet?'

Olivia shook her head. 'I assumed he would continue to be tutored at home like his father until he was ready to attend Cambridge.' Glancing at Gabriel, she wondered if he had other plans.

'Perhaps. However, you'll not know for certain unless the two of you discuss it.' Catherine gave an appraising stare before turning her attention to her son and grandson. 'My husband would build houses out of cards with the boys when they were children. Oh, how he would dote on them.'

She envied the woman. While the memories of the first year of her own marriage were quite lovely, there were none since Nicholas was born. Glancing back at the rug, she watched the playful interaction between father and son. Olivia knew Gabriel loved Nicholas. She just didn't want to witness it.

'Nicholas needs a brother.'

The sip of tea she had taken almost left by way

of Olivia's nose. Her coughing was so fitful that the occupants on the rug looked her way.

'Are you all right, Mama?' Nicholas asked with a wrinkled brow that indeed made him look like a small version of the man next to him.

Nodding her head, Olivia tried to stop the spasms in her throat. When the coughing had subsided and the burning in her nose had lessened, she delicately wiped her eyes.

'Gabriel needs another son,' Catherine reiterated.

Well, Olivia knew that was not about to happen—unless she had an immaculate conception. She would never allow Gabriel in her bed again. 'Nicholas is a healthy boy. We already have our heir.'

'Life holds no guarantees. It is wise to plan for unfortunate occurrences. This family is known for its unbroken line of boys. It should not be difficult for you to have another.'

Olivia refused to look at her mother-in-law. A sharp pain sliced her heart at the thought of the death of her precious boy.

'Certainly you and Gabriel have discussed having more children.'

'Oh, we've discussed it,' muttered Olivia, taking a fortifying sip.

'Then it's simply a matter of nature taking its course?'

'You could say that.'

The realisation that she would have no more children felt like someone had carved out a chunk of her heart. If Gabriel did intend to send Nicholas away to school, there would be another tremendous void in her life that nothing would fill. And then she would be alone with no one to love.

The flames of the candles flickered as Olivia walked towards Nicholas and Gabriel. 'It is time for bed, my love,' she said, approaching Nicholas's side.

Gabriel recalled hearing those words before. It was the last night he had found release inside a woman—the last time he had bedded his wife. He bit the inside of his cheek to stop himself from dwelling on the image of Olivia lying under him, with her soft legs squeezing his sides. All these years of frustration had done nothing to quell his desire for her.

'Look at our fierce fortress, Mama. It's almost as tall as me.'

'Very impressive indeed. I commend your steady hand.'

Nicholas turned his large hazel eyes to Gabriel. 'Do I truly have to go to bed, Papa? I want to stay awake as long as you do. I am almost a man, you know.'

Gabriel glanced at Olivia to gauge her reaction.

Her head was angled down towards Nicholas, obscuring her features. Instinctively, his attention was drawn to the swell of her lovely breasts, hidden in the lemon-coloured satin folds of her gown. How he wished he could trace the curve of one breast over to the next. He curled his fingers into a fist to stop the aching. Being this close to her was always torture. 'If your mother says it's time for bed, you must obey. However, we cannot leave our fortress unattended. Why don't you knock it down before the enemy attacks it while we slumber?'

'Oh, that is an excellent notion.'

Gabriel imagined the sound emanating from his son was something close to the war cry issued by the Indians across the Atlantic when they rode into battle. 'Well done, Nicholas. Now give us a hug.'

His son threw his arms around Gabriel's neck and squeezed tight. When Nicholas relaxed his grip, his wide grin highlighted his two missing front teeth. 'Goodnight, Papa. Thank you again for my prime bit of blood.'

Olivia smothered a laugh behind her hand at the exact moment Gabriel bit his lip to stop his. Their eyes met for an instant before she looked away.

'Who taught you that?' Gabriel asked, before holding up his hand. 'Never mind, I think I know which uncle it was. That is not the way a future duke refers to his horse.'

'Uncle Andrew told me my horse is a real sweet goer. He says for a gentleman to be a bang-up cove he needs to have a prime bit of blood the other gents would want to ride. He said I shouldn't name him something a chit would, nothin' flowery and such. Did you know some day I'll be able to ride him in a foxhunt? A real hunt! Uncle Andrew says he will take me. I will skip my lessons for the day and he will take me on a foxhunt! Will *you* take me riding, Papa? Can I ride my horse tomorrow?'

It was a miracle his son was not out of breath. 'Perhaps we could go riding in Hyde Park before breakfast.'

His son's eyes widened with anticipation.

'But you must rise early,' Gabriel continued. 'I have many things that require my attention and a gentleman always fulfils his responsibilities. Will you be able to rise with the sun?'

Nicholas threw his arms around Gabriel again. 'Oh, yes! Oh, yes! I promise, I will be awake before you.'

Gabriel hugged his son tightly. It was always difficult to disengage his arms from the one person who meant more to him than anyone.

His son jumped back and turned to Olivia. 'Oh, Mama, did you hear that? Papa is taking me riding tomorrow.'

'Yes, I heard. I dare say you and Buttercup will make such a sight.' Her lip twitched, giving away the mischief behind the serious tone of her voice.

Nicholas's features hardened, making him look older than his five years. 'I cannot be calling my prime bit o' blood Buttercup. Uncle Andrew said I need to name him somethin' fierce.'

Olivia chewed her lower lip and appeared to give his comment great consideration. 'Oh, you mean like Rosebush.'

He scrunched up his round face. 'Rosebush? That's not fierce.'

'Have you ever been pricked by a thorn? I assure you, rosebushes are quite fierce.'

Nicholas shifted his gaze between his parents. 'Is she sincere?'

Gabriel stood and caught Olivia's eye before giving Nicholas a slight shrug. 'Your mama is a girl. Girls do not understand manly ideas,' he teased. 'We shall find a very noble name for your steed.'

'Uncle Andrew said I should name him Cazznoah. I told him that was a silly name and he just laughed. Cazznoah is a silly name, isn't it, Papa?'

Gabriel closed his eyes and took a breath. 'Yes, Nicholas, Casanova is a silly name for a horse.'

Olivia cleared her throat and caught his eye. Her disapproving glare at his brother's suggestion spoke volumes. Andrew always did like to have a bit of fun at Gabriel's expense, but telling their son he should name his horse after a man who was known for seducing women crossed the line. Obviously Olivia agreed. It didn't take words for him to see she disapproved.

'Please bid your grandmama goodnight, Nicholas,' she said, turning him away from Gabriel. 'She would be disappointed if she did not get to wish you sweet dreams.'

Following the intimate picture of Olivia and Nicholas as they left the room, Gabriel stared at the doorway. How much longer would he have to wait for news of the interrogation?

His thoughts drifted to a stormy night long ago, when his body was chilled from the drenching rain that did nothing to wash away the sickening smell of blood from the air. He swore to himself that would never happen again. Andrew could be trusted and, God willing, he would be coming back.

Adjusting his cuffs, he walked towards his mother. 'Are you certain Andrew was not given to you by gypsies as an infant?'

She laughed and handed him a cup of tea. 'I do suppose that would explain many things, but I assure you he was not. What a pity he couldn't stay because he was feeling poorly. I believe I'll call on him tomorrow to see if he's improved.'

He sat down beside her. The idea of their

mother fussing over Andrew, when his brother detested the attention, made it difficult to hold back his grin. Unfortunately he knew circumstances forced him to dissuade her. 'I happen to know the bounder is suffering from the ill effects of a questionably spent afternoon.' Now, at least, he could amuse himself imagining the lecture that would be given the next time his brother encountered their mother.

Taking a slow sip of tea, Gabriel closed his eyes and savoured the delicate flavour. He must remember to have James inform Olivia it was an exceptional blend.

'I spoke with Olivia about your need for another child.'

The coughing began in the back of his throat and rapidly moved to his nose. Was there a full moon, or was some other natural occurrence causing illogical things to happen today?

'What possessed you to do that?' he asked when he finally stopped choking.

'Well, it is about time you had another child.' His mother arched a regal eyebrow, which still had the ability to make him squirm. 'Come now, you can't believe that having only one son is a wise decision with the responsibility your title holds.'

'More than anyone I understand the responsibility entrusted to me. I also know I have brothers who may have sons should it come to that.'

Narrowing her eyes, she placed her cup down. 'It is not the same and you know it. You need more sons and you need to do something about it.'

He shook his head at the unusually demanding nature of his mother. 'What possessed you to bring this to my attention?'

'You are thirty-two. Your wife is twenty-six. Soon you both will run out of time. I do not understand this hesitation you both have.'

Gabriel took a deep breath. His mother had told the one woman on earth Gabriel was certain would never let him touch her that they needed to have sex. It's a wonder his mother wasn't wearing her tea. But then again Olivia was always perfectly composed when other people were present. Alone, he discovered, she could be a hellcat.

'You made your opinions known to Olivia?'

'I simply stated there was a need for the required second son.'

'And what was her reaction to your subtle suggestion?'

His mother hesitated before she took a small sip from her cup. 'I do not recall,' she mumbled.

The strip of linen tightened around his throat and he wished it were possible to begin his day all over again. Of course he wanted another child. The memories of his childhood were filled with times he had spent with his brothers. He wanted Nicholas to have that, too, but it was no longer possible. Years ago he'd resigned himself to that fact. 'I know you have the best intentions, but please do not interfere.'

Even though he wanted another child, Gabriel knew Olivia would never want him to get close enough to her to accomplish it. That part of his life had passed.

## Chapter Two

From the doorway to the Blue Drawing Room in Carlton House, Gabriel could see the round table in the centre of the room was set for Prinny's breakfast. And for one man eating alone, there was enough food and drink to easily satisfy four people.

As Gabriel crossed the threshold he was taken aback when the burly Prince Regent pulled him into a hug. The man squeezed Gabriel's rib cage, making it difficult to breathe. Disengaging himself from Prinny, Gabriel placed him at a distance, only to be grabbed again into another firm hug.

When Prinny finally released him, he slapped Gabriel on the right shoulder—the very one bruised from being slammed against the carriage wall the day before. Gabriel held back a groan.

'Leave us,' Prinny instructed the four footmen, dressed in blue livery with gold lace, who were posted around the table.

The men filed out quietly, the last one closing the door behind him.

'I owe you my life, Winter. You protected me with your own person. Bravery and loyalty such as yours is uncommon. You do your father proud.'

Another tight embrace followed and this time Prinny's large meaty hand clamped down on Gabriel's sore shoulder. Bloody hell! He didn't know how much more appreciation he could take.

'I am simply relieved you were unharmed. Please know I'm aware restricting your movements to Carlton House will not be easy for you, but I firmly believe, for now, it's the safest place for you.'

Prinny returned to his breakfast and unceremoniously dropped into a blue-velvet chair. With a wave of his hand he motioned for Gabriel to join him. 'Would you care for anything? If none of this food is to your liking, I will have my kitchen make whatever you desire.'

'Thank you, but I've already eaten.'

'Then a drink, perhaps?'

There were numerous bottles scattered across the table containing wine, champagne and brandy. Prinny appeared to be imbibing all of them. Gabriel shook his head, knowing he needed to keep his mind sharp.

Prinny resumed cutting into his pie. 'I don't understand why you want me to remain here. There

no longer is a threat to my life. Your note said the
scoundrel had been apprehended.'

'He was. However I believe he had assistance
orchestrating your demise. I've come from the
Tower and they have not yet been able to get the
gunman to admit to anything.'

Prinny dropped his fork with a clatter and
reached for his glass of champagne. His hand
shook as he brought it to his lips. 'So you truly
believe there is someone walking around England
who still intends to murder me?' He drained the
entire glass.

'I do and that is why it is imperative you remain here where you are under guard at all times.'

'Very well,' Prinny replied on a sigh, 'but you
must find this person without delay. Devonshire
is hosting a ball soon, it's reported Mrs Siddons
will return to the stage to perform in *Douglas* at
Drury Lane and I hear the new exhibition at the
Royal Academy will be stunning. If I remain here
too long, I shall miss all the fun.'

'I will do my best to ensure this is handled as
quickly as possible. Since the threat could have
come from anywhere, I think it prudent if you
limit your visitors to an approved list of people.'

'Nonsense, no one visiting here would wish
me harm.'

If only life were that predictable. 'Tell me about

the gentleman you purchased the painting from. He appeared surprised to see you.'

'I imagine he was. He expected one of my agents to purchase it for me.'

'It would help if you could recall mentioning our outing to anyone. The gunman was carrying a drawing of my coat of arms.'

Pouring himself more champagne, Prinny appeared to give the question serious consideration. But after a few moments, he shook his head. 'I might have mentioned it in passing to a few people during Skeffington's musical. Capital evening. Selections from *The Marriage of Figaro*. You should have been there.'

'Opera does not appeal to me,' Gabriel said off-handedly. 'Who did you tell?'

Prinny shrugged and took another drink. 'Don't recall, don't you know. Talked with so many people and the champagne was flowing. Astonishingly I didn't have the devil of a headache the next day. But that was before I asked you to join me.'

To steady his exasperation, Gabriel looked up at the massive crystal chandelier and concentrated on the red and blue coloured flecks dancing in the sunlight. If only Prinny didn't like to brag so. 'And your household…who knew I'd be taking you in my carriage?'

'I informed Bloomfield that morning, but he is trustworthy.'

Gabriel knew Prinny's equerry. He appeared as loyal to Prinny as Gabriel was. Nevertheless, he would assign someone to watch the man. 'Very well, I shall let you know the minute you are safe to leave this building.'

'You don't expect me to remain inside on a rare day such as this? The sun is shining. Surely I can enjoy the gardens.'

There was a tightness forming between Gabriel's eyebrows and he pinched the bridge of his nose to transfer his attention to a new discomfort. Why did it feel like dealing with Prinny was the same as handling his young son? He leaned forward and folded his hands on the table. 'Your gardens share a wall with St James's Park. It would be very simple for someone to reach you, if you were out there.'

Prinny let out a snort before pouring the remaining contents of the champagne bottle into his glass.

Gabriel rubbed his eyes. He needed to return home where he didn't have to deal with anyone who was irrational. At least at home his life was predictable.

When Olivia entered the nursery that morning, she found Nicholas restless in his lessons with his new tutor. All he wanted to talk about was his ride through Hyde Park on his new pony. He told her how his father had taken them onto Rotten Row where he saw numerous well-dressed gentlemen out for their morning rides. He wanted to know when he would be old enough to wear a beaver hat of his own.

He was growing up.

For the first time, she noticed the little dimples that kissed the knuckles of his hands were disappearing. And Gabriel might be considering sending him away to school—or, worse yet, Nicholas would ask to go.

Olivia's heart sank with the weight of how much she would miss him.

For the remainder of the morning she thought about how wonderful it felt to hold her nephew. By the afternoon she desperately wanted another child to cuddle and love.

But in order to have that child, she would have to ask her husband to come to her bed.

And she would be forced to endure his company.

Five years ago she told him she could never bear to feel his touch again. If she wanted this, she would have to lower herself to go back on her word to him.

This wasn't something she could tell his secre-

tary to pass on to him when he next saw Gabriel.
Mr James would have an apoplexy on the spot. It
also wasn't something she could pass along to her
maid. Colette would be setting out Olivia's thin-
nest nightrail and placing rose petals on her bed
before he would have even agreed to her request.

Perhaps she should write him a note.

After many drafts, some ridiculous and some
obscene, Olivia decided to simply request a meeting. If she could focus her appeal on the need for
another child they could avoid discussing how the
child would get there.

And maybe that would help scrape the image
of naked bodies and intimate conversations from
her brain.

It was four in the afternoon when Olivia received word from Colette that Gabriel was available to see her. Standing outside the massive door
to his private study, she pressed her hand against
her stomach. What if Gabriel did not want another
child? Or, suppose he no longer found her desirable enough to bed? She would never be able to
face him again.

The answers she needed would not be found in
the hall. She raised her chin, knowing she would
regret it for the rest of her days if she didn't ask
him for this. Her courageous side rallied, her
knock echoed off the oak panel.

The deep rumble of his voice was audible from within as he bid her to enter. Her heart began to pound and she glanced down, praying it wasn't visible through the gauzy fichu tucked into her dress. She rubbed her sweaty palms down her skirt and turned the handle. Upon entering the impressive room, she spotted Mr James standing before Gabriel's desk awaiting a document her husband was sealing. Once the paper was in his hand, Mr James turned to face her and bowed. He appeared nervous, but she found that whenever Mr James was in the same room with Olivia and Gabriel, he always seemed as if he couldn't wait to leave.

'Good day, Mr James,' she said, smiling congenially.

He greeted her with a pleasant reply before excusing himself. The click when the door closed reverberated around Gabriel's private sanctuary. There was no turning back.

For the first time in years, they were alone. Suddenly the generously sized room felt much too small and she was certain he could hear her uneven breathing from across the room.

They stood there staring at each other for what felt like an eternity. Then Gabriel moved out from behind his desk. Her heart hiccupped. He painted a handsome picture with his perfect posture and his fit frame impeccably encased in an expertly fitted Delft-blue tailcoat with a champagne-coloured embroidered waistcoat underneath. Buff trousers and highly polished top boots covered his muscular legs and his light brown hair looked slightly tousled, as if he had been running his hand through it as he worked at his desk.

At his suggestion, they took a seat in the two chairs placed in front of one of the long windows that overlooked the street. As he fixed an expectant gaze on her, she silently debated how to begin.

'I suppose you're wondering what it is I wish to discuss with you?'

He sat completely still, the picture of civility and physical perfection. 'I have some idea.'

'You do?' she asked, unable to hide her surprise. Had his mother spoken to him as well? From his sober expression it did not appear he was going to be amiable to her request.

'This is regarding last evening, is it not?'

Olivia's heart was jumping in her chest. 'It is. I have thought about this quite a bit and believe it is our duty.'

Gabriel nodded thoughtfully. 'The duty lies with me. I will see to it. I expect it to be an exasperating task, but I agree it must be done.'

Did he really say making love to her would be exasperating?

'I assure you, I will find absolutely no pleasure in the task,' she replied drily.

'That is why it's best done quickly.' At the clopping sound of horses riding by, Gabriel shifted his attention out the window. 'It's a logical request to make. I suppose it was inevitable.'

Inevitable and exasperating—this is how he described bedding her! It took enormous restraint not to rail at him. The point was to have another child. If she had to endure this insufferable man to do so, she needed to disguise her anger. She refused to let him see that his words had any effect on her. In that, she could be in complete control.

She stood rather abruptly, needing to get away before she did something rash—such as kick him in the only area of his that she needed.

'The sooner we attend to this, the better. I will see to it this evening.' He stood and walked her to the door, unaware how perilously close he was to having his head knocked into it.

The moment Olivia left his study Gabriel was able to breathe normally. Being close to her always left him restless, as if his body were fighting the knowledge that he was better off without her.

After pouring himself a glass of brandy, he returned to his desk and put his feet up. Their meeting had gone better than he'd anticipated. He knew only something of great importance would compel her to request an audience.

He considered various scenarios before recalling last night. It was no surprise she wanted to address it. He was impressed she thought they should do it together. However talking with Andrew about what was improper to say to Nicholas fell solely on his shoulders. He would be the one to explain to his brother that it was not appropriate for a boy of five to call his horse Casanova. Nicholas would be Winterbourne some day. He needed to begin learning now what it meant to embody the respectable title.

Yes, a talk with his brother was in order. It also gave him the opportunity to hear how the interrogation was progressing.

# *Chapter Three*

As the melodic sounds of the orchestra filled the crowded ballroom of Devonshire House, Olivia stepped through the movements of the quadrille without hearing a single note. Since her conversation with Gabriel, she wondered if she had made the right decision in approaching him about having another child. Oh, she still desperately wanted another child, but after his reaction to her request, she wasn't certain she could bear to be in his company long enough to conceive one.

He had been horrid—and his comments continued to pierce her heart.

*I expect it to be an exasperating task, but it must be done.*

*The sooner we attend to this, the better.*

If she had any hope of having another child, she needed to lock away her contempt for him. Maybe then the thought of Gabriel touching her wouldn't make her want to injure his manhood—

permanently. She would never conceive a child if she did that.

'I hope it is not my company that has caused that expression to darken your lovely face,' commented Comte Antoine Janvier.

Pulling her attention back to her dance partner, Olivia smiled apologetically. 'Of course not, I fear I am not very good company this evening.'

With a few final steps the quadrille ended.

'Perhaps a glass of champagne shall lift your spirits,' he said, escorting her off the crowded dance floor towards one of the many drawing rooms.

As they crossed the threshold, he took two glasses from a passing footman and handed one to Olivia. She took a long drink and he arched a dark brow.

'Shall I fetch another, or would you care for mine?' he asked, tilting his glass towards her.

The warmth of a blush rose up Olivia's neck and she turned away. Her gaze settled on the portrait of the previous Duchess of Devonshire. 'Forgive me,' she said, returning her attention to her friend. 'You are being very kind, considering I have not been an ideal companion.'

He gave a careless wave of his hand. 'It would be tiresome if you were always *plein de vie*.'

Olivia grinned. 'I wasn't aware you thought I was full of life.'

'There is a sense you find enjoyment in your surroundings, but I suppose you can be as selective as you wish with the entertainments you attend since you are the Duchess of Winterbourne.'

'Yes, there are advantages to the title.' Being married to her husband was not one of them.

'I notice you and His Grace rarely accept the same invitations.'

Their friendship was still new. If he wanted to know how wide the rift was between her and Gabriel, Olivia was certain any of the gossips in attendance would be happy to recount the tale of what had driven them apart. It was something she never discussed with anyone, except Victoria. 'His Parliamentary affairs keep him busy into the evening. Oh, look, more champagne.' Olivia didn't wait for Janvier to procure her another glass. She took one off the tray of a passing footman and replaced it with her empty one.

A low chuckle escaped Janvier's lips before he took a sip from his glass. 'Not something you wish to discuss. I understand. Let us change the subject. Tell me, have you heard Mrs Siddons may return to the stage soon?'

'I have.'

'Do you suppose you will attend one of her performances?'

'It would be a shame to leave my box at the theatre empty for such an anticipated return. I don't suppose you are an admirer of hers?' she asked with an amused smile.

'What kind of man would I be if I were not?'

'Would you care to join me on opening night?'

Janvier leaned forward, placing his lips close to her ear. 'I would like nothing better.'

His warm breath fanned her neck and an uncomfortable shiver travelled down her spine. Pretending she had an itch, Olivia stepped back and scratched her left shoulder.

He studied her over the rim of his glass. 'But the royal box would probably be occupied opening night. That would mean there would be such a crush. You would not mind?'

She gave a slight shrug. 'A crush is no bother, if the entertainment is worthy.'

Janvier's dark eyes twinkled mischievously. 'Then I would be honoured to join you.' He scanned the salmon-coloured room. 'I am surprised your Regent is not here this evening.'

'Georgiana told me the poor man is suffering from the gout again. If it is as severe as last time, it would not surprise me if he missed Mrs Siddons's performances altogether.'

By the time she arrived home, Olivia was certain she had drunk enough champagne that she could endure Gabriel's presence in order to have another child. He said he would come to her to-night. Now, she was ready for him.

After sending Colette away, she stretched out on her bed in an excessively large, white-linen nightrail. Her bare feet were cold on top of the blankets, but she reasoned it would be over quickly, and there would be no chance of Gabriel's scent remaining on her sheets.

What was taking him so long? He was home. She'd heard his muffled voice along with that of Hodges through the door that connected their rooms over an hour ago. His strong knock made Olivia jump. Bringing her hands to her chest to steady the pounding of her heart, she called for him to enter.

The door opened slowly and it was difficult to see his expression in the shadows of the room. 'Why is it so dark in here?'

'I thought you would prefer it this way,' she replied, relieved her voice did not give away her nervousness.

Gabriel closed the door behind him and walked further into the room. He was still dressed impeccably for an evening out. Turning this way, then that, he spun in a circle. Finally, he spotted her. 'Are you well?'

'Of course.'

'Are you not cold?'

'No,' she lied.

There was a hesitation, then he cleared his throat. 'It's late. Perhaps we should discuss this in the morning.'

He was leaving? After all this time agonising and waiting for him, he was leaving? How much was she expected to endure? She jumped off the bed and ran to the door, blocking his way. 'I thought we had an agreement.'

'We do... I mean we did.'

'You've changed your mind?'

Gabriel held up his hands, appearing as if he couldn't bear to touch her. 'I simply thought we could do this tomorrow.'

'Oh, no, we will do this now or not at all.' Olivia closed her eyes and prayed he would agree to stay.

'Very well,' he said, sounding as if he was trying to calm a skittish colt.

Olivia nodded and walked back to the bed. When she laid back down, she noticed he hadn't moved from where he stood by the door.

'It will not work with you all the way over there,' she bit out sarcastically.

'I am fine over here,' he said with a raspy voice. 'I can hear you just fine.'

'Well, I do not expect to do any talking so that really should not matter.'

Gabriel cleared his throat. 'You are certain you would like me come closer?'

If he made her explain exactly how this would work, she was bound to strangle him with her sheets. 'I believe that is how this is done—if memory serves me correctly.'

He approached the side of her bed. She waited for him to do something, but all he seemed capable of doing was staring at the landscape by Constable that hung behind her.

Now it was her turn to clear her throat, but this was to get his attention. Once she had it, she motioned to his tailcoat with her finger.

He nodded and plucked a string off his sleeve. 'Yes, it's new. Mr Weston continues to prove himself the finest tailor in London.'

Resisting the urge to smother him with one of her pillows, Olivia took a deep breath and looked at the idiot she married. 'Fine, leave it on. Just open your trousers.'

An odd sound emerged from Gabriel. 'My what?'

'Trousers.' Olivia began to slide the hem of her nightrail up her legs. 'Fear not, I will not look.'

With her eyes squeezed firmly shut, Olivia missed her husband's shocked expression that quickly turned to a heated gaze. Abruptly he grabbed her wrist, preventing her from raising the material any higher than the middle of her thighs.

Refusing to open her eyes, she let out a sigh. 'Very well, you take the lead.'

'Olivia, what exactly are you doing?' he asked in a husky voice.

She threw her forearm over her eyes. 'I thought you said you wanted to get this over with quickly?'

He let out a soft laugh and she peered out from behind her arm.

His face was cast in the shadow of the crackling fire behind him. 'I thought we were discussing Andrew this afternoon. However, I now believe you were talking about something else entirely.'

'Andrew? Why would you think I was talking about having a child with Andrew?' She yanked the yards of material over her knees and sat up, tucking her legs under her. Reaching over for one of her numerous pillows, she hit him with it.

He grabbed it. 'I thought you wanted me to speak with Andrew regarding his behaviour around Nicholas. What did you think we were discussing?' He tossed the pillow next to her on the bed.

Relieved that the room was cast in such low light, Olivia was certain her face was crimson. 'How could you possibly mistake me wanting to have another child with me wanting you to reprimand your brother?' she asked with annoyance.

'A child?' he choked out. 'Is that what you wanted to discuss? Why didn't you simply say so?'

'I did!'

She hit him with another pillow and he caught this one as well.

'No, you did not,' he said as if he were speaking to someone Nicholas's age. He tossed this pillow next to the other one. 'Not once did the word "child" leave your lips.' He cleared his throat again. 'You want another one?'

Olivia was too emotionally spent to say another word, so she simply nodded and closed her eyes.

'You are certain?'

Again she nodded and this time she met his shadowed gaze.

He tossed his head back and closed his eyes. She waited. Any dealings they had with one another from now on hinged on this very moment. Her palms began to sweat.

'Slide over,' he commanded softly.

She shifted towards the centre of the bed and closed her eyes when he began undressing. Was he as smooth and muscular as he had been years ago? Opening one eye, she peeked. He stood there shirtless, tugging off his trousers. She closed her eye quickly before he caught her. Blast it! He looked as good as he had the day she'd married him.

The bed dipped next to her and she felt a tug on the ribbon at the neckline of her nightrail. 'You have too many clothes on.'

She swatted his hand away. 'We can do it like this. I'll just raise my hem.'

He steadied her hand as she began to move the fabric up her legs. 'Is that what you were planning to do? Lay here with your eyes closed and lift your voluminous skirt for me?'

'I won't complain. Just do what needs to be done.'

Gabriel's body jerked back as if she slapped him and he combed his hand through his hair, making the ends stand up in all directions. 'Bloody hell, Olivia, what kind of man do you think I am?'

'Oh, I know very well what kind of man you are,' she spat.

'What does that mean?'

'It means I know you are only interested in your own needs.'

He glared down at her. 'Like hell I am. And how am I to attend to your needs, when you are trussed up like a Christmas goose? It's a wonder you aren't suffocating.'

'I'll have you know this fabric is the finest French linen,' she said through her teeth.

'Then you should have had three gowns made from it instead of one.'

She hit him with another pillow. This time he threw it on the floor.

'Just take me!' she shouted, surprising herself, as well as Gabriel.

They didn't move. They simply stared at one

another as their chests rose and fell in unison. The only sound was the occasional pop from the logs in the fireplace.

Abruptly he jumped out of bed and began tugging on his trousers. 'I cannot do this,' he repeated.

'Wait! Where are you going?' she asked, rising to her knees, stunned by his rejection.

He jerked his shirt over his head and began gathering the rest of his discarded clothing. When he had them all in his arms, he stalked over to the bed. 'Regardless of what you think, Duchess, this is not going to work,' he ground out.

'All the world thinks you are a man of honour, but it's a lie. You only ever think of yourself.'

Gabriel gathered up his boots and stormed to the door leading to his room. When his hand clutched the handle, he paused. 'You are lucky you are not a man,' he said through his teeth before he slammed the door behind him.

A pillow, book and hairbrush hit the door in rapid succession. Just when she thought she was finished crying over him, Gabriel pushed her to the emotional edge—again. The tears were falling and she couldn't make them stop. She would not give him the satisfaction of hearing her cry, so she pressed her lips firmly together as her body lurched with her silent sobs.

He didn't want her. He couldn't even bring

himself to bed her to get a spare. What was wrong with her? Why couldn't she hold the attention of the one man who had once meant the world to her?

Olivia still wanted that child, now more than ever, but now she would never conceive one.

She hated him for that!

She hated him for what he had done to her five years ago!

And she hated him for reducing her to tears by taking away her only chance at experiencing unconditional love again.

## Chapter Four

The next morning before the sun had even begun to rise Gabriel rode his horse around the Serpentine as if the demons of hell were chasing him. He continued to circle the lake in Hyde Park, hoping the pounding of Homer's hooves would knock his brain back together.

His wife had wanted him in her bed after five years, four months and eleven days. That alone should have been cause for celebration. The fact that she wanted another child with him should have made him the happiest of men. But at the moment, he wanted to drown her in the lake he rode around.

If she had been a man, she would have paid for the insults she threw at him as he left her room. Did she really think that little of him? Had she ever understood what kind of man he prided himself in being? His wife was as much a stranger to him as the girl who sold flowers at the entrance of the park.

The idea that she thought he would bed her by throwing up her nightrail and thrusting inside her, while she would have been in obvious discomfort or planning the week's menus, was just too much to bear. Did she really believe he was such a beast? Oh, he knew she did not like him. She had made that very clear, but to think that poorly of him was infuriating. From the day he had entered his cradle, honour and duty were drilled into him. Whether she believed it or not, he was a man bound by honour. And that honour had cost him more than she knew.

Up ahead, three men on horseback cleared the trees. The sun had begun to paint the sky in pinks and yellows, and the rumble of his stomach told him a good breakfast might settle some of his anger. It was time to head home.

Gabriel was sitting in his breakfast room, tucking into his meal and reading *The Times*, when Bennett informed him the Earl of Hartwick was calling. Hopefully his friend was here to tell him something about the smell of the note belonging to the gunman. Glancing up, Gabriel followed Hart's progress as he strolled into the room, his black frock coat fluttering behind him. If he had not handed over his coat to Bennett, Gabriel knew this wasn't a social call.

Hart dropped into the chair next to him and tipped his head towards Bennett. The butler looked at Gabriel for approval before fetching a glass of his best brandy for the Earl. After taking a small sip, Hart ran his hand through his black hair, attempting to move a lock that had fallen over his bright blue eyes. 'It's a good thing you're so predicable that I knew I'd find you here at this hour. I want you to know I had plans last night that I altered especially for you.'

Gabriel cut into his ham and studied Hart. 'A bit early for brandy, wouldn't you say?'

'I've not gone to bed yet. Well, that is not exactly true…'

'So I take it you have something to tell me.'

'I do.' Hart reclined back, a sly smile peaking over the rim of his glass. 'I know who the gunman is.'

Gabriel put his fork down and leaned forward. 'How?'

'Do you not want to know how I reasoned it out?'

'I fear I don't have much of a choice, now do I?'

'Not if you want that name. What has ruffled your feathers this morning?'

'I'm unruffled, now talk.'

Hart studied him and took another sip of

brandy. 'It was a good thing Andrew mentioned the man's accent when he showed me that note.'

'His accent?'

'Yes, he said he recognised it from his time near Manchester. Using that bit of information, I took a trip by the river to the Black Swan. Many of its patrons hail from up north. I simply asked a lively lass of my acquaintance who is a barmaid there if she would take a look at him for me. I was pleased to discover that she did indeed know the man.' He took another slow sip, savouring his drink. 'She also found identifying a prisoner quite exciting. So for that, I thank you.'

'You took someone to the Tower without my consent?' Gabriel tried to relax his fist.

Hart waved his hand casually in the air, which was all the more infuriating. 'Apologies…deep regret…whatever it is you need to hear. But be aware I did not exactly have the opportunity to contact you at the time.'

'And how did you explain your need to identify the man, and why he was being held in the Tower?'

'I told her he attempted to rob me. She believed it, saying he was an unsavoury fellow who was known to annoy the patrons with talk of his disgust of the monarchy and those that serve it. And we played a game of sorts. She was blindfolded for our journey. I never told her we were in the Tower.' Hart removed a folded piece of paper from the pocket of his black waistcoat and slid it towards Gabriel. 'Here. That is his name, an area of town *and* information about the man's family, because I am that good at what I do.'

Maybe now they would finally get some answers. Without opening it, Gabriel tapped his finger on the folded paper. 'So maybe you are as good as you think you are.'

'I will attempt to ignore the surprise in your voice.'

'Had anyone at the Tower overheard the information your barmaid gave you?'

Hart shook his head and surveyed Gabriel's breakfast. 'I thought it best to gather all the details while she and I were alone.'

'Hopefully there is useful information about his family to finally force him to talk. Andrew has been observing the interrogations. He informs me the man has a high threshold for pain.'

'He will break sooner or later. How is our illustrious friend faring?'

Knowing how restless Prinny could be, Gabriel assumed he wasn't handling his confinement well. 'I am sure he can use a good card game or two to lift his spirits.'

'I imagine I can spare some time. Unless you have something else you need me to do. Shine your boots?'

'From the state of those Hessians, I believe I will continue to have Hodges tend to my boots.'

'Some day you'll have to remind me how I became involved with the lot of you and why I continue to remain.'

'My father had said he asked for your assistance because you were cunning and had a greatness inside of you that you weren't aware of. If you decided to end this association of ours, I assure you that you would be quite bored.'

'You're probably right, but I have a feeling I am not the only one who lives for excitement.'

When Gabriel returned home that evening, having more excitement in his life was the last thing on his mind. As he handed over his hat, gloves and walking stick, he noted the sound of laughter drifting into the entrance hall from somewhere else in the house. He raised a questioning brow to his butler.

Bennett cleared his throat. 'It is Wednesday,' he said as a way of explanation.

How could he have forgotten? It was the one day of the week that he and Olivia had agreed she could entertain at home and he would stay out. It had been a long time since he had been in his London residence this early on a Wednesday evening. All this pressure of finding out who was behind the assassination attempt must have caused the normal function of his brain to shut down.

He would go to his study and have a dinner tray sent there. But as he stepped down the hall, a distinct deep male laugh could be heard coming from the private dining room a few doors away. Gabriel moved to the open doorway and peered inside.

His wife was seated at the head of the table, with Andrew to her right. They were leaning close to one another, deep in what appeared to be congenial conversation. It was the very picture of a warm family moment, something Gabriel had not experienced with his wife in many years.

He had never looked to marry for love. Love was a bunch of sentimental drivel some of his classmates at Cambridge would drone on about, usually referring to a local girl who could lead them around by their passions. Thank goodness he and Olivia had been sensible enough not to seek that in a marriage. They'd had a comfortable friendship based on a mutual respect for each other's opinions and interests. That, and the fact that he'd wanted to sink deep inside of her from the moment he saw her, told him this was the woman he needed to marry. She had been the ideal wife for him, until his responsibilities got in the way.

Leaning against the doorframe, he watched her smile widen at something Andrew said. That dim-

ple that he hadn't seen in ages graced her cheek
and the urge to interrupt the quaint domestic
scene overtook him.

'I was unaware you would be dining here tonight,' he called out, crossing his arms.

Olivia's startled expression was a contrast to
Andrew's friendly greeting. Approaching her side,
Gabriel raised an inquisitive brow at his brother
while he snatched a grape off his wife's plate.

She watched him bring it to his lips. 'I didn't
expect you to be home.'

It was the first thing she had said to him since
he'd stormed out of her room the night before. He
was surprised by her attempt at civility, but then
again, they were not alone.

'It is my house,' he replied, taking another
grape. There were so many emotions running
through him that it was difficult to grab on to one.
His only thought was to wonder for the first time
what exactly happened in his house on Wednesday evenings.

'Would you care to join us?' she asked, sounding as if she was chewing on glass.

Gabriel took a seat to her left instead of his customary chair, which was down the table across
from hers. She ran her gaze over him with a wrinkled brow and Gabriel refused to consider why he
felt an odd desire to stay near the warm sense of
companionship. He motioned for a glass of claret

from his footman. 'So, what had you both so en-
tertained when I walked in?'

Andrew shrugged and looked to Olivia. Gabriel raised his brows, waiting for her response,
plucking yet another grape from her plate.

Her nostrils flared. 'Frederick, please bring another place setting for His Grace,' she said, glaring at Gabriel throughout her entire request.

After the words she'd spat at him last night, he
found perverse pleasure in annoying her today.
The footman was about to turn to enter the butler's pantry when Gabriel stopped him with a raise
of his hand. 'No need, Frederick.'

Frederick turned back to resume his place by
the door.

'Nonsense. Frederick, the setting.'

The footman turned again towards the pantry.

'Frederick, I said that will not be necessary.
The Duchess's plate holds just what I desire.'

The footman once again turned back to face
the table, but this time instead of keeping his eyes
fixed straight ahead, he watched Olivia.

'Perhaps you are mistaken,' she said, taking
the last three grapes and popping them into her
mouth in rapid succession. She narrowed her eyes
at Gabriel, challenging him to take anything else
from her plate.

He reached across and broke off a small wedge
of cheese. It was a childish thing to do, but he

could not resist the impulse. 'I do believe you never did say what the two of you were discussing when I walked in,' he said to her.

'No, I do not believe we did.' She lifted her plate and Frederick jumped to take it. 'I know you are a very busy man. We do not wish to keep you from your business.'

Gabriel took a long drink and looked between his wife and Andrew. 'My business can wait.' He didn't like the feeling of being pushed to the side—of not being privy to something that was going on under his roof.

He felt like an outsider.

He caught his brother's eye. 'I'm surprised to find you here.'

'I don't see why. I enjoy Olivia's company.'

'Andrew came here looking for you. I invited him to join me for dinner and he kindly accepted,' Olivia broke in, glaring at Gabriel like she wanted to throttle him.

The gilded candelabra resting on the table a few feet away appeared to be very heavy and Gabriel wondered if he should have one of the footmen remove it.

'I take it your presence here means your health has improved,' Gabriel said to Andrew, wishing he could grab his brother and drag him out of the dining room without causing suspicion. If he had searched Gabriel out, there was a reason.

Andrew narrowed his gaze at Gabriel and leaned forward. 'It has. Even though our mother is under the assumption I was suffering from the effects of too much ale. Now where do you suppose she acquired that notion?'

It took great effort for Gabriel not to sputter his wine back into his glass. He could not, however, hold back his smile. 'I have absolutely no idea.'

Andrew nodded and fell back into his chair. 'Just as I thought.'

'I still cannot believe you were set upon by thieves on your way here,' Olivia broke in. 'I find it astonishing they would consider attacking you with your intimidating size. Hopefully, the bruises on your hand will heal quickly.'

Andrew shot a quick glance at Gabriel before looking at the knuckles of his right hand and flexing his fingers into a fist. 'I'm sure the bruises will be gone in a day or two.' He smiled warmly at Olivia. 'You are very kind to be so concerned.'

'Nonsense,' she replied in earnest. 'I wish you would let me send you home with some healing salve.'

'I will be fine. Stop fussing so. Save your mothering for Nicholas,' he said reassuringly.

The colour drained from Olivia's face. The topic of mothering brought back all the horrid events of last night and Gabriel knew she was remembering them as well. He should be angry with her—hell, he had been. She had insulted his honour. But he couldn't ignore the fact that he was to blame for what she thought of him.

The sight of her in that ridiculously large night-rail had set his blood on fire and made him instantly hard. He knew he would have embarrassed himself if he had managed to get all that fabric off her. It had been so long since they were together. Olivia had the most amazing bottom he had ever seen and over the last five years, four months and eleven days he'd found himself sneaking a glimpse of it whenever her back was to him.

His thoughts were on her curves when he heard his brother call his name. Shaking his head, he looked at Andrew.

'I asked you how Nicholas liked his ride through Hyde Park. Olivia told me you took him.'

'He liked it very much.' He took another sip of claret, needing to redirect his thoughts away from Olivia's soft skin and enticing curves. As he motioned for more wine, he caught Andrew's amused expression.

'What name has he settled on?'

'To my knowledge he is still undecided.'

Olivia looked as if she was about to say something, then took a sip from her glass instead. He stared at her expectantly, but she turned away. There was an uncomfortable silence. Gabriel knew she wanted him to leave. He was not welcome at his own dinner table. She already thought he would take her with no consideration for her comfort. Did he really want her to believe he was a bore as well?

Rising from his seat, Gabriel took his glass and strode to the door. 'Come to my study on your way out, Andrew,' he said, not waiting for a reply.

An hour later, his brother strolled into his study without even knocking. 'Why do I feel as if you do not like me spending time alone with Olivia?'

'Don't be absurd. She considers you her brother.' Gabriel sat back at his desk chair and watched Andrew walk to the table set with crystal bottles and pour two glasses of brandy. 'How often do you dine here?'

'You mean since Nicholas has been born?'

Gabriel nodded and Andrew sighed, sliding the stopper back in the bottle.

'I don't know. I've never counted. You should try it some time. She is vastly entertaining.' He placed a glass of brandy in front of Gabriel and sank into the chair across from him.

Gabriel leaned forward and narrowed his gaze. 'What do the two of you talk about? I was never under the impression you had anything in common. Dear God…has she developed a love of gambling?'

Andrew shook his head, laughing. 'Our discussions are quite varied. Were you aware she recently began acquiring a repertoire of bawdy tales? They're quite good.'

Gabriel's brain almost exploded. 'You're joking.'

'I'm quite serious. Probably from that painter she has been spending time with.'

'What painter?'

'The one she is sitting for.'

Gabriel wondered which painter Andrew was referring to. She knew so many and had been patron to a few over the years.

'You do know she is sitting for a portrait, don't you?'

Did Andrew have to look so smug? Gabriel rubbed his lower lip and looked away. The idea his brother knew more about his wife than he did was beginning to bother him. 'Of course I do.'

'I should hope so, considering the man has quite the reputation.' Andrew sank back further into his chair.

'Reputation for what?'

'You really don't know anything about her or her friends, do you?'

'I do,' he lied. 'We live in the same house.'

Andrew nodded slowly. 'Well, in any event, I'm glad you came home when you did. I wanted to tell you in person our gunman has finally begun to talk. We were able to use the information Hart gathered to convince our Mr Clarke that if he cared at all for his family, he would tell us what we needed to know. It appears thoughts of his sickly mother helped him find his voice. He says he was contacted by a note left for him at the post about assassinating Prinny and he was told that he would find information on Prinny's whereabouts in a book he was to check in each day at Hatchard's bookshop on Piccadilly. He has no idea who leaves the information, just that when he completed his job, he would receive a thousand pounds. Since he has no love for our monarchy, he didn't see a problem with profiting from Prinny's death.'

'I assume we have men at Hatchard's?'

'We do.'

'Let's hope that whoever was providing this information is not aware Mr Clarke is no longer in circulation. That is the only way we will find out who wants Prinny dead.' Gabriel sat back in his chair and took a long draw of brandy, grateful they were one step closer to ensuring Prinny's safety.

There was a long, comfortable silence between the brothers before Andrew had to ruin it. 'Five years is a long time to be apart from your wife.'

'Your point?'

'You still want Olivia.'

'No, I don't.'

'So while you were in the dining room with us, not once did your mind turn to taking her?'

No, he was thinking about running his hands over her sweet round bottom. However now, thanks to Andrew, he was thinking about much more. 'It did not cross my mind.'

'Liar.'

Gabriel narrowed his gaze. 'You are lucky we are family, or I might call you out at such an insult.'

'Fine. Tell yourself you are not calling me out because I am your brother and not because I am a better shot than you.'

'You are not. I bet I could shoot that taper by the window in half and you could not.'

Andrew sat up straighter in his chair, the excitement of besting his brother evident in his expression. 'What if I shoot the taper in half?'

Gabriel removed a pistol from his desk drawer. 'You won't. But if you do and I don't, I'll buy you a new pair of Hessians.'

'Hoby's?'

'Do you truly believe I would even consider purchasing anything else? And if I win, you tell me about your entire conversation with Olivia.'

*What? What an idiotic thing to win!*

'That's what you want?' Andrew asked, as if he too couldn't believe Gabriel's stupidity.

'Just go first.' Exasperation was in his voice as Gabriel handed his brother the pistol.

'That taper is much too close to make this interesting. I propose we try this in your ballroom.'

Once they were settled in the cavernous room, Andrew loaded the pistol and took aim at the gilded candelabra in front of an open set of French windows. The shot rang out, and the top half of one of the tapers fell to the floor, splattering wax on the wood. With a satisfied smile, he handed the gun over.

Gabriel reloaded it and took aim. Hoby's would not be receiving an order for new boots from this house. He also cut a taper in two, but the top of his fell out onto the terrace. The sound of racing footsteps caused both men to turn towards the door.

Bennett skidded to a halt just inside the threshold. 'Sir, is everything all right?' he asked through laboured breath.

'Yes, Bennett, my brother and I were just settling a bet.'

'Very good, sir,' Bennett said still breathing heavily. 'I will inform madam of it, in the event she questions if you are still alive.'

Gabriel wondered if it would even matter to her.

Andrew strolled to the windows and peered

out into the darkened garden. 'We should have checked to see if anyone was out there.'

'If anyone is skulking about in my garden at night, they deserve to be shot,' replied Gabriel, shooing his butler away.

Perhaps if he plied Andrew with enough brandy, he could still manage to get his brother to tell him what made Olivia laugh.

## Chapter Five

Morning sunlight streamed through the large windows of Mr John Manning's portrait studio directly into Olivia's eyes, forcing her to keep them closed.

'Are you certain no one will recognise me?' she asked from her reclined position on the crimson divan.

The artist took a long tendril of her dark unbound hair and adjusted it over her gown on the swell of her breast. 'I assure you, with your head turned this deep in profile, no one will know it's you unless you tell them.'

She felt a pull near her hip at the grey satin gown he had given her to wear. 'It is to your credit that I trust you as I do. I feel quite foolish lying here like this.'

The pressure from his warm hand moved her left leg. 'You look sinful.'

She wished she could swat his hand. 'That is not helping.'

He laughed. 'But it's true. Any man would kill to have you in his bed.'

Now it was Olivia's turn to laugh, knowing just how false his statement was. 'How often do you suppose you have said those words to the women who sit for you in this very room?'

'Not as nearly as often as I'd like.' He retreated back towards his easel. 'Many women require thought to discover what is beautiful about them, but you will make my canvas sing without much effort on my part. Thereby, your allure will help me create a masterpiece all of London is sure to talk about.'

'I already agreed to sit for you for this experiment of yours. You have no need to work your charms on me.'

'I only speak the truth.' He was back by her side again, his warm fingers tilting her neck up just a bit more. When she squinted up at him, his dark brown eyes were smiling down at her and his unfashionably long black hair had begun to come loose from the leather tie that held it back from his face. His unpolished appearance was a sharp contrast to her husband's fastidious grooming habits.

'I am relieved you do not expect me to remember this exact pose each day,' she said, taking note of the position of her arms.

His grin widened, and he moved a strand of hair away from her face. 'My sketch guides me. You are always quite accommodating with all my poking and prodding. Once we are finished for the day, you may jerk my body into any complex tangle of your choosing.'

That created an amusing image and she closed her eyes again. 'What a capital notion! Now if you don't grant me the breaks I require, I will devise painful retribution.'

'My, what a bloodthirsty duchess you are.'

The sound of his chalk scratching as he drew eased some of her tension. 'Are you certain I do not appear large to you?' she asked, trying to imagine what the sketch looked like.

Chuckling, he continued to draw. 'You are far from large. Although even if you were, it would be of no concern. Men enjoy curves on a woman. It gives us something to hold onto when we are in the throes of passion.'

'Then I believe I have so many places for a man to hold onto, he would be at a quandary where to begin.'

He laughed again. 'I know where I would begin.'

How she wished she could turn her head and peak at his expression. 'Where?'

'I am sketching it right now.'

'Well, that was not very forthcoming.'

'No, it was not.'

Olivia began to laugh.

'Do not move,' he commanded.

He adjusted the folds of the silk by her thigh. She bit her lip and prayed he didn't notice the catch in her breath at the unexpected contact.

'You have the kind of body that tempts men to steal a touch.' He moved her left arm a fraction of an inch.

Olivia opened one eye to study him. They had known each other for more than a year. Not once, in all that time, had he exhibited any form of inappropriate behaviour with her. Even now, she knew he saw her only as an object in his painting. He must be attempting to make her feel at ease, since she was sprawled out over his divan in a most unrefined pose. She was well aware what her body looked like and, as she had discovered from her recent encounter with Gabriel in her bedchamber, tempting was not how she would describe it.

'So what exactly is one to interpret from this pose?' she asked, fighting the urge to scratch her nose.

'It is the pose of a woman who has just reached complete fulfilment,' he replied as if discussing the weather.

Olivia raised her head and stared at him aghast, unable to voice a response.

'You must stop moving,' he yelled. 'This will be a masterpiece of movement and light. But each time you shift, you force me to readjust the folds of your gown. I cannot sketch you in a timely manner if I have to continually walk over there.'

She rested her head back down and tried to move her head into the exact position he had placed it. Manning readjusted it a fraction of an inch and then adjusted the hair cascading over her breasts.

He raised his eyebrow at her and pointed his chalk at her in warning. 'Do. Not. Move.'

'Fine, but I honestly do not believe anyone would be interested in seeing how I look after… well, after…' Olivia was certain she could not blush any deeper than she was. 'I am not the best subject for this. You should have asked someone younger. Men would find that much more enjoyable to look at.'

'You believe you know us that well?' The sketching resumed.

'There are many beautiful girls you could have chosen.'

'True—however, I am not interested in girls. Their innocence colours their sensuality. A woman with experience in the activities of the bedchamber has an innate sensuality that is apparent to any man over the age of sixteen.'

'I am not sensual.'

'Of course you are. It's in the way your body moves and the way your eyes acquire a wicked glint, as if you know the secret of bringing a man to his knees.' His voice was so calm and nonchalant.

'So you really prefer women of my age?'

'And older, but if you tell that to any of the young women that sit for me, I will deny it.'

Managing to laugh without moving a muscle, Olivia considered what he said. She had spent years after their estrangement wondering what Gabriel found attractive. The notion of what other men preferred never entered her mind.

When he finally broke the long stretch of silence, it felt as if hours had passed. 'I am almost finished with my preliminary sketch. Have any parts of you lost all sensation?'

'My right arm is beginning to grow numb. This really is an indulgent pose. I believe I may have dozed for a few moments.'

'I believe you did. Your breathing became quite rhythmic.'

He approached her side, then rubbed her right arm. The warmth and pressure felt heavenly.

'What the bloody hell is going on here?' bellowed a deep, angry voice from the other end of the room.

Olivia jerked her head towards the doorway and closed her eyes, pretending her husband was not standing there looking as if he wanted to toss them both out the window.

Manning groaned at her movement and stared daggers at the imposing man who had interrupted their sitting. 'Who are you to intrude in my studio, sir?' he asked.

'I am her husband. Now take your damn hands off her.' Gabriel's voice was commanding with no room for negotiation.

Manning backed away, raising his hand in surrender. 'I am simply adjusting her body for the portrait.'

'I know of no respectable portrait that requires such a pose.'

She would not move her body to inconvenience her friend. 'What are you doing here?'

Gabriel's fiery gaze shifted to her. 'I had an appointment not far away. I thought I would escort you home.'

How could he possibly have known where she was? And, why in the world would he want to escort her home?

'I believe your sitting is over for the day, Duchess,' Gabriel commanded.

'Nonsense, there is still more to do. Isn't that

correct?' She turned her head towards her friend, who appeared pale.

He shifted nervously. 'There isn't much more to do. You are welcome to stay until I am finished for today.'

She was not about to allow that to happen, but before she could voice her opinion Gabriel walked to the easel, crossed his arms and studied the sketch.

'Continue,' he said with a nod.

'I will have to touch her to adjust her form.'

'He does not care,' Olivia murmured.

But the artist's eyes were fixed on Gabriel, who nodded his consent and watched as Manning went back to the easel to study Olivia's pose. He approached her and hesitantly moved her neck and arm. Very carefully he adjusted the folds of her gown.

The sketching resumed and Olivia could hear Gabriel move towards the chair near the door. Suddenly the pose she was in was not as relaxing as it had been a short time before. Why had she ever agreed to sit in this ridiculous position?

Although it probably only took fifteen more minutes of sketching in silence, to Olivia it felt like hours. Finally she heard him toss his chalk onto the table and she picked up her head to gauge his reaction. His grin was infectious.

'You're pleased?' she asked, smiling back at him.

'Exceedingly so. I'll need you to come back to begin painting.' He walked to the divan and held out his hand to help her up.

Gabriel rose abruptly. Both Olivia and Manning turned his way.

Immediately, her friend dropped her hand. 'Will you be able to arrive before eight? I would love to capture the early morning light on the folds of the satin.'

She rolled her shoulders to relieve some of the stiffness. 'Yes, I believe I can.'

Manning walked to a cabinet and began removing bottles of pigment. She was about to enter the dressing room when she paused at the sight of Gabriel approaching his side.

Her husband picked up a dish with something brown resting in it and held it out. 'You smoke while my wife sits for you?' Gabriel asked, arching an intimidating brow.

'No, I would never.'

'See that you do not.'

Olivia shook her head as she walked into the dressing room, wondering why it should even matter to him. A short while later, she emerged wearing her very proper bonnet and cinnamon-coloured walking dress with Colette at her side. As her maid walked towards the door, Olivia approached the easel, curious about the composition. What she saw surprised her.

Her face was turned away from the viewer so only her neck and the outline of her left cheek were visible. Her hair was fanned out around her with one dark curl sloping down her neck and gliding over her breast. The fingers of her left hand appeared relaxed as if they had no strength left in them. True to his word, no one would know who the subject was.

'Well?' Manning asked, approaching her side.

'I do not even recognise myself.'

'I told you to trust me. It will be breathtaking when I am finished. Mr West will be begging me to exhibit it.'

She hoped for his sake that would be true. The man was a highly skilled artist. The more people exposed to his work, the more commissions he would receive.

There was a distinct clearing of a throat from the doorway where Gabriel stood, looking down at his watch. If he was so impatient to leave, he could do so without her. For years he had completely avoided her and last night he interrupted her dinner with Andrew. Now he wanted to escort her home. What was he about?

As they walked out onto the pavement, Gabriel had to squint to adjust to the bright sunlight. After last night's discussion with Andrew, he was curious about this artist Olivia had taken an interest in. Luckily it did not take James long to find where the man's studio was located.

'Where is your carriage?' he asked, scanning the busy road.

'Colette and I walked. One of the wheels of my carriage required some work this morning and I saw no reason to wait on such a lovely day.'

'My carriage is always at your disposal should there be a need.'

He took her by the elbow and steered her around some young boisterous bucks. The moment they passed them, she shifted her arm out from his grasp.

'Where are you planning on hanging the portrait?' he asked, clasping his hands behind his back and redirecting his thoughts away from the idea that she could not bear for him to touch her.

'We hope to have Mr West agree to exhibit it at the Royal Academy.'

Gabriel froze and Colette almost collided with his back. He could not have possibly heard her correctly. That portrait of his wife—looking as though she had just been thoroughly and completely satisfied—was to be on display for all of London to see? Like hell it was!

'No,' he stated firmly and resumed walking. At least that was taken care of.

Olivia caught up to him and did her best to keep pace with his long strides. 'What did you say?' she asked.

He glanced down at her. She was not pleased.

'I said no. That portrait is not leaving our house.'

'The decision is not yours to make. I did not commission it. I am sitting for him as a favour.'

Again Gabriel stopped abruptly, and again Colette pulled herself back from knocking into him.

He must have misunderstood. 'Pardon me?'

'I said that portrait is being painted with the intention for exhibition to show the breadth of his skills as an artist.'

'And you agreed to be his model? Why would you agree to such a thing? That portrait is indecent.'

She snorted. His refined wife actually snorted at his statement. 'You are one to say what is indecent?'

They were turning onto Bond Street, bustling with servants and members of the *ton*. He was aware they were garnering attention simply by walking together. The last thing he needed was gossip about this argument—and this was going to be an argument. She was much too stubborn for it not to be.

He directed his attention ahead of him. 'We will discuss this at home.'

'I'm not going home.'

'Yes, you are. We are going home to finish this discussion.'

'Then I suggest we finish it now because I. Am. Not. Going. Home.'

His nostrils flared when he looked down at her. 'When did you become so defiant?'

'When you showed your true colours,' she replied with clipped movements.

She didn't know him at all. If she believed he was going to allow that portrait to hang in the Royal Academy, or anywhere else outside one of their homes for that matter, she was sorely mistaken. 'Very well, you want to discuss this now, we will.'

Guiding her by the elbow, they walked past Gentleman Jackson's Boxing Salon and into William Gray's Jewellery Shop. The moment the bespectacled proprietor spotted the impeccably dressed couple, he came hurrying over.

'Leave us,' Gabriel commanded.

The mouse-faced little man retreated behind the curtain to the back of the store.

Next he turned his attention to her maid. 'You are to wait outside.'

It was of no surprise that Colette glanced at Olivia for her approval before she walked out the door. He was surrounded by women who seemed to have forgotten he was the Duke of Winter-bourne.

Now he would settle this matter with Olivia once and for all. He tugged her into a corner of the shop away from the windows overlooking the street. 'You are the Duchess of Winterbourne, a respected member of the *ton* and my wife. You cannot display yourself for all of London in such a fashion.'

'No one will know it is me.' Her voice was low but strong.

'*I* will know.' He kept his voice down as well, but it wasn't easy.

When he had walked in on the roguishly dressed man standing over his reclining wife and touching her, Gabriel wanted to carve out the man's bollocks with a butter knife. 'You are not to go back there.' There! Now there would be no question where the painting would be hung since it would not be finished.

'You are mad and have lost all sense of reason,' she whispered sharply.

He wasn't foolish enough to deny what this was. He was feeling proprietary over a woman he hadn't taken to bed in years. And maybe he was just a little bit mad. 'No one should see you that way. I am the only one who should see you that way,' he bit out.

Yes, mad. He was definitely mad.

'But you don't. You cannot even bear to take me to bed.'

'Now who is mad?'

She fisted her hands at her sides and leaned closer so their foreheads were almost touching. 'It's true. So what if he thinks his study of movement and light is also a testament to female sensuality? So what if he believes I am striking? You do not.'

Now, *she* definitely was the one who was mad. He grabbed her by the back of her neck and crushed his lips against hers in a claiming kiss.

Olivia intended to push him away, but she had forgotten the feel of the curve of the muscles in his arms. A slow glide of his tongue against her closed lips had her weakening. And when he pressed his body into hers, all rational thought left her brain and her body took over.

She had missed him—missed the time they'd spent together early in their marriage.

Reluctantly she slid her hands over his shoulders and threaded her fingers through his thick hair. It was shorter now than it had been years ago. She deepened the kiss.

He groaned low into her mouth and slid his hands over the curve of her bottom. And then, just as quickly as it began, he let her go.

'Let that put to rest your false assumption,'

he said, breathing deeply. He stepped away from her, spun on his heels and stormed out the door.

Olivia peered at him through the large shop window as he walked down Bond Street as if he owned the world. She rested her hand on the display case beside her, trying to steady her wobbly legs.

What had just happened? One minute he was being the most insufferable man and the next he was kissing her senseless.

And she'd kissed him back.

She pressed her hand against her forehead, silently berating herself for her foolishness. It must have been her discussion about sensuality with Manning that had caused her to give in to his unusual behaviour. It definitely was not the taste and feel of her husband. Those feelings of wanting him were long dead.

Weren't they?

# Chapter Six

That evening, Gabriel sat at his desk and reread Andrew's letter. It was just three lines, informing him they had no new information at this time. At least that was what Gabriel thought the letter said. He would have to reread it yet again since his mind was preoccupied with reliving a kiss— a kiss with his wife of all people. And he could not stop smiling.

What the hell was wrong with him?

He should not be smiling. He should be furious that she would even consider having that painting hung in the Royal Academy. But instead of being blindingly angry, he was smiling simply because for the first time in ages he'd kissed his wife— and she'd kissed him back.

He *was* mad!

There was something about Olivia that always stirred such strong desire in him. It might be that she was beautiful, but many women were and he had no interest in bedding any of them. It was something else—some irresistible combination of beauty and a sharp mind. But for a man with secrets, her cleverness was more of a curse than a blessing. It was best he remember that.

Gabriel pressed his thumb against the bridge of his nose. He needed to reconfirm his priorities. Someone had threatened Prinny. His duty was to find out who it was and to prevent them from making another attempt on the man's life. The weight of keeping Prinny safe and the safety of his people were heavy on his shoulders. He refused to allow anyone else to be killed on his watch. The last thing he should be thinking about was the taste of his wife's lips and the feel of her bottom as he held her against him.

At least there had been one benefit to her sitting for Manning. Their subsequent argument had led to that kiss—the kiss that he'd initiated and she'd participated in.

Gabriel closed his eyes. The taste of her lips had opened a floodgate of memories of what it felt like to be inside her. It had been so long since he'd had a woman—since he'd had Olivia. His thoughts drifted to one of his favourite memories, which included a warm bath and firelight. All of his attention now was firmly fixed on the image in his head. The letter in his hands fell to his desk.

\* \* \*

Olivia was enjoying a 'ladies' dinner', as her hostess liked to call them. Periodically Katrina, the Duchess of Lyonsdale, would invite a few female friends to dine at her home in London while her husband would make himself scarce for the evening. This evening she'd invited Olivia, Victoria and Sarah Forrester, the daughter of the American Minister. Olivia found she looked forward to these ladies-only dinner parties where the conversations were often boisterous and they did not have to wait for the men to finish their port after the meal was over.

Tonight, Olivia stood next to her sister, staring up at the enormous portrait of Katrina, which hung above the fireplace in the library of Lyonsdale House. In the painting, Katrina sat in an elegant bergère chair with a book dangling gracefully from her long fingers and staring directly at the viewer. Manning had perfectly captured the hint of amusement that often crossed her face, and he had done a spectacular job with the shining folds of her ice-blue silk gown. Off to the side of Katrina's chair, an old globe sat on a small table, a silent nod to the fact the Duchess of Lyonsdale came from the United States.

'It arrived this morning,' Katrina said, looking up at the portrait. 'I did not anticipate it being so grand.'

The serious expression on Katrina's face while she studied the painting made Olivia smile. 'You are an English Duchess now. It should be grand to reflect your station.'

'I know, but it's just so…so…'

'Enormous,' Sarah added helpfully, placing her fingertips over her lips to stop from laughing. 'You're fortunate there was enough room to hold a life-size portrait of you.'

'Sarah, I've only just begun carrying this child.'

'I was simply referring to the size of the wall, not your size. Even you admitted it's rather large. It's as if there are two of you,' Sarah continued, looking between the portrait and Katrina. 'Although it is a beautiful likeness of you, I think I'm relieved I will not be immortalised as such.'

'I'm relieved as well,' came the voice of the Earl of Hartwick as he swaggered into the room alongside Lyonsdale and tossed a lock of his shiny black hair out of his eyes. 'One of you is more than sufficient in this world,' he drawled.

He was sinfully handsome, with a strong athletic build and the finest blue eyes God had ever placed in a man. Olivia had heard his name spoken quite often by women of her age. Delicious and virile were words that were frequently used in those conversations.

'It truly does amaze me that the women of this

town find you so alluring, Hartwick,' Sarah said. 'I believe it will remain one of life's mysteries.'

'Perhaps it's because you are rarely in my company.'

'No, I am certain familiarity would not clear the reasoning.'

Lyonsdale came to stand beside his wife and kissed her hand. Witnessing the love they shared always filled Olivia with regret—regret that she had not found a man who loved her even just a little.

'We are off to White's,' Lyonsdale said, looking up at the painting. 'However, I wanted to show Hart your portrait.' The pride was evident in his voice. 'I told you that gown was the best choice.'

'You said you wanted me to wear the gown I was wearing the night we met. Fortunately for you, it is one of my favourites.'

'I envisioned you in it for so long, it will always be my favourite.'

Sarah and Hartwick rolled their eyes in unison while standing next to each other. Then the Earl walked closer to the portrait and took in the work with his hands fixed on his hips. He tilted his head a number of times before turning around and nodding to Katrina.

'He is right,' Hartwick said. 'The artist has captured you perfectly. Now be a good duchess and bear a child that looks more like you than it does my friend.'

Olivia thought the child would do well resembling either parent and wondered if she would ever conceive another. Gabriel's kiss today confused her. Instinctively her hand went to her stomach.

'You looked a bit pale, Sister. Some fresh air might do you wonders,' Victoria said, taking Olivia's arm. 'Would you mind if we went outside for just a bit?' she asked Katrina.

'By all means, there is a door to the terrace just down the hall,' Katrina replied with a sympathetic smile. 'We shall be returning to the Crimson Drawing Room shortly. Why don't you take your time and meet us there.'

Victoria guided Olivia into the portrait gallery outside the library and Olivia pulled her to a stop. 'What are you about?' Olivia demanded quietly. 'Now Katrina will think I couldn't bear to witness the affection she shares with Lyonsdale and you were trying to spare me the pain.'

'Nonsense,' Victoria said, tugging Olivia to begin walking. She lowered her voice to a whisper. 'I have wanted to get you alone and couldn't wait another minute. How is it that I hear of surprising actions of yours from Lyonsdale's grandmother and not from you, my own sister? Don't look at me like that. You had to know there would be talk of your unusual stroll down Bond Street with Winter. She mentioned it before we went in for dinner.'

Olivia's stomach dipped uncomfortably, recalling the last time she and Gabriel were the topic of *ton* gossip. 'If that mundane fact has people talking, they aren't paying close enough attention to the scandals around them. I cannot believe a simple walk between a husband and wife is cause for discussion.'

'When those two people act as polite strangers for years, I'd say that is cause for gossip. And how is it you did not see fit to tell me?'

'I did not think it noteworthy.'

Victoria looked about ready to stamp her foot on the parquet floor. 'How could you say that? A few days ago you wanted your cook to roast him for the inconsiderate way he delayed Nicholas's breeching. Now you are walking with him down a main thoroughfare and he is buying you jewels. Something is going on and I demand you tell me what it is.'

'Jewels? He did not buy me any jewels.' Olivia opened the door to the unoccupied terrace and stepped outside. The scent of rain was heavy in the air and thick clouds moved swiftly in the moonlight. 'I was sitting for Manning in his studio when Gabriel arrived quite unexpectedly. He said he was attending to matters close by and decided to accompany me home.'

'Why would he care to escort you home? You barely speak with one another.'

Olivia shrugged and rolled her eyes. 'The man is a mystery and always has been. As to be expected, on our way home we had a disagreement. The only reason he dragged me into a jewellery shop was so people would not witness our row.'

Victoria's eyes narrowed. 'Nevertheless people did witness you together and are speculating on a reconciliation.'

'That is absurd. You of all people should understand our marriage could never go back to being what I thought it was, not after what he did.'

'Well, something has changed and I believe you have some notion what has altered his behaviour.'

Olivia rubbed her forehead. Victoria had always been her deepest confidant. Hopefully she would not make her feel worse. She took a deep breath and let the words spill out. 'I told him I wanted another child.'

Victoria's eyes widened considerably.

'But, he has rejected me,' Olivia amended. 'At least I think he rejected me...please do not tell Mother. I could not bear to hear her prattle on about how relieved she is that I've cast aside my pride and started comporting myself like the Duchess I am. I believe my estrangement from him has been a cause of embarrassment for her.'

'I will not say a word to her—however, how

could you not know if you were rejected? I would think it would be fairly obvious.'

'Well, I thought he had rejected me. We did not…that is to say he could not…'

'When did this happen?'

'A few nights past. Oh, it was so humiliating. I cannot believe I even considered it, but now I am so confused.'

Her sister placed a comforting hand over Olivia's. 'Like all men, he is a selfish beast who has no notion of how fortunate he is to have a lovely wife. What is confusing about that? We've known that for years.'

'He kissed me today. Do not groan.' Olivia closed her eyes and dropped her forehead into her palms, not wishing to see Victoria's next re-action. 'And what is worse, I kissed him back.' She was such a fool.

'Oh, no, Olivia, you didn't,' moaned Victoria. 'What in the world possessed you to do such a thing? You know he cares nothing for you. How could you be so foolish?'

'I know. I know,' she whispered back harshly. 'You do not have to remind me. I was the one lying in bed, weak and in pain, when he came to me from another woman's bed.' Why had she been foolish enough to believe he would remain faith-ful when most of the men in their circle, including all the men in her family, were not? Because she had been foolish enough to believe he might have been falling in love with her. He'd never said as much, but his actions spoke of a man who cared for her deeply.

'Why don't you tell me exactly what happened? Leave no detail out.'

'I do not know what happened. One minute we were arguing, the next we were kissing. And it changed everything. Now I have no idea if he rejected me or not.'

'You love children. You are a wonderful mother to Nicholas and a doting aunt to my three. I understand why you would want another child, but you know what will happen. Men cannot remain faithful. It is not in their nature. I know that for certain. However, I never fell in love with Haverstraw and care not about his indiscretions. You were foolish enough to fall in love with Winter and the moment he turned to another, you could barely speak to him. It pained me to witness how much he hurt you. I beg of you, do not let him do that to you again. I am telling you, he will never be satisfied with just your bed.'

'But do you not see? I'm not the same naïve girl I was. This time I have no false illusions. I know he does not love me. I have thought this through. During my confinement, I will leave for the country. Gabriel will remain in London and I will be spared hearing about his liaisons. It's the ideal solution.'

'It would be if you had not kissed him back. I know you, better than anyone. If you try and have another child together you will not be able to re-press your feelings for him. I saw how much he meant to you. I told you when you married him not to expect him to remain faithful. I told you it is a rare man that can be satisfied with only one woman. You should have heeded my warning, but you seemed to expect more.'

Olivia had never expected more, until she met Gabriel. And she'd never felt more alone than the day she realised she meant nothing to him.

'I have you to turn to for comfort. Who will Nicholas have? He should have someone dear to him if his world should fall apart.'

Victoria squeezed her hand. 'He will have his cousins. I am begging you. Be content with the way things are. You do not need another child.'

Olivia released Victoria's hand and walked a few feet to the balustrade overlooking the garden. Thunder rumbled in the distance. She rubbed the goose pimples on her arms. Was Victoria right? Maybe she did not need another child. But why then did the thought of not having another one leave her with an ache in her chest? And why had Gabriel kissed her?

# Chapter Seven

The next morning Gabriel leaned silently against the doorway of Mr Manning's studio and watched Olivia recline along the divan, appearing to be a woman completely at ease in her surrounds. She was back here again, and he knew he had only himself to blame. If only he had been less interested in her when they were first married, he wouldn't be standing here with his arms crossed to prevent himself from dragging her out.

When they had first met, it was evident Olivia had too great a mind for it to remain idle. That was why when he saw how much she enjoyed going to the Royal Academy and admiring the artwork, he'd encouraged her to pursue her interest. It was why he'd introduced her to Mr West and spoke with the man about having Olivia study art under his tutelage. She'd had no desire to create art, but she had a burning need to understand why certain pieces were revered. With her enthusiasm and intelligence, it was no surprise she became a well-respected expert of the Italian masters. His reward came from the luminous joy that shone from her each time she would talk about what she was learning. It didn't occur to him until now that seeing her happy had meant that much to him.

And all these years later, she'd thanked him by posing for an indecent portrait that she intended to share with all of London. He should have encouraged her to pursue horticulture.

His thoughts were interrupted by Manning, who continued speaking with Olivia while mixing more paint. 'Were there any scandals of note at the musical?'

'None that I heard of,' she said on a sigh. 'Although, I try not to pay attention to such speculation.'

'No one was compromised? No one was challenged?' He approached her with a smile and adjusted her arm slightly.

'Not that I witnessed,' she replied grinning.

'How about the Prince Regent? Any interesting tales of his exploits?'

'None. In fact, he was not in attendance. I understand he is suffering terribly from the gout.'

'That must make getting around rather difficult.'

'I would think so.'

'Has he been about?'

'If he has, I've not seen him.'

Gabriel pushed away from the doorframe. 'That is probably because you are devoting too much of your time to charitable causes such as this.'

There was a soft gasp from his unmoving wife.

'Your Grace,' the artist said in an uneven voice, bowing deferentially. 'What a surprise.'

'I decided to show myself in...again.' He walked to the easel and crossed his arms. Today the canvas had paint on it. 'Do you always begin your portraits there?' Gabriel asked, looking at how Manning had captured the creamy skin of his wife's neck and shoulders.

Manning tilted his head and studied the canvas. 'No, it depends where my mood takes me.'

Gabriel's attention was drawn to the top swell of his wife's breasts, painted much too accurately. His fingers dug into his biceps. 'My wife has sat long enough. She needs some refreshment.'

'We have been stopping as often as she requires.'

'You have painted quite a bit. I am certain she needs another.'

'You may continue. I can assure you, I am well.' Olivia's voice rang out from across the room.

Manning shifted his gaze from his subject to Gabriel. Then his brown eyes widen momentarily.

At least the man was not a complete nodcock. 'The light has shifted. I believe we are finished for the day,' he said, turning away from the canvas.

Olivia picked her head up and looked from the painter to Gabriel. 'It was fine a few moments ago.'

'It was shifting even then. I was only trying to finish the last few strokes.'

'There will be no more strokes today,' Gabriel said drily, strolling towards Olivia.

She glared at him but allowed him to help her to stand. 'What are you doing here?' she whispered sharply, adjusting the skirt of that enticing gown.

'I told you,' he whispered back, handing her a glass of wine that had been placed on a table near her, 'I have come to see you have some refreshment. Now go and change. I am taking you to Gunter's for ice.'

He expected her to argue, but she took a sip of wine and narrowed her eyes at him. He could tell she was up for a good row. He was starting to learn the signs.

A short while later, they sent Colette home in Olivia's carriage, and Gabriel helped his hesitant wife into his high-perch phaeton. When he climbed into the box from the other side, he looked over to find her eyeing his new equipage. It was an exceptional piece of craftsmanship, with

its highly glossed black finish that reflected the
London streets like a mirror.

'Is your artist always such a washer-woman?'

'If you are asking if he enjoys gossip, I suppose
he does. Talking, as you are well aware, helps to
make portrait sessions bearable.'

'I would not think a man like that would be interested in the social life of someone like Prinny.'

'Come now, are you truly that jaded? Most everyone is interested in what he does. Manning is
like most aspiring portrait artists. He would love
to have the cache to say the Prince Regent sat for
him. To have his work displayed in a royal residence would be quite the accomplishment.'

'You have introduced them?'

'Not yet.'

'But you plan to?'

'If the opportunity should present itself, I do
not see why I would not. Manning is extremely
talented. Surely you can see that from the pieces
displayed in his studio? He has even painted Nicholas for me.'

'I will agree the man possesses talent, however did I not tell you that you were not to sit for
him again?'

'You did.'

A scruffy dog darted out into the road, and Gabriel expertly manoeuvred the phaeton around it.
The carriage rocked back and forth on its wheels.

'If you heard my command, why were you in his studio today?' He glanced over at Olivia, who was sitting with her hands gripped tightly together.

'I never agreed to your request.'

'It was not a request, and you knew that.' Now he pulled abruptly to a stop as a newsboy ran across the road.

Olivia made an odd sound. 'I honour my commitments, and I told him I would sit for him.'

'Now you must tell him you've changed your mind.'

'I cannot do that.'

'You mean you will not.' He snapped the reins, making the phaeton go faster.

Her hands moved to grip the seat.

'Tell him I forbid it,' he continued.

'You forbid it?' she ground out.

Gabriel nodded, glanced down at her hands, and focused his attention back on the road. If she was not wearing gloves, he was certain her knuckles would be white. 'Why are you so nervous?'

'I find I do not like sitting this far above the ground.'

He took the reins in one hand and pulled her closer to him. 'Do you feel safer away from the edge?'

Olivia nodded a fraction of an inch.

'I will not let any harm come to you.'

Her eyes searched his and everything fell away

around them. Then she quickly turned away and watched the people strolling in and out of the shops. 'You should be looking at the road,' she advised him.

'But the view next to me is infinitely more appealing.' How he wished he could see her face past the rim of her bonnet.

'The road please,' she reminded him with a crack in her voice.

It was a good thing they were close to Gunter's. If he continued to be tempted to stare at her, he was sure to crash into something. They turned onto Berkeley Street, and the trees of the square came into view. 'We have not settled our discussion,' he reminded her, searching for a place to park.

'Yes we have. You do not want me to have my portrait done, and I do.'

'Just to clarify, I do not want you to have *that* portrait done for an exhibition.'

'I realise it is rather bold. However, you've seen the preliminary sketch. No one will know it's me.'

'Rather bold? It is much too provocative.' How could she not understand that?

'If I did not know you better, I would think you were jealous.'

He parked the phaeton along the garden across from the confectioner's shop. There was nothing he could say to her comment, so he chose not to acknowledge it. 'What flavour of ice would you care for?' he asked, purposely changing the subject.

She gave a slight shake of her head. 'I have no preference. You choose.'

Gabriel studied her passive features. If he selected a flavour she hated, would she turn that into an argument? He addressed the waiter that approached his side of the phaeton. 'I shall have bergamot ice and Her Grace will have pineapple.'

Olivia's eyes widened momentarily. He was certain he guessed incorrectly, until she granted him a small smile. 'How did you know that is my favourite?'

'You would order it when I would take you here years ago.'

'I'm surprised you remembered.'

So was he. They sat in silence, Gabriel recalling the times they'd sat under this very tree before their marriage fell apart. When the waiter arrived with their order, Gabriel relaxed and began to enjoy his ice.

'I never knew you liked bergamot,' she commented, sliding a delicate spoonful of ice into her mouth.

Gabriel shrugged. 'I have recently become partial to the taste. Have you ever tried it?'

'Yes, I found it rather good.'

'Well, this is mine. Enjoy your pineapple, and

next time I will order you bergamot.' The thought of taking her here again made him grin.

Her forehead wrinkled before she turned away. Now what had he done wrong? He was only teasing her.

For the remainder of their time at Gunter's neither spoke. They were almost home when Olivia broke the heavy silence that hung over them. 'Why does it really matter to you if I sit for that portrait? For years you have made it quite clear you have no interest in me. I could have walked through the house in animal skins, and you would not have noticed. Now, you are concerned about a portrait and buying me ice. Why?'

Gabriel turned the phaeton into their drive and with the lift of his hand he dismissed the footman coming down the steps towards them. He faced her, staring into her brown eyes that were flecked with gold. 'You were the one who told me you never wanted me to touch you again. For five years I have had no notion if you still feel that way, or if you spoke those words in haste and have since regretted them. You would not speak to me, so I had no way of finding out. But the other night when you assumed I would take you with no regard to your comfort… I had no idea your opinion of me was that low.'

She looked at him as if he had sprouted a second head. 'The day I suffered through hours of birthing pains to have our son, you were with a harlot in her brothel. They searched for you for hours and could not find you. When you finally arrived home, no one had to tell me you were with a woman. I knew. Her scent was all over you. God, I can still smell that cloying perfume. What kind of man do you think that makes you? I believed you when you told me you cared for me.'

'I did care for you. I still do—'

'Apparently, not enough. I know what kind of man you are. The entire *ton* knows what kind of man you are. The very first ball I attended after giving birth to Nicholas I was plagued with pitying looks and whispers behind fans. I was the woman whose husband was bedding another while she was bearing his heir. And that name swarmed around me for weeks. *Madame La-Grange*. Everyone knew—everyone,' she said vehemently. 'Occasionally her name will still drift into conversations around me. Now you buy me ice and fuss over a portrait?'

Hearing Madame LaGrange's name on her lips made him want to vomit. No one should know of their connection—not even Olivia. And somehow, someone saw him leave her room that day and word spread among the *ton* like fire through a wheat field in autumn. Even the servants knew. He would not allow anyone to find out that Madame LaGrange worked for him. He had made that mistake once before with Matthew, and it had cost the man his life.

For a moment it was years earlier and Gabriel was back in the garden in Richmond, flashes of lightning were slashing the inky blackness around him, rain poured onto Matthew's bloodied body that was seeping his life out in Gabriel's arms, and the last person on earth he thought would betray him was standing over him, pointing a gun at his chest. It had become his reoccurring nightmare ever since.

How could he possibly explain to Olivia that he'd never bedded Madame LaGrange without divulging the woman's secret? A secret he would take to his grave. No one was ever going to die again because he placed his trust in the wrong person.

The pain dulling her eyes sliced through him. 'I never meant to hurt you.'

It was all he could say.

She lowered her head, her face now obscured by her bonnet. Although they were married just a few months before Nicholas was born, in that time he had come to care deeply for her. His lies of omission had cost them both.

When she raised her head, he caught the determination in her eyes. 'If you ever had any kind regard for me at all, you will grant me one thing.'

'What is it that you want, Olivia?'

'I want another child.'

That was not what he expected her to say. His thoughts had been on the portrait. 'Olivia, I've always wanted more children with you.' Now hopefully Nicholas would know what it was like to grow up with a brother or sister.

## Chapter Eight

Olivia stared sightlessly at her reflection in the mirror on her dressing table while Colette brushed her hair. Her thoughts kept returning to her conversation with Gabriel earlier in the day. Confessing how she felt about him had been liberating. For years she wanted to tell him what a scoundrel she thought he was. Instead she'd stood silently by pretending she was indifferent to him when deep down she despised him for his betrayal.

She despised him for making her believe he might have had tender feelings for her. She despised him for making her feel as if she were not good enough for him. And she despised him the most for being the man she had fallen in love with.

Now that she'd told him what she truly thought of him, some of her hatred had lifted. She understood what place she had in his life, and now he knew what place he had in hers. She could not allow her feelings for him to return. It would be too painful.

'There's no need to plait it, Colette,' Gabriel's deep voice rumbled from the doorway connecting their rooms.

The hairbrush Colette was using fell to the floor. Perhaps she should have warned her maid that Gabriel would be coming to her room tonight.

'That will be all, Colette,' she said, finding it hard to stop staring at him. He was lounging in the doorway with casual elegance, wearing a navy silk-brocade banyan and holding two glasses in one hand. In the other, he held a bottle. It had been years since she had seen him out of his impeccable attire and it took her a moment to remember to breathe.

'I did not hear you open the door,' she said.

'Perhaps you were too wrapped up in your thoughts,' he replied, pushing off from the doorframe and advancing towards her. He poured out the ruby-red liquid into each glass and handed her one. 'It is the ninety-eight Château Lafite. As I recall, it was your favourite.'

'How is that possible? Bennett has been searching for that vintage for years.'

'That's because Bennett does not know about the bottles I have hidden away.'

'From me?'

'No, I simply have a few bottles left locked in my study.'

'And you have not drunk them?'

'The Lafite was your favourite. I had no desire to indulge until now.'

'I thought that might have been port. I remember thinking I was quite bold when we would drink it together in our rooms,' she replied. The wine tasted just as rich and smooth as she remembered.

'You always enjoyed trying new things.' His eyes dropped to her mouth as she licked the taste of the wine from her lower lip.

'You never made me feel self-conscious.'

'I enjoyed your enthusiasm for things I long took for granted.' He stepped closer and poured more wine into her glass.

'Are you attempting to get me tipsy?'

'I thought both of us could use something to relax us.' He took a slow drink from his glass, his eyes not leaving hers.

'You expect me to believe you are nervous?'

Gabriel shook his head. 'I did not say I was nervous. Apprehensive might be a better word.'

'Because?' Oh, she really needed this wine. He was much too close and smelled wonderful.

'Because I want to depart from your bedchamber without having a piece of porcelain flung at my head.'

So he wanted to lay the cards on the table. That was fine with her. 'Continue to be your delightful self and we should have no problems. I do have two requests, though.'

'Of course, how may I be of service?'

'Since this is a temporary reconciliation of sorts, there is no need to pretend otherwise to the *ton*.'

'You wish for our accord to remain a secret.'

'I wish to avoid the questions that will arise when our behaviour towards one another returns to its usual state.'

He studied her as if she were a complex puzzle he was attempting to decipher. 'It may not.'

Her heart couldn't bear for it to be otherwise. Getting closer to him would only open the wounds that were just now starting to heal. 'I have no doubt it will.'

'And your other request?'

She swallowed the remainder of her wine to gather the courage. 'While we are here—' she motioned between them '—I would like your word as a gentleman that you will not have any intimate encounters with other women.'

'Here?' he asked, purposely pretending ignorance.

Dealing with him could be so exasperating at times. 'While we are trying to conceive a child, I would like you to refrain from bedding anyone else.'

'I see no problem with your request. Very well.'

She searched his eyes for a clue he was being sincere. 'Consider my request carefully. Make certain you can comply.'

He took a sip and nodded over his glass. 'I have no doubt I can comply.'

Was he telling the truth? He had a strong sexual appetite. Olivia knew this first hand. Did that mean he planned to bed her—a lot? She poured more wine into her glass. 'So then you will be monogamous.'

'I will expect the same from you,' he said, narrowing his gaze.

She had not strayed from their wedding vows—he had. Could she throw her wine in his face and still expect him to bed her? Probably not. 'I assure you I have honoured my marriage vows.'

Gabriel looked as if he were about to say something, but instead downed the rest of his wine. He lifted Olivia's glass out of her hand and placed it on the dressing table beside his. 'We need to get you out of that,' he said, looking down at her dressing gown.

This was it then. Now she would know if she could give him her body without opening up her heart. She turned away from him to avoid his gaze and prayed this would not be a mistake. Slowly she slid off her dressing gown. The warmth from his fingers as they brushed her hair forward over her shoulder made her skin tingle. Her body had changed since she'd had Nicholas. It was softer and rounder. Would he still find it pleasing?

'At least you are not wearing enough fabric to supply all the upstairs maids with aprons.'

'Your seductive skills are as impressive as ever,' she muttered and could not help but grin at his laugh.

'And yet I have only begun exercising them. Take care, you may swoon when you hear what I will say when I finally spring you from that be-witching garment.'

This time she did laugh. Maybe it was the wine. Maybe it was the realisation that they were going to have to do this a number of times before she actually conceived—perhaps for months. The very notion made intimate parts of her flutter.

'I am certain you will have me shaking with need,' she teased. But when she slipped her night-rail over her head and turned around, the smile fell from her lips.

His heated gaze left her practically without breath. He took one finger and trailed a line of warmth from her ear, down her neck, across her collarbone and finally between the curves of her breasts. His eyes traced every movement of his finger. It would be impossible for him not to feel her heartbeat quicken with each area he touched.

'You are even more beautiful than I remembered,' he murmured, cupping a breast.

It was all coming back to her. Every touch. Every kiss. Every time she'd cried out his name. When he lowered his lips to hers and coaxed her with gentle nips to open her mouth, memories of the times they'd spent together flooded her mind. She squeezed her eyes shut, trying to push images from the past out of her head. Part of her wanted to remind herself that he could not be trusted, but another part of her wanted to believe he truly wanted only her as much as she wanted only him. During this time together she would take her pleasure, but she would not allow herself to fall in love with him again.

The kiss deepened and a sense of urgency replaced the initial gentleness.

'We both want this, Olivia.' His words filled her mouth with his breath. 'I do not wish to fight with you any more.'

She tasted his familiar lips, sweetened with the delicious wine. She missed this—missed him. He groaned into her mouth and she could not resist unbuttoning his banyan to feel the heat of his hard smooth skin.

While they were together, she would take as much pleasure as she could stand. Then she would lock these memories away when their time together was over. She could resist the spell of his body.

When she slid her hands up his chest, the banyan fell to the floor. He stepped closer. Their bodies fit together like pieces of a puzzle. It had been so long. She traced the bumps of his ribs. How had a man who sat behind a desk all day remained this muscular?

As he caressed her bottom, he groaned again. Lifting her into his arms, he released her gently on the bed and his body followed hers.

'Are you comfortable?' he asked, trailing hot kisses along her neck.

Trying to breathe somewhat normally, she skimmed her hands along his spine and rested them at the curve of his lower back. 'I am quite well,' she managed to reply.

He bit gently into her neck and slid his thumb around her nipple. It was growing painfully hard and she didn't want him to stop.

'You feel very well,' he rasped.

'So do you,' she said with a moan.

He smiled against her neck and she lowered her hand even more. His weight shifted slightly, pressing her into the mattress. Sliding his tongue along the upper swell of her breast, he groaned loudly as he sucked her nipple into his mouth. She had forgotten how good that felt and gripped his head with both her hands. After giving her right breast exquisite attention, he kissed his way over to the left. She could feel the heat pooling between her legs and ground her pelvis into him. Then he kissed a path down to her stomach…

It was becoming difficult to remember how much she disliked this man.

He nipped at her thigh. 'I want you ready for me.'

'I am ready,' she managed to say through strangled breath.

He shook his head and his soft hair tickled the inside of her thighs. Fluttering her eyes open, she met his gaze.

She struggled for air as their eyes locked and he lowered his mouth between her legs. His eyes closed momentarily, as if he were savouring his favourite dessert. He placed long, slow licks while his gaze bore into her.

The air in the room disappeared as her body responded to the amazing things his mouth was doing to her. She did not want him to stop. He continued to torture her with his mouth until she began to tremble, then she let out a loud cry as she came. His strong arms held her down, as he continued to lick and suck her. She had to push his head away to make him stop.

Her eyes would not open. Struggling to catch her breath, she felt him rise above her.

'I believe you're ready now,' he whispered against her neck.

Before she could think of a response, he was

sliding inside her. Her back bowed. How she had loved feeling this filled. Within moments she was meeting him thrust for thrust. He was bringing her to the edge all over again, watching her as sweat formed on his chest.

'You feel even better than I remembered,' he said, brushing the hair out of her eyes as he continued to thrust inside her.

She did not want to remember, did not want to be reminded of everything that happened between them up to this moment. 'Don't. Stop.'

His movements became more urgent.

She dug her nails into his back.

'Hurry,' he ground out.

He was waiting for her and that lovely gesture set her over the edge again. As he let out a loud groan, he came and soon afterwards collapsed on top of her.

Gabriel's heavy weight was nearly crushing her. As if somehow he knew he rolled, taking her with him so her head rested against his chest. The rapid staccato of his heartbeat matched her own.

She could not move. Moreover, she did not want to.

'Livy, you still turn me inside out.'

Oh, no, not that! Why did he have to ruin it and call her that?

She opened her eyes. He was smiling down at

her—smiling that smile that made the corner of his eyes crinkle and lit up her world.

That smile that he had given only to her, all those years ago.

She stumbled out of bed and reached for her nightrail. Throwing it over her head, she caught his bewildered expression. She needed to get him out of this room as fast as possible. If she did not, she did not know if her heart could stand it. She pressed her hand against her lips to prevent herself from saying anything foolish.

'Livy, what is the matter?'

Why did he have to keep calling her that? It was what he had called her when he was being all sweet years ago.

'You need to go.'

He closed his eyes and draped his arm over his face, showing her the curve of his biceps. 'I am tired, Olivia, and it is late. I just want to sleep.'

'Here?' she squeaked.

Picking up his head, he peered at her through one eye. 'Yes, here, I have done it before. Now come back to bed.' He closed his eye and settled into the blankets.

Now what was she to do? He was much too big to drag out of bed. She picked up his banyan and held it out to him. 'We never agreed you would sleep here.'

He lifted his head again and eyed her. His hair

was tousled and there was a slight shadow on his face from his evening whiskers, giving him a roguish quality. 'I was not aware everything we do would be up for negotiation.' He rolled to his side, propping his head in his hand and exposing his hard muscular chest. 'We just had a brilliant time together, and to be truthful my legs are not quite steady at the moment. Let us not ruin tonight by arguing. Please, come back to bed.'

Olivia felt herself weakening, but if he slept here she feared it would be harder to keep him out of her heart. Especially when he was all sweet and rumpled. He eyed her expectantly.

Pushing back her shoulders, she took a deep breath. She could do this. She could sleep with him without it affecting her in the least. Many women slept with their husbands without even liking them. It was just sex, two bodies responding to one another. That was all it was. It had nothing to do with feelings of any kind.

She folded his banyan carefully and placed it at the foot of her bed. Reluctantly, she slid under the covers. If she laid on her back with distance between them, she would be fine.

Gabriel slid beside her and pulled her close. This would never work. Squeezing her eyes shut, she turned on her side to get away from him, but his arm tightened as he spooned his body against her.

'Go to sleep, Livy,' he mumbled into her hair.

The ice around her heart melted a little bit more. Oh, good heavens! There had to be a way to resist him.

# Chapter Nine

'Mama, Mama, you won't believe—'

There was a little voice in his dream. What was a little voice doing in his dream about Olivia? Gabriel shifted his weight and breathed in her honeysuckle scent.

'Papa, is that you? What are you doing in Mama's bed?'

The warm softness below him began to shift and then poke him. Gabriel tightened his arm around it to get it to stop.

'Wake up,' Olivia whispered sharply.

Why was she telling him to wake up? She should be telling him that she wanted to feel him deep inside her. Gabriel groaned, rubbed his whiskers against the soft linen draped over her enticing breast and cracked one eye open to the faint morning light.

And was met with his son's curious expression an inch from his nose.

Startled, Gabriel jerked away from Olivia.

'Hello, Papa. Good morning, Mama,' said Nicholas from where he was standing beside the bed, playing with Olivia's sleeve.

She turned and kissed their son. In an attempt to wake up his muddled brain, Gabriel rubbed the back of his head and stretched.

'Your hair looks silly, Papa, and why aren't you wearing a shirt?'

Olivia arched her brow at Gabriel, leaving the explanation to him.

'It was very warm last night,' he replied, rubbing his eyes.

'No, it wasn't. There was a fire in my room all night.' Nicholas crawled up on the bed and sat cross-legged next to Olivia. His doe-like eyes widened with excitement. 'Did you hear the rain? There was a mighty storm. Why are you here? Did the thunder scare you?'

She gave a small snort and glanced at Gabriel. At least she believed he was manly enough to withstand a thunderstorm without retreating to the inside of his wardrobe.

'Your papa came to enquire after me and was too tired to return to his rooms so I let him fall asleep here.'

'That was nice of you, Mama. What's that?' Nicholas asked, poking Gabriel below his ribcage.

With bleary eyes Gabriel looked down to the

puckered scar from his old gunshot wound, his constant reminder of his costly mistake. 'It's an old fencing injury.' One more lie in that chain of many he was forced to tell.

'Uncle Andrew says chits like men with scars.'

'You have spent entirely too much time with your Uncle Andrew,' he mumbled.

Olivia traced the outline of his round scar with her delicate finger and caught his eye with a curious expression.

'Do you like Papa's scar, Mama?'

She turned to Nicholas. 'Would you like to see *my* scar?'

'You have a scar?' Nicholas asked with eager anticipation.

'I was thrown from a horse.' She rolled her sleeve up over her elbow.

Gabriel peered over and saw a jagged white line about two inches across. He had never noticed it before. When was she thrown from a horse? James should have informed him of any injury she had sustained.

Nicholas gave a low whistle. 'Did it hurt? Did you cry, Mama?'

She ran her fingers through their son's hair. 'For just a bit, my love. Now up you go so your father and I can begin our day.'

'Will you have breakfast with us too, Papa?' Nicholas asked with a wide smile. 'You never do and I would like that very much. I am rarely with you and Mama together. I rather like this.'

And lying there in bed with his wife and child, Gabriel realised he liked it too. They were shut away from the problems and whispers of the outside world. It felt like they were a true family and it was awfully intimate. Suddenly going back to sleep in his room and having breakfast alone held no appeal.

Olivia shook her head and began to say something when he interrupted her. 'Of course we will take breakfast together,' he replied, noticing his wife's surprised expression. Was she at all happy about his announcement? 'Run off and tell Bennett we will dine together in the breakfast room.'

Nicholas's smile brightened his face. 'That's a capital idea,' he said, before jumping off the bed and running out the door.

'Is this part of your ritual each morning?' He rubbed his eyes and looked at the clock on the mantel. 'My word, it is barely six o'clock!'

She laughed. 'From what I recall you also rose with the early streaks of dawn. He does not come in every morning, but a fair amount.'

He had forgotten how sinful she looked when she had just woken up. The lids of her eyes were a bit lower and those loose tresses of her dark hair reminded him of how she looked after a rather vigorous bout of lovemaking—like they'd had last night.

'Why are you looking at me like that?' she asked, moving her head away from him.

He climbed on top of her and propped himself up by his elbows. 'Like what?' he countered, rubbing his nose on the side of hers, needing to touch her in even the smallest of ways.

'Please move. We must get dressed.'

'But I like the way you look without your dress.'

'Gabriel.'

He placed coaxing kisses along her mouth. If he could only get her to kiss him back, he was certain he could easily convince her to let him enter her again. When her lips parted to accept his kisses, he hardened in anticipation. She was heaven and sin wrapped all in one. Mornings such as this came flooding back to him. 'I love being inside you when we are both half-asleep.'

The loud crash startled them both and they swung their heads to the doorway in unison.

Colette stood frozen, the remains of Olivia's chocolate and a broken cup at her feet. Gabriel let out a low curse and jerked the sheet up to his waist. This day was not starting out as he planned.

'I... I...knocked but... I saw his lordship leave and thought you'd be needing my assistance getting dressed.'

'I will ring for you shortly, Colette,' Olivia murmured while covering her eyes. 'You may tend to the mess later.'

The maid dashed from the room and thankfully closed the door behind her.

Gabriel sighed and dropped onto his back. Hopefully the remainder of his day would not hold any more unexpected interruptions.

When Gabriel entered his breakfast room at the unusually early hour to the smells of chocolate, coffee, eggs, ham, warm bread and strawberry jam, he found it hard not to smile. Olivia had shooed him from her room without one more taste of her tempting lips. If he was not able to make love to her this morning, at least he would eat well. He went directly to the sideboard, filled his plate with his favourite morning fare, then took his seat at the head of the table between his wife and son.

As Bennett poured him coffee, Gabriel could have sworn he heard the man humming. 'Can I get you anything else, sir?' he asked with an unusually cheerful lilt to his voice.

'No, that will be all, Bennett.' Gabriel scanned the freshly ironed copy of *The Times*. Thankfully there still was no mention of the assassination attempt. The fewer people who know about it, the safer Prinny would be.

'This just came for you, madam,' Bennett said, handing Olivia a missive sealed with red wax.

Who would send his wife a note so early in the day? Was that common as well? How was it that he knew the exact time Prinny rose each morning, but he did not know the most mundane things about his own house? Gabriel surreptitiously looked at the handwriting and tried to identify the imprint on the seal. Without tilting his head to the side, he would not be able to distinguish the mark.

'You do eat a lot of food in the morning, Papa.'

Olivia placed the note down and pursed her lips. His opportunity was lost.

'Nicholas, it is not polite to comment on what other people place on their plates,' she corrected him.

Their son turned to her in amazement. 'But do you see his plate?'

Olivia picked up her cup of chocolate. 'I see it. Grown men have rather large appetites.' Her fine dark eyes met Gabriel's over the gold rim of her blue Sèvres cup and she took a slow sip.

If he didn't know any better, he'd think she was being flirtatious. The very idea of it made him smile.

'Lord Andrew is here to see you, sir,' Bennett announced from the doorway. His previous cheerful demeanour seemed to have got lost on his way to escorting Andrew to the breakfast room. Apparently, this morning, when he wanted his family all to himself the outside world seemed determined to disrupt their private moments.

It was just after seven o'clock. Gabriel hoped the urgent news that brought his brother to his doorstep would be good.

'I realise I am calling early, but—' Andrew froze in the doorway and his wide-eyed gaze travelled from Gabriel to Olivia and finally to Nicholas.

'Uncle Andrew,' Nicholas screamed. Jumping out of his chair, he hurled himself at his uncle. Andrew easily caught him and spun Nicholas around so that the boy rested around his neck like a scarf.

There was no indication from Andrew's demeanour the direction this visit would take. From the playful attention Andrew was paying to Nicholas, it was impossible to tell the urgency of his call.

'Is everything all right, Andrew?' Olivia asked with concern.

He stopped trying to drop Nicholas to the floor. 'Yes. Forgive me for the early hour.' His gaze darted to Gabriel and back to Olivia. 'I found I could not sleep and I know that Gabriel is an early riser. I thought a good ride through the park would clear the cobwebs from my head.'

Patience was a virtue. As much as he wanted to

ask the reason for Andrew's visit, Gabriel would bide his time so as not to draw undue attention from Olivia. 'Would you care for breakfast, or have you eaten already?'

'I would never refuse to dine at your table.' Andrew dropped his nephew into the seat Nicholas had vacated and strolled to the sideboard as if the domestic scene was commonplace and he was in no hurry to speak with Gabriel.

While Gabriel watched Andrew sit next to Nicholas with a plate full of food and accept coffee from Bennett, he fought the urge to lean past his son and swat his brother on the head. He had offered food to Andrew to appear polite. The arse wasn't supposed to accept it.

Andrew was halfway through eating an enormous serving of ham and eggs when he finally noticed Nicholas, watching him with an openmouthed stare. The acknowledgement pulled Nicholas out of his stupor, and he studied his bowl of porridge.

'Mama, may I have eggs and ham instead of porridge?'

Olivia shifted a glance between Andrew and their son. 'If you'd like.' She signalled for a footman to bring another plate to Nicholas and opened the note that had been taunting Gabriel since it arrived. Her brow wrinkled as she scanned the paper.

'Have you received distressing news?' Gabriel asked.

The footman re-entered the room with a plate for Nicholas as she turned to Gabriel. 'It's a note from—'

'Papa never eats breakfast with us, Uncle Andrew, but since he slept in Mama's bed last night we asked him.'

The plate slipped out of the footman's hand, landing on the table with a thud as Gabriel choked on his coffee and Olivia turned crimson.

Andrew leaned closer to Nicholas and arched a brow. 'You don't say,' he said through a devilish grin.

Nicholas opened his mouth to continue when Olivia quickly chimed in.

'Your bruises have not improved. Perhaps now you will agree to take some healing salve home with you.' Bless his wife's polite diversionary tactics.

Andrew shot Gabriel a meaningful look and removed his hand from her inspection. 'It is nothing.'

'Papa has a scar. Mama and I saw it this morning since he wasn't wearing a nightshirt.'

Andrew was quite familiar with that scar. It was thanks to his brother's quick actions that Gabriel's body hadn't received another wound—a fatal one. Still, he needed to speak with his son about the importance of keeping certain aspects of their family life a secret. The sooner he learned that lesson, the better.

Meanwhile Andrew seemed to be thoroughly enjoying Nicholas's loquaciousness and propped his head in his hand. 'It seemed rather cool last night to be sleeping without a nightshirt.'

'I said the same thing,' Nicholas said in astonishment as his stomach rumbled loudly. Excusing himself, he hopped off his chair to fill his plate at the sideboard. It seemed discussing his parents' private activities was not as interesting as selecting the perfect slice of ham. Thank heavens for small miracles.

Andrew went back to eating his breakfast and Olivia returned to that mysterious note.

'I hope the news you've received is not too distressing,' Gabriel said. 'I gather from your expression that you have not received happy tidings.'

She eyed him intently. 'I suppose it depends on who you ask. Mr West is not well and has asked me to go to the Royal Academy this morning to settle the arrangement of the paintings for the upcoming exhibition in his place. I will have to cancel my sitting for today.'

'That is unfortunate. Did he say what is troubling him?' He took a sip of his coffee to hide the smile that was about to spread across his face at the very notion his wife would not be continuing that bloody portrait session.

Shaking her head, Olivia leaned close enough that he could smell her honeysuckle perfume. 'I am certain this pleases you immensely,' she said for only his ears.

'I would not wish ill on Mr West. You should know that.'

Olivia leaned back in her chair and rolled her eyes. She took a sip of her chocolate and her soft pink tongue slipped out to lick her lip. It was almost impossible for Gabriel to hold back a sigh of yearning.

Andrew shifted in his seat, taking Gabriel's attention away from Olivia's lips. Prinny's safety was his priority. Why was he having difficulty remembering that? 'I have appointments today, Andrew. What say you we go for that ride now?'

Andrew gulped down the remainder of his coffee before he tossed his napkin on the table. 'Excellent. Thank you for breakfast, Olivia.'

Nicholas stuck out his lower lip. 'You're leaving already, Uncle Andrew?'

'I'm afraid so. However, I'd venture to say you will see me again.' He ruffled Nicholas's hair as he walked past him.

Gabriel crouched next to his son and Nicholas gave him a tight hug. 'I rather like having breakfast with you, Papa,' he said, releasing his hold.

And Gabriel realised how much he rather liked having breakfast with his wife and son. It was an improvement from eating alone, reviewing paperwork. Without thinking, he kissed Olivia on the forehead on his way to the door.

# Chapter Ten

Why was everyone riding so slowly down Piccadilly at this hour? Even Gabriel's horse was pitching forward, trying to poke his nose past all the slow goers. If they did not arrive at the park soon Gabriel feared he would no longer possess any patience at all. In the meantime he continued to scowl at every driver, rider, merchant and pedestrian he saw.

When they finally turned into the park, they steered their horses sedately onto Rotten Row. At this hour, the only people on the bridle path were a few servants exercising horses some distance ahead. Finally, he would get some answers.

'Tell me what brought you to my door.'

Andrew guided his horse closer to Gabriel's. 'You will not be pleased.'

'Is that meant to soften the blow?'

'Mr Clarke is dead.'

Gabriel's blood ran cold as he jerked the reins to hold his ground. 'Care to explain?'

'Dead. I think that just about explains it.'

'I beg to differ. How in the bloody hell is the man dead when he is being hidden away in the Tower under lock and key? No one was to be informed he was there.'

Andrew rubbed his lips together. 'We were all shocked by the news. He was alive last night when they brought him his food. Hours later they found him dead on the floor.'

'Poison?'

'It appears so. We have questioned everyone involved and have no leads. It's as if some spectre appeared and disappeared just as mysteriously.'

'Then no one involved in holding him and the interrogations can be trusted. Perhaps this is why they have been unable to uncover any tangible leads. Say nothing of what we suspect and keep me apprised of anything suspicious.'

'Of course.'

'From this moment forward, finding out who wants Prinny dead falls solely on our shoulders. We must make certain he is not harmed. I do not know how much longer I can keep him safe inside Carlton House. Each day he becomes more and more restless. He is like a child and I cannot force him to follow my directions. I only wish he were not so trusting.'

Gabriel went to turn Homer around when his brother stopped him.

'We are not finished,' Andrew said. 'I believe there is one more thing that requires discussion.'

What more could they have to discuss?

'You are honestly not about to acknowledge that ideal family portrait I just witnessed? I believe an explanation is in order.'

Gabriel did not agree. Pulling the brim of his beaver hat low over his forehead, he shaded his eyes from the sunlight filtering through the branches above them. 'Olivia and I are attempting a reconciliation of sorts.'

'Of sorts?'

'Yes.'

When Andrew raised an expectant brow, Gabriel let out a sigh.

'You did not arrive at my doorstep so early to discuss the state of my marriage.'

'No, I did not, but after that unusual display, I find myself too intrigued not to. Now why is it normally you barely speak to her, the other night at dinner she was throwing daggers at you with her eyes and today you are kissing her goodbye? And please note, I am not even mentioning the entertaining information which Nicholas kindly provided.'

'It's complicated.'

'Women always are.'

Andrew had no idea. 'Olivia and I would like to have another child.'

'Well, it's about time.'

'Pardon me?'

'You know it is best for you to have more boys for the ducal line. Don't count on any of us to help you fulfil your obligation. Michael broods too much. No woman would ever want to marry him. And by the time Monty is old enough and finds a woman who can ignore his exasperating nature, you will be long dead.'

Gabriel narrowed his eyes at Andrew. 'Skeffington is in his dotage. When he gives up the ghost, I am certain his Duchess would be more than happy to lower herself to marry you. In fact, it would not surprise me if she attempted to pull you behind a tree while he was being lowered into his grave.'

Andrew visibly shuddered. 'Do not even jest. That woman is becoming more and more difficult to avoid. But we are getting away from our discussion of you and Olivia.'

'No, that discussion is over. I told you why this morning's events were a bit unusual.'

'A bit? I would say the events I witnessed were monumentally unusual.'

Gabriel could feel Andrew studying him and he kept his gaze fixed firmly ahead of them. He'd had a remarkable night with his wife. He did not need Andrew poking him with a stick to make him analyse what it meant.

'Have you told her that you have always been faithful?'

He knew this would happen. 'Of course I have not told her.'

'She is your Duchess.'

'It is not that simple. I would need to reveal everything to her. Our father never disclosed anything to Mother. To this day she does not know what we do and what responsibility he had. I put my trust in the wrong person once. I will not let it happen again.'

'Olivia is not Uncle Peter and the situation is vastly different.'

'Is it? Is it truly different? Tell me how?'

'She is your wife.'

'And he was our beloved uncle. A man I looked up to all my life, much as my son does you. *I* went to him for advice after Father died. *I* told him what we do, foolishly believing he already knew. When Father said to suspect everyone and trust no one, he was right. My mistake cost Matthew his life. I was the one who felt his life slip away in my arms that night. No amount of rain could have washed his blood from my hands. Every day it eats away at me that I continue to allow his family to believe he was the victim of a robbery that night. Lord Scarbury should have known his youngest was a man of heroic actions who gave his life protecting the Crown. Matthew deserved at least that.'

'You had me give his widow a substantial amount of your money and say I was settling a gambling debt to help support her and their son. You did all you could do considering the circumstances.'

'I couldn't bring him back!' It was the first time he allowed Andrew to see how deeply he had been affected by the events of that night. If he could help it, it would be the last.

'You are not the only one to feel the sting of one's actions where that night is concerned.'

And now he felt even worse. 'Forgive me. I didn't mean to imply it had been easy on you.'

The muscle in Andrew's jaw twitched. 'I'm glad you realise that.'

They rode in silence towards the path out of the park. Eventually, Andrew cleared his throat. 'If you explained you never tupped that woman, she would not think you're a bounder.'

'And tell her what exactly? She knows I was with Madame LaGrange. Shall I tell her that I was, in fact, with the woman in her brothel while Olivia's life was in danger bearing our child, but I did not bed her? Then the question becomes what was I doing there? Olivia is an intelligent woman.

You cannot give her half-truths. I will not reveal Madame's secrets. Not now. Not ever.'

All this talk of Olivia had distracted him. He needed to readjust his priorities—quickly. Prinny was in danger and he had no idea from whom.

Olivia dangled a small basket from her hand as she stood in the Blue Drawing Room of Carlton House and smiled at the man seated before her.

'You are truly an angel, my dear. Have I mentioned that to you?' the Prince Regent said, his eyes fixed on her basket.

At times he could be so easy to please. 'You are only saying that because I brought you marzipan.'

'That is simply not true. I would have said it if you brought me macarons instead.' He motioned for her to sit near him as he took the basket she held out and began to sample the sweet confections.

'I called on you to enquire about your health—however, you appear quite well. Much better than the last time the gout struck,' she remarked, noticing neither of his feet was bandaged. 'I am surprised you are not in bed.'

Prinny's mouth was full and he mumbled something, but it was impossible to distinguish what it was. He shifted on the sofa and studied his next morsel. 'My physician says I am to stay off my feet. He didn't say where.' He gestured with his head towards the tea tray on the table next to them. 'Why don't you pour yourself some tea and we can have a nice chat.'

The deep red liquid in the glass that rested on the table caught her attention. Certainly he wouldn't be drinking port. Not if he had the gout.

She gripped the ebonised wooden handle of the silver teapot and poured the aromatic liquid into a Sèvres cup. She had seen the white Sèvres tea set before with its gilding and its bucolic scene of a young man gazing adoringly at his lover. What she hadn't seen before was the oval straight-sided silver teapot with the swan-head spout that was engraved with Napoleon's imperial coat of arms.

'This is a new acquisition. I've lost count of how many items of his you own. Are you determined to collect all of his possessions?' she asked, placing the teapot back on the tray.

'That little man thought he could conquer the world—that he could best me. Well, I showed him. I defeated him and now I get to enjoy the things he held dear.' He popped a piece of marzipan into his mouth.

She narrowed her eyes. 'You never sent word about the painting. Did you go to purchase it? I hope you did not encounter any trouble.'

There was a hesitation to his movements. 'It went well. I am deciding where to hang it. I still do not understand why he would not loan it to you so you could show it to me while I decided if I wanted to purchase it.'

'I imagine he was concerned he would not receive payment and the artwork would remain here.'

He gave a careless snort. 'Why don't you tell me what I have been missing?'

'There is not much to tell. I've come from the Royal Academy where Mr West has asked me to assist him in determining the placement of works for the latest exhibition. I hope you will be feeling better by the time it opens. The works are quite moving. And, if you were planning on attending the Nettlefords' ball, I understand they will be serving lobster cakes. That alone should tempt you enough to leave this house.'

Prinny's hand stilled over the treats, and he cleared his throat. 'I hope to be…feeling right as rain by then,' he mumbled.

Evidently the prince was feeling better, since he was eating the marzipan as if it were his last meal. Perhaps she should have brought him a smaller selection. Eating that many pieces in rapid succession could not be good for one's digestion.

'I'm glad you're enjoying the marzipan.'

Prinny looked down as if he hadn't realised he had eaten nearly the entire basket and held it out to her. 'Would you care for one?'

She selected the smallest piece. 'I assume you

will be well enough to attend the opening of *Douglas* at Drury Lane. They say Mrs Siddons will be returning to the stage.'

Prinny's smile dropped. 'I hope so.'

'Then I look forward to seeing you there. I assume you will not bar me from your box,' she teased.

He smiled affectionately at her. 'I would never do such a thing to you.'

'I have the notion that a small stroll would serve you well, since you did finish that entire basket of marzipan. What say you we take some air in your gardens?'

Prinny's eyes darted from Olivia, to the guard by the door, and back to Olivia again. 'I suppose one short stroll outside could do no harm.'

# *Chapter Eleven*

Gabriel had arrived home from Parliament and been sitting at his desk, staring at his only clue for what felt like hours. Something about the handwriting on the note found on the gunman tickled his brain, but he could not for the life of him determine what it was. Hopefully a quiet evening at home would lift his spirits.

By the time he emerged from his rooms dressed for dinner, he was looking forward to a pleasant meal and another night in his wife's bed. From the staircase landing, his gaze travelled down and settled on Olivia, who was speaking with Bennett in the entrance hall.

Her shiny dark hair was swept up, exposing the creamy skin of her neck and graceful shoulders. Her gown was the colour of irises and her arms were visible through the long semi-opaque sleeves. As she turned towards the staircase, the diamonds around her neck sparkled in the candlelight and Gabriel was blessed with a delicious view of the upper curves of her breasts. His lips rose, knowing he would have her all to himself for the entire evening.

Then he spied the wrap Bennett was holding out for her. As he dashed down the stairs, she spotted him.

'Where are you off to?' he asked without even offering her a greeting.

She dismissed Bennett with a slight nod and their butler disappeared down the hall. 'I am going to Vauxhall to meet friends for dinner and to see a performance of Madame Saqui.'

Was he acquainted with these friends? Deciding she looked much too enticing to be strolling about Vauxhall without him, he pulled the sides of her wrap together over her breasts. The fabric was warm and soft, and reminded him of her skin. To stop himself from touching her, he held onto the edges of her wrap.

'What are you doing?' she asked, looking down at his hands.

'Making certain you do not catch a chill.'

She narrowed her eyes, but did not push his hands away. 'That is very considerate of you. I suppose this concern has nothing to do with any late-night activities you are anticipating.'

'I have no notion of which activities you are

speaking of,' he replied with what he hoped was an innocent expression. 'You look quite beautiful this evening.'

Her body stiffened. 'Thank you,' she replied, backing away from him so he was forced to release her wrap.

Had he offended her? He had not intended to. 'It is a cool evening. I shall inform your coachman to place a warm brick in your carriage.'

'Comte Janvier has kindly offer to take me in his carriage, so there is no need to concern yourself.'

Every nerve in Gabriel's body snapped to attention. Her phrasing could not have been worse. 'He is to be your escort for the evening?' he asked, raising his chin.

'Yes, he was invited as well and offered to accompany me weeks ago.'

'Well, I believe I shall wait with you and greet the Comte when he arrives.'

'There is no need. You should go about your affairs.' She walked away from him to the gilded mirror next to the door and adjusted her hair.

'Dinner and a good book await me this evening. I am in no hurry.' Not wanting her to witness his jealousy, he turned away and met the condescending gaze of his great-grandfather, staring down at him from a life-sized portrait of the man on horseback. Gabriel wanted to tell him to mind his own business. It was quite evident he was behaving like an overly protective bore, but she was his wife. His. He simply needed to be certain that Comte Janvier understood that.

A knock echoed through the marble hall and drew Gabriel's attention to the front door. As he adjusted his cuffs, soft footsteps filled the hall, announcing Bennett's arrival before he appeared.

'You can leave now, Gabriel. I am certain that is Janvier and Bennett can manage the door.' She addressed his reflection in the mirror and raised her brows expectantly.

'I believe I will remain right where I am.'

She looked as if she was about to speak, but there was no time since Bennett had opened the door. Gabriel was standing out of Janvier's line of vision when the man walked inside. Not that it would have mattered anyway since the Frenchman's eyes were firmly fixed on Olivia. He couldn't blame him. She was stunning. It was apparent to Gabriel that Janvier was considering the different ways he would like to take her. The man was perilously close to losing consciousness.

Gabriel cleared his throat. Janvier turned and his head snapped back as he realised Olivia's husband was standing a few feet away.

'Ah, Your Grace, what an unexpected surprise.' He held out his hand.

Gabriel took his gloved hand and squeezed the

man's long, slender fingers tightly, wishing he could break a bone or two. When he released his grip, he was pleased to see Janvier wiggle his fingers around before placing them at his side.

'It's kind of you to accompany my wife this evening, since I will not be available to attend to her until she arrives home.'

He was staking his claim and Gabriel was satisfied to catch the understanding that crossed Janvier's face.

'I shall make every effort to ensure Her Grace's every need is met.'

*French bastard.* 'I shall have to recommend my tailor to you. Mr Weston cuts a very fine coat.'

A forced smile rose on Janvier's lips. 'That is very kind of you. However, I believe my tailor does an exceptional job.'

From the corner of his eye, Gabriel could see Olivia cross her arms. So they weren't exactly being subtle. They were men. He turned to her and held out his hand. 'I will see you into the carriage.'

He knew she was fighting a desire to turn around from both of them and stomp back up to her rooms. She placed her white-gloved hand onto his arm and, for the briefest instant, the pressure of her fingers dug through the sleeve of his tailcoat. He bit back a smile at her subtle silent statement.

They stopped a few feet from the carriage and

waited for the footman to open the door. Gabriel leaned down and let a small puff of breath float over his wife's ear and neck. 'Hold on to some of that fire till you return, Livy. It will make for a most enjoyable night in bed.'

She glanced at her friend, but he was busy speaking with his coachman.

'You are presuming I will allow you in my bed after that display,' she scolded him in a low voice.

'In order to have another child, I believe I need to be in your bed—frequently—if we are truly intent about this. One time probably was not sufficient.'

'Perhaps it was sufficient. Perhaps I am already carrying a child.'

*Our child. The child would be ours.* Gabriel looked over at Janvier and wanted to plant a facer for all new reasons. 'I believe it is best to keep trying until we are certain,' he whispered back, taking her gloved hand to his lips, searching her eyes for even the slightest reaction.

Immediately, she pulled her hand away and re-adjusted her wrap. 'You believe I can be so easily charmed after that display of male dominance? I am not a bone to be fought over by two dogs.'

'No, you are not a possession. You are the woman I chose above all others to marry and would do so again without hesitation. I was simply reminding him that you are my Duchess and should he offend your honour in any way, he will answer to me.'

Janvier approached Olivia's side and she shifted her attention to adjusting her gloves.

'Shall we?' Janvier asked, moving his gaze between Olivia and Gabriel.

'Yes, let's not keep our friends waiting.'

She allowed Gabriel to help her into the carriage. His eyes were still on her when Janvier edged past him.

'I shall have her home before sun up,' the Frenchman said as he entered the carriage and took his seat across from Olivia.

Gabriel gave a curt nod before he stepped back, allowing the footman to raise the step and close the door with a click. Within minutes, Comte Janvier's carriage pulled away with his wife inside.

Striding into their house, Gabriel went directly to the dining room, needing to focus on the food and drink set before him and not on the fact that his wife, who might already be carrying his child, was out with another man. As Gabriel settled into his chair, Bennett nodded to one of the footmen to begin serving the first course.

'Bennett, has Comte Janvier been a frequent guest of the Duchess?'

'He has attended a few of her dinner parties.'

'And has he escorted her anywhere else in his carriage.'

'No, sir. This is the first time.'

Gabriel sat back on the red-velvet cushion of his chair and watched one of his footmen ladle turtle soup into his bowl. He knew that he and Olivia had lived separate lives under the same roof. In regards to his responsibility to the Crown that situation had made things infinitely easy for him. Yet seeing a man drive off in his carriage with Olivia had set the pulse in his temples pounding.

He knew they'd agreed to be monogamous with each other while they were trying to conceive another child. He trusted Olivia to hold to their agreement. What he did not trust was that slippery Frenchman.

Gabriel scraped his chair back suddenly, startling the footmen and Bennett. He walked to the window and looked out at the cobblestone street below. The sound of carriage wheels and men on horseback going to and fro could be heard through the glass. He had not lied to her. He would marry her all over again, even knowing it would lead to their estrangement. The time they had spent together during their courtship and before Nicholas was born was some of his happiest, before things went horribly wrong. Would it be possible to have that again?

He should have insisted on going with her. He

should not have handed her into the care of that wolf. It was too late now.

Drawing in a deep breath, Gabriel turned and slowly walked to the table. Sitting back in his chair, he reminded himself that Olivia was very capable of handling men.

By the time Olivia and Janvier left Vauxhall a soft rain had begun to fall. In the dim light and the gentle sway of the comfortable carriage Olivia should have felt completely relaxed. She'd had a pleasant dinner with friends and enjoyed an entertaining performance. Unfortunately the spectre of her husband had hovered over her all evening.

When Gabriel had asked her about her plans, good breeding had almost prompted her to suggest he join their little party. She'd had to bite her lip to prevent the words from escaping. There was no reason to foster a friendship with him when their reconciliation was only temporary.

Then she heard his voice rattling around in her brain once more. *You are the woman I chose above all others to marry and would do so again without hesitation.*

She rubbed her brow and mentally berated herself. Giving in to thoughts of Gabriel could only lead to confusion and heartache. She couldn't trust him. Those were simply pretty words that fell from his lips to charm her. He was not sincere.

If only being around him hadn't felt so wonderful.

Her thoughts drifted to the kiss he'd placed on her hand. She could not deny that simple kiss on her gloved hand had left her body anticipating more of his touch. What was wrong with her? She hadn't even felt the warmth of his lips through the kidskin, just the pressure, and suddenly she felt eager to be home. She rubbed her knuckles, trying to erase the sensation.

'I shall venture to blame the hour on your silence and not my company,' Janvier said with a smile as he watched her from across the carriage.

Pulling her thoughts from Gabriel's lips, Olivia gazed at her friend. 'Forgive me, your carriage is quite comfortable and the hour is late. I fear the combination of the two has made me rather sleepy.'

'It pleases me that you are so relaxed in my presence. I could sit beside you and you could rest your head on my shoulder. I would gladly be your cushion.'

'That would not be proper though, would it?'

'No one will see. We are alone. My staff is trained to knock before they open the door. Do not concern yourself with what they would think if we are discovered together.'

Before she could object, Janvier moved across the carriage and settled himself next to her, pressing his thigh against hers. The scent of bay rum followed his movement. There was no denying he was an attractive and charming man who probably would make an ideal lover if she were so inclined. Wondering about how his kisses would compare to Gabriel's, Olivia let her gaze drop to his smooth, full lips.

A small devilish grin creased the corners of his mouth. 'My shoulder is at the ready.'

'I do not believe I am that tired.'

'Shall I return to my side of the carriage?'

She shook her head. 'I am no longer the young ingénue.'

'Were you ever naïve? Somehow I think you were born with an air of sophistication.'

'That is because we met when I am already at such an advanced age.'

Janvier's laughter improved her mood. Friends could do that. 'You are far from your dotage.'

'That is reassuring to hear. I simply meant you did not know me when I was a young girl. I suppose, like most, I harboured romantic fantasies.'

'And now?'

'And now I understand the realities of life.'

He shook his head. 'In life there is always room for romance.'

'Is there? I do believe I have long disregarded that notion.'

'Perhaps you need to be reminded.'

His lips were touching hers before she even realised he'd moved. The only sound was the raindrops pinging off the carriage roof and the turning of the carriage wheels over the cobblestones.

She was so stunned by the soft, coaxing seduction that it took her a few moments to react. Realising he was actually kissing her, Olivia pushed against his chest and pulled her head back.

Before she could issue him a set down, Janvier spoke. 'Forgive me. I misunderstood the direction of our conversation. I assure you, I meant no disrespect.'

The sly man had already stopped her from accusing him of being insolent and issuing a slap across his face. Years of wearing a polite mask made it easy for her to appear completely composed. 'Let us be clear, I have no intention of beginning a liaison with you. I enjoy your company, but if you are seeking something more we should part ways.'

Janvier slid across the carriage and resumed his seat. 'I understand. I hope you will continue to allow us to be friends.'

'As long as we understand one another.'

'We do. It will not happen again.'

The carriage came to an abrupt halt and as predicted there was a knock on the door. Once Janvier uttered his consent, the door to the carriage

opened and the steps were lowered. 'Until I see
you again,' he said, tipping his head respectfully.

Olivia nodded and allowed the footman to assist her onto the wet pavement as he held a large
umbrella over her. Placing a hand on her stomach,
she took a deep breath of the damp air and looked
up at the vast expanse of her house. There were
times when thoughts of retreating to the country
with no men for miles appeared to be an excellent notion.

By this time of night, the fire in Gabriel's study
had died to a low flame. Hours before, he'd discarded his coat and reclined in his most comfortable chair in casual elegance, resting his feet on
an embroidered footstool. Tonight he had chosen
to reread the *Iliad* while he sipped his favourite
port. He should have been completely relaxed.
Except every so often, his attention was drawn
to the bracket clock on the mantel.

Eventually Bennett informed him that Comte
Janvier's carriage had pulled up to the house.
Glancing at the clock, Gabriel snapped his book
shut and took note of the late hour. He walked
into the entrance hall just as Olivia began to climb
the stairs. She appeared lost in thought. He called
her name softly, but she continued her ascent. He
called to her again, this time a bit louder.

She jumped and turned towards him. This was

not the way he would have preferred to begin seducing her. She approached him slowly, her concentration fixed on unbuttoning her gloves.

He searched for something to ask instead of questioning why she had remained out till such a late hour, making him worry for her safety. 'Did you enjoy Madame Saqui?'

'She was exceptional as always.' The buttons on her right glove seemed to hold great interest and he realised she had yet to look him in the eye.

'Would you care for my assistance with those?'

Her eyes finally met his and she smiled politely. 'No, thank you. Were you on your way upstairs, or did my arrival disturb your work?'

He wondered if he was persistent in questioning her, if she would tell him what was occupying her thoughts. It was obvious something was troubling her.

'I was just reading and heard you come in. Would you care to join me?'

She hesitated before she nodded and walked past him towards his study. Once inside she dropped those troublesome gloves on the table beside the chair he had vacated and walked towards the fire to warm her hands. Her delicate profile was illuminated in the soft glow and Gabriel took advantage of the opportunity to study the slope of her nose and her enticing bow of her lips.

Realising Janvier must have done nothing to

warm her during their ride home, Gabriel went to the table near his desk and removed the stopper from the crystal decanter housing his favourite port. His gaze continued to shift to her as he poured the wine into a glass. By the time he reached her side it appeared her attention was back to her surroundings.

He held the glass out to her. 'This should warm you.'

'Thank you, although I truly am not that cold.'

Could her quiet demeanour be a result of his actions with Janvier? If he wanted to regain her favour, he needed to extend an olive branch of sorts. He was not accustomed to apologising, but there were times it was necessary.

'Please forgive my behaviour with the Comte earlier this evening. I only wished to ensure that he would treat you with the utmost respect.'

She looked up from her glass. 'You had said as much before I left. I accept your apology.' Their eyes held as she slowly took a sip. Her small smile peeked out from the rim. 'Giving a woman port while entertaining her in your study, what would people say?'

'Some might say I am a man bent on seduction,' he said with a quirk of his lips.

'Only some?'

'The others would just be shocked.'

'For inviting a lady into your sacred domain or for plying her with port?'

'Could I ply you with port to seduce you?'

Olivia slowly shook her head, her eyes never leaving his. 'You forget that I am quite familiar with your methods.'

Their verbal sparring matches always made him smile. She looked away suddenly. He placed a finger on the side of her jaw and directed her gaze back to him.

'And what are my methods?'

'You will see that I drink just enough wine to lower my inhibitions sufficiently so that I agree to do things that, in the light of day, I would never consider.'

The air left Gabriel's lungs and he laughed. 'Well, Duchess, I am *very* familiar with you and know even without the assistance of drink you have done things no proper Duchess would ever consider doing in the light of day. You cannot blame wine for your actions.'

'I have no idea what you are referring to,' she said, raising her brows innocently. 'I believe you have reached an age that causes one's memory to falter.'

'Is that so? So you never swam naked with me in a pond in Kent and then ravaged me on the shoreline?'

'Ravaged is such a strong word.'

'And you never tied me to your bed with your stockings while I slept, so I would be late for my morning appointments?'

'As I recall you were late for all your appointments that day.'

'Because we never left your bed.'

'That was not entirely my fault.'

'And then there was the time you dismissed the staff from serving dinner in the dining room.'

'I simply wanted to converse with you without being overheard.'

'Because you wanted to discuss which dessert tasted better on your skin.'

'A discussion that should not be had in the presence of servants. Every Duchess is aware of that rule.'

'What about the time you crawled onto my lap in a moving carriage of your own volition and whispered sweet suggestions in my ear, leaving me no choice but to take you then and there?'

She stilled, then sauntered to the chair he had recently vacated. His gaze was drawn to her shapely bottom, the curve of which would appear as she moved.

'You appear to remember quite a bit of what I did years ago,' she said.

'You did some very memorable things. In fact, if memory serves, during one visit to see my parents did you not—'

'Yes. Yes. You made your point. You had your moments as well.'

The annoyance in her tone made Gabriel laugh. He stepped closer, and she pick up his leather-bound book and cocked her head to read the spine.

'How many times have you read this?'

'I have lost count. In any event, that is Cowper's version. It's closest to the original text,' he replied defensively.

She tossed the book on the table and reclined back in his chair. 'I had forgotten how comfortable this chair was. It almost begs one to curl up with a book and not be proper.' There was sadness in her eyes, as if she too had missed the happy times they had spent together.

'And how improper did you want to be?' he asked as his body was pulled by an invisible force to stand in front of her.

She rolled her eyes and shook her head. 'I was referring to my posture.'

'So was I,' he replied, flashing her a devilish grin.

She shifted her gaze back to the fireplace. If only he knew what was whirling through that mind of hers. Perhaps he could distract her enough to erase the sadness in her eyes.

Slowly he removed the glass from her hand and placed it on the table. This didn't seem to improve her mood, but he wasn't finished. Lifting her effortlessly into his arms, he resumed his seat and settled her on his lap with her legs draped over the armrest. Then he handed her back her glass.

'You were in my chair.' It was as much an explanation of his action as he was willing to admit to her. He guided her hand with the glass to his mouth and took a sip of port.

'I did not agree to share that with you,' she said with a furrowed brow.

'Would you care to have the wine back? I believe if you slip your tongue into my mouth you may taste some of the remnants.'

A smile tugged on the corner of her lips. 'I am in a generous mood. You may keep the wine you have stolen.'

'Unlike you, *I* do not mind sharing.'

She hid her smile with the rim of the glass and was forward enough to lick her lips slowly after taking a sip. It would be miraculous if she didn't feel his arousal underneath that beautiful bottom of hers.

He wanted her. He wanted to taste those lips. He wanted to feel the softness of her skin. He wanted to bury himself deep inside her and not pull out until they both were completely spent.

Taking his finger, he angled her face towards him and lowered his lips to hers. At first he had to coax her to open up to him, but it didn't take long before she was participating fully in the kiss—

tasting like hot cherries from the port. Could he ever be this close to her without wanting to lose himself in her?

She pushed against his chest and he reluctantly pulled back.

'I have no desire to ruin my gown with wine.' She sat up and placed her glass on the table next to them. But instead of resuming their kiss she rested her head on his chest.

Did that kiss have no effect on her at all? Gabriel stared up at the ceiling debating if he should kiss her again. Then he felt Olivia's fingers work on the knot at his throat.

'Do not assume I am doing anything more than ensuring that I am not the only one who is slightly dishevelled,' she said.

'I would not dream of it.'

She wasn't dishevelled in the least, but he wasn't about to point that out.

As she sat up, she unwound the linen from his neck and carelessly dropped it over the side of his chair. 'You looked a bit uncomfortable,' she explained, placing her head back on his shoulder, her soft hair tickling his neck. 'You are not considering picking that up and folding it neatly, are you?'

Surprisingly he hadn't been, until she mentioned it, and then he sneaked a glance towards the rumpled linen on the floor and resisted the urge to pick it up. The graceful fingers of her left hand parted the opening of his shirt and she softly combed her nails around his neck.

He should not be the only one missing some attire. That hardly seemed fair. Knowing where he would begin, he trailed his hand over the curve of her hip, down her lovely leg to her dainty feet, where he removed one and then the other shoe.

'What are you doing?'

'I am simply returning the favour.'

'Your heart is beating rather quickly. Are you well?' she asked in an amused voice.

He skimmed his fingers up her leg to the back of her knee and was rewarded when she shivered. 'I am well. Although I could be very well.'

'Is there such a thing as being very well?' Her warm fingers slid along his collarbone and traced the veins of his neck.

Closing his eyes at the sensation, he knew for certain there was such a thing as being very well. She enjoyed playing the unaffected minx, but when his fingers slid between her thighs he was pleased to discover she was slick.

Her body stilled and she parted her legs further for him. As he slid one and then a second finger inside her she clenched his collar. He slowly pumped his fingers in and out, spreading her wetness.

'I believe this might constitute being very well,' he commented with a satisfied grin.

'It might,' she moaned, moving her hips to his rhythm.

'Now that hardly sounds promising. I think I need to try harder.'

'Harder, yes.'

He pumped his fingers more forcefully. Her legs began to tremble. She was rubbing her face on his shoulder like a kitten and he was uncertain who wanted her to come more. He loved knowing he could make her feel this way.

'Come for me, Livy.'

She crushed her lips to his. The kiss was urgent and demanding, and within seconds he swallowed her cry.

Gabriel kissed her softly. The small kisses she gave in return gave him hope that she still felt this burning attraction whenever they were together.

He cradled her in his arms. There were nights early in their marriage when he had held her in unguarded moments just like this. 'I want you, Livy. I want you now.'

Her eyes met his. 'Then let us go to bed.'

'I cannot wait.'

'Where would you like me?'

'Here, in this chair.'

She appeared amused by his statement—amused and intrigued. 'In this chair?'

'You did say it was comfortable. I believe you remember how it is done.'

She glared at him until the corner of her lips twitched. 'I do believe that would be highly improper for people of our station.'

Gabriel lowered his mouth so his lips were less than an inch from hers. 'Blame it on the wine.'

He kissed her again, savouring her sweet taste. As she shifted on his lap, the friction did wonders for what was inside his breeches. Her hands were in his hair and his hands held the sides of her face, not wanting her to pull away.

She shifted again. Now she was straddling him, with her gown tangled up between them. He always loved this position and slid his hands around her to cup her bottom. She undid the buttons of his waistcoat as he trailed slow kisses along her jaw on the way to her neck. His tongue licked her skin. Every inch of her tasted like heaven.

Olivia worked frantically on the last few buttons of his waistcoat before she cried out in frustration. A gentleman's duty was always to assist a lady in need. Pushing her hands aside, he pulled hard at the opening of his waistcoat. Buttons popped and flew to the floor.

Before long his waistcoat was off and all he could think about was losing himself inside her. She pulled his shirt over his head and it went sailing somewhere to his left.

They were kissing again and her warm hands slid over his chest. She had too many layers of clothing on. He reached for her breasts. Her stays had pushed them up so a good amount of them were already exposed. His hands were trying to lift them from their confines, but Olivia's bloody dressmaker had her body secured tightly in her gown.

Gabriel moved his hands and tried to unfasten all the tiny corded loops on her back. It felt like hours before he was able to slide the sleeves of her gown down her shoulders. She pushed against his chest, stood and shimmied out of her gown till it pooled at her feet.

If their heated kisses hadn't made his body burn, the outline of Olivia's curvaceous form through her chemise with the light from the fireplace behind her was incinerating him.

Jumping to his feet, he kissed her hard, trying to give his body time to calm down enough so he wasn't throwing her over the chair and pounding into her.

She moaned and it almost did him in.

He tugged on the silk ribbon of her stays and she broke the kiss to remove it. Their eyes locked. He took hold of the linen near her thigh, lifted her chemise over her head and threw it behind her. A faint *whoosh* sound came from the fireplace and the firelight flared. They looked in unison as the remnants of her chemise were swallowed up by the flames. She shifted her open-mouthed stare to him, then pressed her lips firmly together.

'I'll buy you twenty more,' he said and sucked on the tip of her breast until her back bowed.

She was so warm—and tasted so good. He practically tore off his trousers before he lavished attention on the other breast. He needed to be inside her and he was going to do it now in that chair. Olivia let out a soft gasp when he picked her up and tugged her down onto his lap.

Within minutes she shifted and straddled him again. The feel of her warmth as she slid down over him brought a groan from his lips. He didn't even need to move her. She was setting a rhythm on her own. He was in heaven. Nothing existed outside this room and the only thing he was aware of was the woman above him. He dropped his head back as she picked up the pace and rotated her hips. His hands fell away at his sides. She could do anything to him at that moment and he would let her. He would grant her any request.

It was impossible to steady his breathing when he watched himself enter Olivia—again and again. The delicious friction would soon be his undoing.

He needed to go deeper inside of her and coaxed her to shift positions so she was kneeling on the seat of the wingback chair facing away from him and he was standing behind her. The first time he entered her, he drove himself so deep he almost came with that first thrust. He tried to hold back his release as long as he could, entering her again and again. Eventually his mind shattered into a million pieces as he came. When she let out a raspy cry and her body collapsed against the chair, he knew she had found her pleasure again.

Dropping his head down on her back, he wrapped his arms tightly around her limp form. The erratic pounding of her heart matched his own. He had no notion how long they remained that way, just that he had the strongest desire not to let her go—ever. It was a notion that unsettled him.

Eventually he released her. Her cascading sable hair shone in the firelight, the pins were lost somewhere in and around his chair. She looked sinful. She looked like a woman thoroughly satisfied. She looked like a woman he would have an impossible time putting aside again.

He sat back in the chair, cradling her on his lap.

When her lips rose into a mischievous grin, that dimple he always adored appeared on her left cheek. 'This was entirely your idea.'

'I take full responsibility for the state you are in,' he replied, placing a kiss on her nose.

'Good. I am glad we agree I was the innocent party in this episode.'

'If I do not contradict that statement, will you agree to such episodes in the future?'

She ran her fingers through the strands of his hair. Gabriel was positive it was standing on ends, making him look rather ridiculous. 'You burned my chemise,' she stated simply.

'You made me ruin one of my favourite waistcoats and I have a neckcloth lying on the *floor.*'

'What will the servants think?' she teased.

He trailed a finger down her neck to the swell of her breasts and then the valley between. 'I'd venture to think the maids will be shocked to finds buttons and pins scattered around this rug come morning.'

She really had beautiful breasts. Just as he began circling the tip of one with his finger, it hardened to a delicious bud. He would never grow tired of eliciting a reaction from her.

'We should go upstairs,' she suggested. 'The staff will be up and about soon, and I would not want them finding us like this.'

She was just too tempting. He lowered his mouth and ran his tongue around her nipple. 'Like what?'

She pushed his shoulder playfully. 'Do stop, Gabriel, unless you can finish what you are attempting to start.'

He placed his hand over his heart. 'You wound me, madam.'

'Your sense of self-worth is quite large. You can easily withstand the small wounds I can inflict.'

But could he? And why did Gabriel get the sense that the wounds she could inflict on him were worse than those given by anyone else?

He helped her to stand. 'The rain has stopped.' Then he glanced down. 'I am still wearing my shoes and stockings.'

'It appears so. At least you will have an easier time dressing. What will I do without my chemise?'

'Here.' He picked up his shirt and lowered it over her body. The hem came down to her knees.

'I am not even remotely respectable in this.'

He looked up from buttoning his trousers. She was right. If anything she looked wanton—like a woman who knew how to coax a man into her bed and keep him there for days. Her breasts were visible through the linen of his shirt, and he instinctively licked his lips.

'See.'

'It's late. No one will see you. However if you truly are that concerned how you look…' He took his waistcoat with the missing buttons and helped her into it. Then he picked up his cravat and draped it loosely around her neck a few times. 'That's better.'

She eyed him sideways. 'Somehow I do not believe I would be admitted to Almack's dressed like this.'

'Dressed like that, it would be best if I never saw you anywhere near Almack's—or anywhere else for that matter.' Thoughts of her in Manning's studio flooded his brain and he unclenched his fist.

'Never fear, I can assure you this will be the last time I will be wearing your clothes.'

The statement, uttered so casually, left him disconcerted. Focusing his attention on his wife's bottom as she bent down to retrieve her slippers and gown, Gabriel ran his hand up the inside of her thigh, making her jump.

'Are you trying to seduce me, Gabriel? At your age, I would think you would not have the stamina.'

'I think we should find out.'

When he grabbed for her as she ran to the door, her laughter filled the room. He cursed his stupidity for not locking the door earlier when he invited her inside.

He was about to throw her over his shoulder to take her up to his bedchamber and prove to her that he had the stamina of a young buck, when he noticed she stood frozen in the open doorway.

Stepping behind her, he looked over her head and saw a flustered Bennett with one of the upstairs maids. The young girl's eyes were wide as she looked at Olivia and they opened wider when she spotted Gabriel's bare chest.

Quickly he pushed Olivia behind him and motioned for them to enter the room as if nothing unusual had occurred. Turning slowly while keeping Olivia behind him, he backed her out into the darkened hall and closed the door.

'I wonder if Bennett will ever recover?' she mused.

'He has been exposed to our scandalous ways in the past.'

'Yes, but I do not recall him ever finding us in such a state.'

'Colette appears to have recovered nicely from her shock. The last time I saw her, she bobbed her curtsy to me with only a slight blush.'

'Well, she did see a rather different side of you.'

Gabriel shifted uncomfortably, recalling how much of his backside his wife's maid saw.

'What time do you suppose it is?' she asked.

From the window at the end of the hall, faint rays of light were casting bluish squares onto the floor. 'Four?'

'No, that cannot be possible.'

'You did arrive home rather late. It must be

four. Bennett watches over the cleaning of my study every morning at four.'

Olivia stopped ahead of him on the stairs. 'Why?'

He gently prodded her to keep walking. 'Why what?'

'Why does Bennett oversee the maid?'

'There are times I leave my papers about. He makes certain they are left undisturbed.'

'But why not Mrs Mitchell? She is our house-keeper. I would think she would oversee the clean-ing of your study.'

Why did she have to be so astute? 'Because Bennett has been seeing to the study of the Duke of Winterbourne ever since I can remember. It is simply his domain.'

When they reached her bedchamber there was a distinct hesitation before she looked up at him. 'Will you be coming inside?'

He reached around her and opened the door. As much as he wanted to, Gabriel knew he could not sleep for long. He had much to do. If he left her bed two hours from now, he might disturb her sleep. Or worse yet, sleeping next to Olivia might cause him to oversleep. He shook his head and kissed her cheek. 'I will only disturb you when I rise.'

Was that disappointment he saw cross her face? In the dim light it was difficult to tell.

'Very well, but I will be awake before seven for my portrait session.'

Muscles that had been wonderfully relaxed suddenly tightened up. He was just about to ask her why she was torturing him, when she placed a finger to his lips.

'I assure you. No one will know I sat for it when it is exhibited. There is even the slight chance Mr West will not agree to include it.'

One could only hope.

They entered her room and he closed the door behind them. 'Does Colette know she is to tell no one of your association with the painting?'

'Of course.'

He should forbid her from continuing to sit for the artist, but it was clearly something that brought her joy. How could he cause her any more sorrow?

He tasted her lips one last time before pulling away and striding to the door to his bedchamber. As he placed his hand on the cool metal of the handle, he had the strongest urge to have one last look at her. She had not moved from where he had left her. 'I may allow for these sittings, Livy, but I do not have to like it.'

When the door closed, Olivia's slippers and clothes fell from her hands. Squeezing her eyes shut, she tried to erase the memory of him standing near her bed without his shirt. His scent was on the shirt he'd placed on her, and she rubbed her arms over the soft linen. Instead of tearing it off, she decided it would be comfortable to sleep in.

She lit one of the candles flanking the mirror on her dressing table and peered at her reflection. She looked like a woman who'd spent the night rolling around in bed with her lover—only they had not used a bed—and those memories would not be easy to forget.

Closing her eyes and rubbing her forehead didn't help. Breathing deeply made no difference either. Every nerve in her body was tingling because she couldn't stop thinking about having Gabriel deep inside of her. She groaned and lowered her head to her arms.

Going back to a celibate life after they conceived another child was supposed to be the easy part. Now Olivia wasn't sure that would be true. Her body felt alive again. Making love to him made her feel desirable. It made her feel powerful. It was addictive—or perhaps that was Gabriel.

Janvier had kissed her. Olivia knew if she showed the least bit of encouragement he would take her to his bed—or in his carriage. She did not believe he would be very particular.

But she felt nothing from his kiss; no spark of passion, no desire to straddle him and no fierce need to have him all to herself. Those feelings were reserved for her husband.

Gabriel had said some lovely things to her tonight. He'd even apologised for his behaviour—an act that was unprecedented. Why was he being so nice?

Olivia grabbed her hairbrush and pulled it through her hair with forceful strokes, attempting to rattle her brain enough that she would stop considering his feelings about her. She was a grown woman who understood how the world worked. It was rare to have a marriage based on love. There were only a few marriages she knew of that were. While it might be painful to witness the looks those men gave their wives, long ago she'd accepted her husband would never look at her that way. She had been dealt a different hand in life and now she accepted that.

She was giving herself a headache, not to mention her eyes were having trouble staying open. Blowing out the candles, she crawled under the blankets and arranged all the pillows snugly around her. Their weight and warmth made her feel secure. Closing her eyes, she wondered if she really would manage to wake before seven o'clock.

# Chapter Twelve

It felt as if she had been asleep for only five minutes when Olivia heard Colette humming. Placing one of her many pillows over her head to muffle the noise, Olivia rolled onto her stomach. There was definite activity in her dressing room with the splashing sound of water being poured into her tub. She would never fall back to sleep now. Tossing the pillow aside, she opened her eyes.

She spied Colette shaking out the dress that she had worn last night and then retreat into her dressing room. Peering over the edge of her bed, she scanned the floor and saw no other evidence of how she had spent the evening.

Her maid re-entered the bedchamber and stopped when she saw Olivia was awake.

'Why are you humming?'

Bobbing a respectful curtsy, Colette had no luck suppressing her smile. 'Please forgive me if I woke you. It's a lovely morning.'

Olivia thought it would be better if she were able to sleep longer. 'What is the commotion in my dressing room?'

'His Grace ordered a bath to be ready for you at seven. He said you were not to be disturbed until then.'

Olivia rubbed her brow and stood, allowing Colette to help her into her dressing gown. 'What about Nicholas? Surely he did not bar Nicholas from entering my room.'

'I do not believe so. However, His Grace did have breakfast with his lordship in the nursery already. Perhaps that is why he did not wake you today.'

'The Duke ate in the nursery?'

'Yes, madam.'

Her world was becoming a very strange place. First her husband appeared to have suddenly grown attracted to her again and now he was eating breakfast with their son.

The heat from the bath water was a balm for the areas of her body that were a bit tender after the vigorous activities of last night. She was not going to think about the thoughtful gesture on Gabriel's part. She was not going to reminisce about the times after rather spirited nights of love making, when Gabriel had ordered a bath drawn for her in the morning. And she absolutely was not about to consider why he'd left William Cowper's translation of the *Iliad* on the table next to her bath.

Gabriel was in excellent spirits as he made his way to see Prinny at Carlton House. Although he checked on Nicholas each morning, today he'd decided to have breakfast with him. Spending time with his son in the nursery brought back fond memories of when his own father had sat in that very room playing with Gabriel and his three brothers.

Perhaps his house might once again be the very noisy place it had been when Gabriel was a child. The image of playing blind man's bluff with Olivia in her picture gallery with four or five children dashing about made him smile. There was no reason they needed to stop at two children.

His carriage rocked to a stop under the *porte-cochère* of Carlton House and he looked out at the immense Corinthian columns. He needed to shake her from his mind long enough to focus on his duty to protect Prinny. But as he made his way down the hall to Prinny's private apartment, Gabriel couldn't help wondering if Olivia was enjoying the bath he had arranged for her. He glanced at his watch and pictured her smooth skin glistening in the water at that very moment.

Once again he arrived as Prinny was sitting down to breakfast, this time in the Gothic Dining

Room. The Regent painted a lonely picture, sitting by himself at the enormous table in the long panelled room normally used for dinner parties. As Gabriel crossed the threshold, Prinny motioned with his fork for Gabriel to sit.

'This marks a change for you,' Gabriel said, taking the seat to his right. 'I had not thought you ever took breakfast in this room.'

Prinny swallowed a mouthful of ham and reached for his glass of wine. 'I never do. But you have me held up in this fortress for a week and I am growing bored of my rooms.' A bored Prinny was not a good thing. 'Fill up a plate and join me, Winter.'

'Thank you, but I have already eaten this morning.' There was no mistaking the meaning behind the pursed lips of his host. 'However, I am sure I can find something to tempt me.'

That appeared to appease Prinny, because his mouth curved into a smile for the first time since Gabriel had entered the room. A plate and utensils were laid out before him and he accepted a cup of coffee to be polite rather than quench his thirst. Stirring sugar into his cup, Gabriel tried to find the perfect way to break the news that they were no closer to finding the person who wanted Prinny dead. He decided to be direct.

'You have said nothing about my new painting,'

Prinny said, motioning with his fork to a painting that hung over the sideboard.

So they would make small talk first. Gabriel took a cursory glance at the painting of people. 'It's quite nice.'

Prinny snorted. 'Quite nice, he says. Quite nice is that cup in your hand. That, my friend, is a stunning example of an Italian master. Part of a collection owned by Boney's sister, Pauline.'

Gabriel looked back at the painting and then at Prinny, who had shifted his attention back to his breakfast. 'How in the world did you acquire that?'

'Olivia.'

'My Olivia?' Gabriel choked out, his eyes widening.

Prinny's hand paused with his glass halfway to his lips. 'What ho? *My Olivia?* Careful or you may catch yourself sounding like a man who actually cares for his wife.'

Not up for being baited, Gabriel knew enough to ignore the comment. For years Prinny had admonished him about the state of his marriage with Olivia while he went about ignoring both of his wives and taking a number of mistresses.

How was it that Olivia would know about a painting that belonged to Napoleon's sister? 'How did Olivia help you acquire that?'

'She was approached to authenticate the piece

and told me about it. Capital gel, that wife of yours. This is the painting you took me to purchase. In fact, she was originally to accompany me to Mr Owen's that day, but she needed to be home to personally see to the last-minute arrangements for your boy's breeching ceremony.'

Olivia would have been in the carriage that day? Ice crept along Gabriel's veins as he thought how close she had been to lying dead in a pool of blood.

'I suppose,' Prinny continued, breaking into his thoughts, 'I could have postponed the purchase, but I was too eager to see it so I contacted you instead.'

'I am surprised you did not go on your own.'

'Olivia said Owen was skittish and the royal carriage would have attracted too much attention in that area.' He began cutting into his ham and eyed Gabriel's untouched plate. 'I imagine you ate something delicious for breakfast. I always enjoy a meal at Winterbourne House. Say…what if I stay with you until you catch the villain trying to do me in?' His expression held all the excitement of a little boy with a master plan.

'That's not an option. We want people to believe you are forgoing all your engagements because you have the gout. If it becomes known there was an attempt on your life, it could provoke others to try to do the same. Have you forgotten that eighteen years ago your father faced two assassination attempts in one day? That second attempt might have been driven by the first. I will not take that chance with you.'

Prinny sucked his teeth, determination shining in his eyes. 'Well, I could have the gout at your house. That would not be unheard of.'

'No, you cannot. Have you already forgotten you were shot at riding in my carriage? You are safest here with the Guards protecting you. You also do not even appear to be a man afflicted. I believe people would notice.'

'Oh, pish!' he said, waving a fork in the air. 'Olivia already knows I do not have the gout.'

Gabriel's heart stopped. 'How do you know that?'

'Because she came to call on me.'

'When? You are not supposed to have any visitors outside the few people we agreed upon. Who else have you seen?'

'Only Hart and Andrew, but they are on the list. Really, Winter, I realise you do not speak to her, but she is your wife. I assumed you would give your consent and it was safe. More importantly, the dear gel brought me marzipan.'

'Which you should not have eaten because you have the gout,' Gabriel said with more force than he should have.

Prinny looked down at his plate and cut into

more of his ham while he mumbled something under his breath.

'You did not eat any of the marzipan in front of Olivia, did you?'

Prinny tossed his fork on his plate. 'Demmit, man, I rule this country and if I want to eat marzipan, I damn well will eat marzipan!'

Gabriel closed his eyes and pressed his thumb against his brow. He counted to ten. When he opened his eyes he caught Prinny's pointed stare. How was it possible that this man did not realise the danger he was in? He wanted to chastise him like a child. Instead he took a deep breath and composed his voice.

'You ate all the marzipan.'

Prinny looked away. 'I might have.' Digging into the butter with his knife, he looked back at Gabriel. 'It is only Olivia. And since she already knows I am not afflicted with the gout, what say you I stay at your house? You can protect me there.'

'No, and why do you believe she knows you do not have the gout?'

'Well I did eat all the marzipan, and she told me I appeared to be doing quite well when we went for our...'

'Your what?'

'Oh, bloody hell, this is ridiculous. I defeated Napoleon, for God's sake. I went for a walk. In my garden. With your wife. There, I said it.'

Gabriel pressed his thumb against the bridge of his nose, praying it would prevent his brain from exploding onto the table. 'Your gardens are adjacent to the park.'

'You do not have to tell me that. I'm the one who lives here!'

'And whose idea was it to go for a walk in the garden?'

'It was Olivia's. But in all fairness, the gel is unaware of the danger I am in.'

The hairs on the back of Gabriel's neck rose and he rubbed them through his collar.

'I cannot look at these walls for another day,' Prinny continued. 'You must find whoever is behind this and put their plans to rest. Olivia believes Nettleford will have lobster cakes at his ball next week. Lobster cakes! I have things to attend to and places I need to be. The world is moving and I am standing still.' He buttered a slice of toast. 'At least tell me you are closer to finding out who is behind the shooting.'

'The man who shot you is dead.'

Prinny's knife clattered to his plate. 'Dead? How is that possible? He was being held at the Tower. To my knowledge there was no hanging.'

'He did not face the gallows. Although there was no blood nor sign of a struggle, it appears he was murdered.'

The colour left Prinny's face and beads of sweat formed on his forehead. 'Poison.'

'We believe so.'

Prinny looked down at his food as one would a gutter rat and pushed his plate away.

'You are safe here,' Gabriel tried to reassure him. 'And if that were poisoned, I assure you, you would be dead by now.'

'Murdered? But how is that possible when he was being held at the Tower?'

'I am not entirely certain, but I assure you I will find out.'

Prinny drained his wine and motioned for more. 'You need to find him.'

'We will. But for the love of all that is holy, do not leave this house, do not see anyone else and trust no one.'

Gabriel entered his house frustrated they hadn't yet uncovered who was behind the assassination attempt. There was unrest up north and in the streets of London. Many people were unhappy with Prinny for the cost of his extravagant life-style. The threat could have come from anywhere.

He was about to walk into his study and write a note to Andrew when Bennett gave a discreet cough.

'Lord Hartwick is waiting for you in the Gold Drawing Room, sir.'

'The Gold Drawing Room?' Gabriel echoed, reconfirming the location.

'Yes, sir. I felt it was the safest place to keep his lordship while he waited for you.'

Striding into the room, he found Hart seated at one of the game tables with a row of cards laid out before him. He was just about to lower the Queen of Hearts onto one of the piles when he spied Gabriel.

'It's about time. I don't know how many more rounds of patience I could play before I grew bored enough to begin searching for hidden passageways.'

This was why Bennett was so indispensable. 'There are no hidden passageways.' At least none that he wanted Hart to know about.

Hart lowered the card and picked up a glass of what Gabriel assumed was his finest brandy. 'Bennett would not allow me to wait in your study, which I believe would have been infinitely more interesting than poking about here. By the way, one of your gardeners enjoys taking a nip from the bottle as he prunes your shrubbery. If Her Grace has noticed a lack of blooms recently, it's because he is cutting them off and disposing of them along with the dead branches.'

'I take it this is not a social call?'

'At this hour? While I do enjoy our amusing

conversations, you are correct. I have news. You may wish to lock the door.'

By the excited gleam in Hart's blue eyes, Gabriel knew the news he had uncovered was of no trivial matter. He took his friend's suggestion and locked the door before he took a seat at the table and waited for him to continue.

'Have you determined who was providing the information on Prinny's whereabouts to Mr Clarke?' Hart asked, tossing his head to the side to shift a lock of hair out of his eyes.

'I have not.'

'Well, I have,' he said through a smug smile.

Gabriel leaned forward and rested his arms on the table. 'Who is it?'

Hart sat back in the chair and stretched his legs out. 'I was at Lyonsdale House recently, when Julian mentioned the wedding portrait of his wife had been completed. Always the polite guest, I asked to see it.'

'I do not understand what this has to do with the gunman.'

Hart leaned forward, their knuckles almost touching, 'Because the signature on that portrait matched the handwriting on your note.' He reclined back again and arched an arrogant brow.

'You are certain?'

'I wasn't at first. Something about the signature looked familiar, but then today I realised where

I had seen such handwriting before. Are you still in possession of the note?'

Gabriel nodded.

'Let me see it and I will prove to you I have found your match.'

When Gabriel returned from retrieving it from his study, Hart spread the paper out on the game table.

'See here the swirled loop of the "m" and the down stroke of the "j"? I tell you, I have found your match.'

Although Hart was known to have an uncanny memory, Gabriel was not completely convinced. However, this was as close to a lead as he had had since the attempt on Prinny's life. He had to pursue it.

'Whose signature is it?'

'A Mr John Manning of Hanover Square.'

Gabriel's heart dropped to his stomach and the hair on the back of his neck rose. That man spent time with his wife…with his child.

'You have grown quieter than usual,' Hart said. 'What are you not telling me?'

'The gunman is dead.'

Hart's previously casual pose was replaced by one of rapt attention. 'How is that possible? He was under guard.'

Pushing away from the table, Gabriel stood and walked a few paces in agitation. Spinning back around, he ran his hand through his hair. 'I do not know. You are certain Manning might be involved?'

'I tell you, that is the man's hand. If only you had a painting of his, we could…' Hart's gaze bore into him as if he could read Gabriel's thoughts. 'Your wife is his patron. Surely there is a painting of his here?'

Dear God, this couldn't be happening, not again. *Never discount the obvious.* His father had pounded it into his head. The more he considered the facts, the harder it became to steady his breathing. Olivia had arranged the meeting between Prinny and Mr Owen. She told him not to take the royal coach and that she would take him in hers. Her carriage had the Lyonsdale crest on the side, just as his did. Just yesterday she'd persuaded Prinny to go for a walk outside in his garden where anyone in the park beyond would have had an easy shot at him. And he had heard her discuss Prinny with Manning.

He did not believe in coincidences. He knew first hand anything was possible. His past had taught him that—at a great cost. An icy chill ran through his veins.

If she were part of this, she would be tried for treason and swing from the gallows. He tried to scrub the image from his mind, but it would not go away.

'Winter, did you hear me?'

He could not do this with Hart present. 'I will search for one of his paintings. With the collection my wife is amassing, surely you can see it will take some time for me to locate his work.'

'I have solved the informant's identity before you did and yet you will not look me in the eye. If he is the person who hired Mr Clarke, you will be able to put the mystery of this assassination attempt to rest. The vile criminal will swing.'

And that was what Gabriel was beginning to fear.

## *Chapter Thirteen*

Once Hart was on his way, Gabriel rang for Bennett. 'Is Her Grace home?'

'No, sir, I believe she is at Mr Manning's studio for her sitting.'

Gabriel closed his eyes and prayed he was wrong. 'Do you know when she is expected to return?'

'No, sir, I do not.'

'Is Colette with her?'

'No, she was granted the day to visit her mother. I believe Lady Haverstraw is with Her Grace today.'

Gabriel rubbed the ring that had belonged to his father, not at all comfortable with what he was about to do. 'If she arrives home in the next hour, I need you to keep her from our rooms.'

Bennett did not look pleased and he knew it was taking all of his butler's control not to say what was on his mind.

'Do I make myself clear, Bennett?'

'Yes, sir,' Bennett replied before Gabriel took the stairs, two steps at a time.

Olivia had mentioned Manning had painted something for her. He paused in the doorway of her bedchamber and knew once he entered, his life with his wife might be changed for ever.

Taking a deep breath, he turned the handle and was met with the faint scent of honeysuckle. He had not been in the room without her in years. The curtains were drawn back, letting the light stream in through the mullioned windows. There were miniature portraits on her dressing table.

That appeared to be as good a place as any to start. He picked up each frame and squinted at the signature on each one. If any of these were painted by Manning, it would be anyone's guess from the small size of the writing.

He ran his hand through his hair and turned about the room. There was a landscape over her bed and two smaller ones flanking the large one. Who did she say Manning painted?

His entire body froze and his gaze shifted to the fireplace. There it was. Over the mantel was a portrait of Nicholas. His son was sitting on a bench wearing a blue-velvet gown, his arms wrapped around Gabriel's mother's spaniel, Caesar. Walking slowly towards it, he found the signature of the artist in the lower-right corner. His stomach dropped when he took note of the distinct curve of the 'm'.

There was no denying it. Hart was correct. Olivia's friend was the man who'd supplied the gunman with Prinny's whereabouts. However, the scrap of paper he held in his hand would not prove a thing in court. They needed to monitor Manning's movements and hope he revealed his actions.

He knew he should not waste the opportunity to try to find something that might tie Olivia to Manning's crime. His stomach rolled at the idea.

On the table beside her bed was a stack of books. He went through each one, looking for hidden notes, but found none. Her dressing table held the usual items a woman kept on hand. He checked and found no hidden compartments. Where would a woman hide her secrets?

He entered her dressing room, where just that morning he knew she'd reclined bathing in the warm water he had arranged for her. Even in the early years of their marriage, he had never had a reason to look inside his wife's wardrobe. Seven shelves of pristinely folded silks, satins and muslins were available for his perusal. How many gowns did one woman need?

Rummaging around the bottom of the immense painted cabinet, his hands touched a wooden box approximately one foot by eight inches. It didn't take long before he picked the lock. Pausing for a moment, he prepared himself for what he would find. When he lifted the lid, he stopped breathing.

Perched atop a stack of letters that were tied with a red ribbon was the miniature portrait of himself that he had given Olivia shortly after he had asked for her hand. At one time it had resided on her bedside table. Untying the packet, he thumbed through the many letters he had written to her during their betrothal. At the time, he found himself writing to her simply to receive a letter from her in return—a letter he could read over and over again.

She'd kept them. The way she had looked at him these past five years had made him believe she had burned them long ago—probably in a bonfire on one of their estates—or while singing a merry tune, drinking bottles of wine with her friends.

But she had kept them, tied with red ribbon.

There also were pressed flowers and the elaborately designed diamond-and-sapphire brooch he had given to her as a wedding present. He recalled having the brooch reset three times before he was completely pleased with the way it looked. And now it sat in a locked box at the bottom of her wardrobe.

Gabriel placed the contents back inside their wooden tomb and made certain to relock it. Standing up, he surveyed the room again. Going back into her bedchamber, he walked over to her bed and looked underneath. There he found another box. This one was unlocked and held his correspondence with her since Nicholas was born.

There were letters granting permission to order new furniture for the drawing room, his enquiries on the state of Nicholas's health when he was sick and notices to when he would be leaving town. She'd kept them. But these letters held no love tokens, no gentle reminders of pleasant memories. She hadn't even tied them with ribbon.

There they sat, the remnants of the last five years of his life—efficient, impersonal and orderly. For five years he'd buried the memory of the morning Nicholas was born. Now he could see her lying in her bed, exhausted. He thought she'd never looked more beautiful. But as he'd kissed her, she'd pushed him away and began demanding he tell her where he had been. He was not about to confess that he had been in a brothel with Madame LaGrange, so he'd said nothing.

Then she began throwing things at him—anything she could get her hands on that was close to her bed. He was so taken aback by this unprecedented outburst that he was stunned into silence.

She told him she had no wish to speak to him or let him touch her ever again. Gabriel was not the type of man to demand conjugal rights of an unwilling wife. So for five years he'd left her alone, waiting for a sign that she had forgiven him. It had appeared in these last few days that she might have found a way to move past his supposed indiscretion. Now that was the least of his concerns.

There was nothing here. He'd looked everywhere and there was no evidence that Olivia had plotted anything with the artist. She considered Prinny a friend. But she had known where he would be the day the shots were fired. Part of him believed Olivia could never intentionally harm anyone. But another part of him knew anything was possible.

Andrew walked into Gabriel's study looking like a man who needed to spend a week in bed— and not in the company of a woman. His eyes were glassy and he blinked a few times from the opposite end of Gabriel's desk as if he was having a difficult time remaining awake.

'I hope this is important enough to have James drag me here when all I have is a desire to crawl back into bed,' Andrew said.

'I take it you had a late night?'

'Hart ran off and left me to play cards alone with Prinny until sunup. I believe I owe him a decent sum, but I could not tell you for certain since I think I fell asleep in the middle of the last hand.'

'I spoke with Prinny this morning. He appeared no worse for wear.'

'Yes, well, I imagine he went to sleep when I left. I, on the other hand, had a meeting with Mr Donaldson of Bow Street, apprising him of the investigation, followed by a meeting with Colonel Collingsworth. Yet again, he offered the services of the Guards should we have need. I had finally fallen asleep, when James came knocking upon my door.'

'I believe I know who the man behind the assassination attempt is.'

That appeared to have woken Andrew up. 'How? Is it anyone I would have heard of?'

'The artist, Manning, supplied Prinny's whereabouts to Mr Clarke.' Gabriel's hands grew clammy as he said it out loud for the first time.

Andrew's eager expression fell. 'Are you certain? Olivia's Mr Manning?'

Gabriel curled his right hand into a tight fist. 'He is not Olivia's Mr Manning.' He took a deep breath. 'I want to believe she is not involved in any of this, but I never thought our uncle would do what he did. Olivia knew where Prinny would be the day of the shooting. She was the one who told him not to take the royal coach. Hell, she even arranged the meeting.' He rubbed the back of his neck.

'If what you are saying is true, she will be

charged with high treason. You are her husband. She could possibly implicate you, saying it was done with your directive.'

'I am well aware of the law, Andrew. There is no need to remind me.'

'What will you do?'

'We need proof Manning is indeed the man we are looking for. I want to know his comings and goings. If he leaves, I want him followed.'

'I take it you would like my assistance in this?'

Gabriel nodded. 'Devise a schedule for the watch. Have the men report to you and come to me the minute you uncover anything. Should you have enough evidence to take him into custody, bring him to the house in Richmond. We will hold him there for his interrogation. I want him far from the Tower and the danger that is there.'

Andrew stood. 'Of course.'

'And, Andrew, do not breathe a word of Olivia's connection to the man to anyone.'

Olivia was convinced it had been hours since anyone had uttered a word in Manning's studio. Didn't they realise how boring it was to lie still for this long? She opened her eyes and focused on the chipped wooden frame of the large mullioned window. From this angle, she could see the tops of the trees in Hanover Square. Unless someone was planning on climbing any of them, nothing outside held her interest. Surely it had to be close to the time they'd agreed her sitting would end?

Her friend had been uncharacteristically quiet for most of the morning as he painted. She had no desire to interrupt his concentration. Her sister was another matter.

'What are you reading, Victoria?' Olivia called out to where she assumed Victoria was still sitting on the sofa near the door.

'*Nightmare Abbey* by Thomas Love Peacock.'

Olivia stifled a laugh. 'Truly? What possessed you to read such a thing?'

'Who could possibly pass by a book by someone named Love Peacock? It is rather satirically amusing. I'm rather enjoying it. You may borrow it when I am finished, if you like?'

Olivia's right arm began to grow numb and she wiggled her fingers. The sound of a page being turned broke the silence of the room. Was it possible to die of boredom?

'You might want to mention to Lady Nettleford the next time you are together that I spoke to Prinny regarding her ball. I expect he will be attending.'

Victoria sighed and closed her book. 'You realise if I do mention it to her, she will talk of nothing else.'

'Yes, but she tends to become all befuddled

around the man. Perhaps this will give her time to prepare herself.'

'I thought he was suffering with an unusually severe bout of the gout. Do you think he will be recovered in five days?'

He was completely recovered, as far as Olivia could tell. It was perplexing why he continued to maintain this ruse, but she had long given up trying to understand Prinny's motivation on most things.

'I believe he will be well enough by then. Please be sure to inform her that he is partial to lobster cakes.'

'I shall send a note off to her later today,' Victoria replied with amusement in her voice.

There was no feeling in her arm. She needed to move. 'Do you have much more to paint today?' she called out, hoping that Manning was paying enough attention to hear her.

A rustling sound came from behind the canvas, then a grunt. 'I am finished for the day. The light is changing.'

When Olivia lifted her head and turned towards him, she found him scratching his pencil upon a scrap of paper at one of the tables that held his pigments. She stood and arched her spine, relieving some of the stiffness. Finally she could go to Victoria's for luncheon and stimulating conversation.

With her sister's help, Olivia changed into her own dress before they walked out from his studio onto the pavement to look for her carriage. In its place, they found a black town coach, the lacquer dulled to a matt finish, drawn by grey horses. It was unmarked, with no crest. She would have not given it further consideration except her driver was perched atop the coachman's box. She exchanged perplexed looks with Victoria before turning to her footman. 'Where is my carriage?'

He cleared his throat and shifted slightly on his feet. 'This one belongs to the household, madam. We were preparing to return for you when one of the stable hands noticed a wheel on your carriage was loose again. In order to arrive in a timely manner, we decided not to wait to have it adjusted. Unfortunately, this was the only carriage available for your use.'

She glanced at the coachman who had been recently hired. 'Why did you not bring His Grace's carriage?'

'His Grace left shortly before we did in it.'

Victoria backed away from the offending carriage and removed a handkerchief from her sleeve. 'Why do you even have such a thing? I cannot believe Winter would stand for something so decidedly worn. He probably changes his shirt at least five times a day. Why would he allow such a carriage to be kept in your stables?'

For the life of her, Olivia had no idea. She had never seen it before. She walked to the steps and climbed inside. Considering the outside of the coach looked unremarkable, the inside cushions were clean and rather plush, with black-velvet coverings. The windows, on the other hand, could use a bit of a cleaning.

Victoria sat next to her and wrinkled her nose. 'I shall send you home in my carriage.'

'Nonsense, I shall take this one. It is just for the day.'

The rain from the night before had left the roads in poor condition. Even though the cushions were plush, a number of times Olivia and Victoria had to hold on to the leather straps to keep from being jostled off the bench.

During Olivia's ride home from her sister's the road conditions had not improved and as the carriage turned a particularly sharp corner Olivia was thrown from her seat onto the rear-facing bench. She righted herself and began to adjust her skirts when she noticed a rectangular panel had opened near her feet. Assuming it was a storage area for firearms in the event of a robbery, she bent down to close it. Her attention was immediately drawn to a wooden box inside. Curious as to the contents, she lifted it out and placed it on her lap.

Expecting to see a pistol, she was confused when she looked inside. She had seen boxes like this before. Usually, the households who favoured entertaining their guests with theatricals used them. Inside she found a small mirror the size of her palm, tufts of grey, black, and red hair, pots of glue and facial paint, eye patches and glasses with plain glass lenses. Why in the world would it be in this carriage?

She had just enough time to return the box to its hiding place when the carriage slowed to a stop at her home. By the time her footman had lowered the step and opened the door, no one would've guessed Olivia was riddled with questions. Did Gabriel know about this? Surely he must since the carriage belonged to them.

Striding off towards his study, Olivia wanted answers. She raised her hand to knock and then thought better of it. She turned the handle and the door swung open. The ticking of the bracket clock was the only sound to break the silence. Her gaze skimmed over his desk to the long windows and, finally, to the chairs by the fireplace. Her husband and his secretary were nowhere to be found.

Walking further into the room, she dropped down into the chair behind his desk. Her eyes travelled to the portrait of her father-in-law, which presided over the room from his position above the fireplace. The distinguished-looking man sat regally, with his chin raised. On his pinkie he wore the ring he had given to Gabriel shortly after they were married on the night he died. A familiar pair of hazel eyes stared down at her. She could almost feel his disapproval that she was sitting in his son's chair. Well, she had a reason. His son was becoming quite an enigma.

The more she thought about that box, the more her brain filtered through the other odd things she had noticed about Gabriel over the years. The scar that Nicholas had pointed out was the most recent one. He had said it was from a fencing accident. Olivia was not convinced. There were also letters that she had seen arriving for him at strange hours of the day and night, their butler's presence during the cleaning of this room and the times he would not be in attendance at events she was sure he would have wanted to go to.

The more she thought about it, the more questions she had.

Her gaze travelled to the silver inkstand on his desk—the only object on the polished wooden surface aside from the silver Argand lamp. When she gave a pull on the brass handles of the drawer of his desk, it didn't budge.

Resting her forearms on the desk, she drummed the surface with her fingers. Something tugged at the back of her brain. It was as if she was staring at an unfinished portrait, unaware who the sitter was.

When she was a young girl, she had been adept at picking the lock of Victoria's letterbox. Did she remember how it was done? She pulled out a hairpin and lowered it to the small keyhole of the drawer.

'Olivia?'

She jerked her head up. There, in the doorway, stood Gabriel.

It was just her luck.

## *Chapter Fourteen*

After closing the door, her husband advanced towards her. She was not about to show him that she was rattled by his presence. While holding his stare, Olivia dropped the hairpin. It landed silently on the rug under his desk. Thankfully, he didn't appear to notice.

'Hello,' she said, folding her hands on the desk's gleaming, wooden surface.

Her greeting was met with silence and she felt like a child caught taking sweets intended for guests. She was a grown woman. This was her home. And she should be able to wait for her husband in any room of her choosing.

As if nature disagreed, rain began to plink a steady rhythm on the windowpanes.

'Would you care to sit down?' she asked, rising from his chair.

From the opposite side of the desk, he held up his hand to stop her. 'No, by all means.' He took a seat in one of the two cabriole chairs across from her, crossed his legs and raised a speculative brow.

Slowly she sat back down. 'I came here looking for you.'

'And you thought I would be hiding in the drawer of my desk.'

Blast it, he did see her trying to pick the lock!

She attempted to appear composed while her heart beat wildly in her chest. 'Why do you keep the drawer locked?'

'Because I do not want anyone to see the contents,' the annoying man replied, crossing his arms over his chest.

'Why?' she asked, mimicking his movement.

'I value privacy.'

'Would I find the contents shocking?'

'That depends. Suppose you tell me what you were hoping to find and I can save you the trouble of attempting to pick the lock tonight while I'm asleep.'

'I have no idea how to pick a lock.'

'Forgive me if I say I do not believe you. If you do not intend to tell me what you were hoping to find, perhaps you can tell me why you are here?'

'I sat for my portrait today.'

'I see. And is there a reason you are telling me this?'

'Yes, because the oddest thing occurred when I left the studio.'

His entire body stilled and Olivia was almost certain he was holding his breath.

'Apparently my carriage was in need of repair,' she continued, 'and when my driver returned at the designated hour to collect me, he arrived in what could only be described as a hackney coach.'

It was refreshing to know she could still shake his composed demeanour.

'He collected you in a coach for hire?'

'No, I was told it was a spare carriage that we keep. They brought it out since you were using yours.'

He leaned forward. 'What did this carriage look like?'

'As I said, it resembled a hackney coach. It was a dusty black with no coat of arms and the windows were decidedly dirty.'

'And John Coachman took you home in this?' he asked, fiddling with his ring. There was no mistaking he knew of this carriage. And he was not happy she was now aware of its existence, as well.

'He did. Why do we keep such as a conveyance?'

He shrugged nonchalantly. 'I imagine it to be one of the carriages the staff uses to move between town and the country.'

Olivia had seen those carriages before and this was not one of them. And there was also the matter of the box. She was certain there was more to it than her husband was letting on. 'There was something else odd about the carriage,' she said.

'What?'

The slightest reaction on his part might be the only clue she would gather. She leaned closer. 'I discovered a trapdoor at the bottom of one of the benches and inside I found a box.'

He broke their gaze for just a moment. If she wasn't looking so closely, she might have missed it.

'What kind of box was it?' he asked, appearing nonchalant.

'It was a box quite similar to the ones that are used for amateur theatrics.'

Not one bit of surprise crossed his features.

'Isn't that odd, Gabriel? Why do you suppose such a box as that is stored in one of our carriages? To my knowledge we do not even own a box for that purpose.'

He remained composed—too composed for her liking. 'I could not say. However, you are correct. There appears to be no reason we would own such a box.'

'So you have no explanation why it would be there?'

He shrugged again and picked an unseen string off the sleeve of his navy tailcoat. He knew something.

'Perhaps Bennett would know,' she said, as if she truly thought she would find out the answer from a man so loyal to Gabriel that he supervised the cleaning of this very room. Then it occurred to her. There was something in this room Gabriel wanted to make certain wasn't discovered by a maid while she cleaned away the dust and ashes.

Olivia glanced at the fireplace. It would be an ideal place to destroy letters he did not want other people to see.

She rose abruptly, knowing he would not give her any of the answers she needed. 'I will leave you now Gabriel. I am certain you have many matters that require your attention.'

He stood up and nodded at her—always striving to appear the perfect gentleman. 'Good day, Olivia,' he replied and she felt his gaze follow her until she crossed the threshold and closed the door.

Demmit! Gabriel shoved his chair back. Who in the hell thought it best to place her in that carriage? Very few members of his household even knew of its existence and those that did knew it was only to be used for surveillance.

Someone would be made to answer for this. Now, more than ever, they had to be operating with extreme caution. One small blunder could lead to Prinny's demise. the

Olivia wasn't foolish. She knew there was significance behind the contents of that carriage and he was fairly certain she knew it led back to him.

He took a seat at his desk, scanned the room and took in her perspective. His gaze settled on the portrait of his father. He rubbed the Pearce coat of arms on his ring. His father knew enough not to trust anyone with what he did. He was even wise enough not to trust his closest brother. Gabriel had learned that lesson the hard way.

Olivia had been about to pick the lock to his desk drawer. Of that, he was certain. He just had no notion of what she would have been searching for.

Taking off his ring, he slid out the small shaft that was hidden within a well behind the stone and twisted it until it clicked securely in place, forming a small key. He used it to unlock his desk drawer. His gaze skirted past the loaded pistol and sheets of blank paper to the small red box tucked into the corner—the box that held the reason he always kept this drawer locked. He placed it on the centre of his desk and stared at the square that was smaller than the palm of his hand. It hadn't been opened in years.

Letting out a deep breath, he raised the lid and stared at the gold oval pin, outlined with seed pearls. His attention was drawn to the centre of the brooch, to the painting of his wife's fine brown eye. He removed the lover's eye from its silk nest and held it between his thumb and forefinger. It had been painted from her wedding portrait and delivered to him in this very room the day after their son was born—the day after Olivia told him she no longer wanted him in her life.

It was purely sentimental drivel that made Gabriel wear it on his waistcoat every day for a year. She had just delivered their son. It was his way of honouring her for that. Originally he believed Olivia would eventually forgive him for his supposed indiscretion, just like most women of the *ton* were apt to do. However, by the time Nicholas turned one year old, it became apparent she would not. The day he returned the trinket to its box and locked it away, he understood the level of sacrifice he would have to make in order to continue his work and protect his people. Now he was relieved he'd never wavered and told her about Madame LaGrange.

At the soft knock on the door, he returned the brooch to its hiding place and called for his intruder to enter. The door slowly opened, and Bennett hesitated before walking into the room. Good. The man should be nervous to approach him after that carriage had been used to fetch Olivia.

It wasn't until Bennett was a few feet away from the desk that Gabriel noticed the missive in his butler's hand. All thoughts of railing at the man left him when Gabriel spied the smooth, black seal used by Andrew for confidential communications. Surely Manning could not have tipped his hand this quickly. Then he remembered Olivia had been there to sit for the man that morning. His heart thundered in his chest. Dismissing Bennett with a nod of his head, Gabriel waited until he was alone once again before he slid his knife under the seal and unfolded the paper. It was only one line—but it said so much.

*An urgent package has arrived for you in Richmond.*

He crumpled the note as he walked to the fireplace. Knowing they were one step closer to finding out who was behind the assassination attempt should have filled him with relief. Instead he was filled with trepidation.

The watchful gaze of his father looked down at him as he tossed the note towards the fire. Then that familiar voice rang in his head one last time.

*Trust no one and suspect everyone.*

Gabriel approached the observation room in the small brick house in Richmond to find Andrew waiting for him outside the doorway. To expedite his journey, Gabriel had taken Homer and raced him through London. Even though it took him about an hour, it was the longest ride of his life.

'I assume this means my suspicions were correct,' he said, approaching his brother.

Andrew nodded. 'There is a bottle of your favourite claret on the other side of this door. Colonel Collingsworth has already arrived with members of the Guards should we require them. He is eager to help with the interrogation. I expect Mr Donaldson will arrive shortly.' He pulled Gabriel by his elbow to a nearby alcove behind the stairs. 'I still believe this could have been accomplished without anyone else present. You are placing yourself at great risk.'

'That is not the way of the law. In order to have a proper trial, we must proceed accordingly. If it appears we tampered in any way with the investigation, he will be released and all of this will be for naught. Prinny's life comes before all else.'

'But—'

'I appreciate your concern, little brother, but I am firm in my conviction. Now tell me about our guest.'

'You had the right of it about Manning. He was providing information to Mr Clarke regarding Prinny's whereabouts.'

Gabriel tried to steady the pounding of his heart. He should be relieved that they were one step closer to eliminating the threat to Prinny. Instead, he might be one step closer to condemning Olivia.

'What was observed?'

'I left your house earlier today with Spence in tow. I stationed him across from Manning's studio with a stack of newspapers to sell so no one would question his presence. Approximately an hour later, Olivia and Lady Haverstraw were seen leaving his studio in our carriage. Not her carriage, mind you, our carriage.'

'Yes, yes, I know, just tell me what the bloody hell happened.'

'Fifteen minutes after their departure Manning left and Spence trailed him to Hatchard's.'

'Who was inside Hatchard's?'

'I happened to be in Hatchard's to check on Williams when we saw Manning place a note into a copy of Dante's *Divine Comedy* tucked under a bookshelf on the second floor. Immediately after he placed the paper inside the book, Manning left the premises. Once I was secure in the knowledge we were alone, I removed it from the book and read it. It was evident it was penned by the same hand as the other note. I left Williams to see if anyone will retrieve it. Harris and Spence were able to subdue Manning in his studio and they brought him here. The note referenced Nettleford House on Park Lane.'

*Nettleford?* Gabriel tried to steady his heart,

which he was certain was going to crash through his chest. This was the second time a letter intended for an assassin referenced a location Olivia knew Prinny would be.

His stomach turned. In his heart he didn't want to believe it was true.

'What is it?' Andrew asked, lowering his voice further. 'You know something.'

He needed to remove his emotions and think logically. First and foremost was his responsibility to the Crown. He ran his thumb over his ring. 'Olivia spoke of Nettleford's ball to Prinny. He told me she tried to persuade him to attend.'

Andrew looked as if he wanted to send his fist into the wall. 'Demmit, Gabriel! Do you see why inviting Bow Street to this inquisition was not in your best interest?'

'That is precisely why Donaldson needs to be present. If she is involved in this, she needs to face the consequences of her actions.'

'And as her husband, you might pay for her crimes as well.'

'Then I will face the hangman's noose if that is God's will.'

'But, Gabriel—'

'Not another word, Andrew. If this is to be my fate, so be it.' But he prayed to God it was not. And he prayed even harder that his wife wasn't a murderer.

## Chapter Fifteen

Olivia had watched Gabriel ride off from behind the curtains of her bedchamber. His impatience to arrive at his destination was evident by the speed with which he mounted Homer. In the past she would not have cared in the least about any trip he took. But today, after discovering that mysterious box in the odd carriage, Olivia wondered what was so urgent that Gabriel needed to race away on horseback this late in the day. Her need for answers was driving her to distraction.

Convinced the answer to the riddle about him would be found in his study, she made her way downstairs. When she tried the handle to the door she found the blasted man had locked the room—probably because he knew she would be back. The only thing that prevented her from kicking the door in frustration was the knowledge she would do more injury to her foot than to his massive door.

Well, she was not about to let a mere lock stop

her from finding answers. Removing one of her hairpins, she inserted it into the keyhole and after several attempts she managed to open the door.

The shutters were closed and the only light came from the glow of the dying embers in his fireplace. As she bent down at the hearth to light a candle, a small scrap of burnt paper caught her eye. Dragging it out of the ashes with the poker, Olivia picked it up and blew off the soot. Returning the unlit candle, she walked to one of the tall windows, cracked open one of the shutters and read the words on the paper in her hand.

*...package...in Richmond...*

So whatever had caused him to speed away from their home, at least she had an idea of his general direction. The question was, what was inside this package that made his departure so urgent? And exactly where in Richmond had he gone?

The sparsely furnished, windowless observation room in the house in Richmond was lit by one small candle placed on a table in the corner. It took Gabriel a moment before he spotted Colonel Collingsworth and shook his hand.

'Well done, Your Grace. I understand from Lord Andrew that man, Manning, has much to answer for.'

'We believe so, Colonel. My brother tells me you brought men to guard him in the event we need him to remain here until a trial?'

'I have. If you have a secure room, my men will make certain no one has a chance to kill this one before he is brought before the court.'

Just then Mr Donaldson entered the room and Andrew slid a glance at Gabriel.

'I say, Winterbourne, what the devil is so important you took me away from Bow Street so urgently?' His eyes skidded to Colonel Collingsworth and then Andrew, before a look of comprehension settled on his face.

While Andrew relayed the events of Manning's capture, Gabriel peered through one of the small holes in the wall and took his first look at the prisoner. Although the long white shutters on the windows were closed, the candlelight from four large, silver candelabras illuminated the room in a bright glow.

Manning was sitting in a chair with a strip of white cloth covering his eyes and his hands were cuffed behind his back. Brennan, one of Gabriel's men, lounged against the wall behind the artist with his arms crossed over his massive chest, watching silently.

'Although he has questioned where he is, we have not said a word to him since we removed him from his studio,' Andrew offered, approaching Gabriel's side.

Manning repeatedly licked his lips and periodically turned his head, as if listening for even the slightest sound.

Gabriel stepped back from the wall. 'He appears rather skittish.' He turned to Colonel Collingsworth and Mr Donaldson. 'My man Brennan is inside with Mr Manning. Should you require his assistance, do not hesitate to let him know.'

Mr Donaldson nodded. 'Is there any further information about the prisoner that Lord Andrew has not told us that might assist us in interrogating him?'

Gabriel's hands began to sweat and he purposely avoided his brother's eyes. He should tell them about Olivia's association with the man. He should tell them she had been prompting Prinny to attend Nettleford's ball just a few days ago. And, he definitely should tell them Olivia had been to see Manning prior to the artist's departure for Hatchard's.

Instead he shook his head and firmly pressed his thumb into the stone of his ring, feeling more protective over her than he expected. 'As far as I know, my brother has given you all the relevant details.'

Mr Donaldson peered briefly into one of the holes in the wall. 'Very well.' He gestured towards the door. 'Colonel, I believe it is time to see what he knows.'

After the door closed, all the air in the room appeared to leave with them. Gabriel wanted to take a deep breath to steady his nerves, but found the tight pressure on his chest prevented him from drawing in much air. He caught Andrew's concerned expression before he sat down in the chair and focused his attention on the prisoner on the other side of the wall. Through the vent near his boots, he heard, rather than saw, when Mr Donaldson and Colonel Collingsworth entered the room. So much had come down to this very moment.

They took seats across from a very alert man, who shifted in his chair.

'I know there is someone there,' Manning said with a shaky voice.

Mr Donaldson nodded to Brennan to remove the man's blindfold. Manning blinked a number of times before narrowly studying the well-dressed men in front of him and then eyed Brennan from his scuffed boots to his sturdy legs, broad shoulders and black hair that fell past his collar. Once he had sufficiently taken his measure, he turned back to the men seated across from him.

Eyeing Colonel Collingsworth's scarlet uniform with gold trim, he addressed him first. 'You're a

Guard to the King. What business do you have with me? Why was I brought here?'

Colonel Collingsworth leaned his tall, athletic frame closer and folded his hands on the top of the table. 'Is your name John Manning?'

Manning's gaze shifted between his inquisitors and he blinked four times before he nodded. 'I am.'

'John Manning, you are charged with high treason, for conspiring to murder the Prince Regent of the kingdom of Great Britain.'

All the air missing from Gabriel's lungs appeared to push its way out of Manning's with a loud *whoosh* and the man fell back against the chair. 'I have done nothing of the sort. Surely, sirs, you are mistaken.'

'Do you deny visiting Hatchard's bookshop today and placing information about the Prince Regent's future whereabouts into a copy of Dante's *Inferno*?'

The colour drained from Manning's face and his chest visibly rose and fell as if he had been running instead of sitting for so long. 'I… I…'

'You should be aware before you attempt to deny it that you were seen doing so by noble men who protect the Crown,' the Colonel informed him.

Manning sat up tall and cleared his throat. 'Even if I did place a paper with the date and location of a ball, that does not mean I am conspiring murder.'

'And what if I told you that someone with your hand recently provided an assassin with the location of the Prince Regent the very day someone tried to kill him?'

The colour drained from Manning's face and his wide-eyed gaze moved from Colonel Collingsworth to Mr Donaldson and back again. 'Assassin?'

'That is the term for a person who attempts to kill someone.'

Under the table, the artist's right leg began to tremble. Pressing his lips firmly together, he lowered his head and stared at Colonel Collingsworth through his lashes. His chest rose and fell rapidly, matching time with Gabriel's.

From behind the large mural on Manning's right, Gabriel rubbed the stone of his ring, praying that Olivia was not part of this treachery. It would destroy him to find out the woman he had chosen to marry had the heart of a murderer. The image of Olivia being led to the gallows was making him feel sick.

Gabriel focused his attention on the scene before him.

'Do you know the penalty for treason, sir?' This time it was Mr Donaldson who spoke. 'You will be sentenced to death. You will swing within a fortnight.'

Manning's head jerked in his direction, but he remained silent—except for the sound of the rapid tapping of his boot.

'Tell us about Hatchard's. Tell us why you placed a note into that book. Who were you attempting to contact?'

The tapping sound was now replaced by the sound of heavy breathing, as Manning appeared to struggle with his decision to talk. Finally, he let out a shaky breath. 'I have no notion of who takes the information I leave. I was told to place the information in that book each time I learned of somewhere the Prince Regent would be. I swear to you I had no idea what they would do with the information.'

*They? Dear God, there was someone else involved.*

'Who told you to do this?'

'I do not know. I am innocent of any treachery against the Crown. I had no notion what they would use my information for.'

'Why should we believe you?'

'I am telling you the truth. I have no idea who has been retrieving my notes. They never told me their names.'

'Who told you where to place this information of yours?' Colonel Collingsworth asked.

'I do not know. You have to believe me. I never met them. A note was delivered to my studio one afternoon, early in the month. This person knew of a child of mine—a child that is far from London with his mother. If I did not provide them with the information they wanted, they threatened to harm my child. They told me they would mutilate him so badly that his life would be a living hell.'

'Were you contacted by one person or were there others?'

'I only received the one note.'

'How long were you to supply them with information?'

'I do not know. They said they would notify me when they no longer required my services.'

'Do you still have the letter?' Mr Donaldson asked.

'No, I destroyed it as they directed.'

'How many notes have you deposited at Hatchard's?'

'Four... I think.'

'And the information on the Prince Regent's plans, where did you get it?'

Manning looked away.

The pounding of Gabriel's heart was so loud, it almost blocked out the noise from the other room. From of the corner of his eye he saw Andrew turn his way. He sucked in a deep breath and squeezed his eyes shut, forcing a sense of calm to steady his frantic heart.

Manning shifted in his seat. 'Are these handcuffs necessary? I have answered your questions and they are chafing my wrists. Surely with that mountain of a man behind me and the two of you between me and the door, you don't believe I could actually escape. Do you?'

Colonel Collingsworth nodded to Brennan and the cuffs were unlocked. Immediately, Manning began rubbing his wrists. The men sitting with him might have missed his tactic for avoiding the last question, but Gabriel had not. Why did he not want to reveal where he had gathered his information? Was he protecting someone or fearful of them?

'The information on the Prince Regent's whereabouts. How did you acquire it?' Mr Donaldson asked again, and Gabriel almost wished he had forgotten that he hadn't received an answer the first time.

'They will know you have me and that I have told you things. They will want retribution. Please, sirs, I beg of you. Please do not let any harm come to my child and his mother. They have had no part in this. They should not be made to suffer because of me.'

'You are in no position to make any requests,' Colonel Collingsworth said, clearly disgusted.

'Then I have nothing else to say.' Manning leaned back in his chair and closed his eyes.

'Cooperate with us fully, Mr Manning, and should you be found guilty, transportation might be an option.'

Manning said nothing as he stared at his captors.

'Then I believe this interrogation is over,' Mr Donaldson said, rising to his feet. 'Colonel, you may take the prisoner now.'

He walked to the door and it wasn't until he touched the handle that Manning called to him.

'Sir, I shall tell you everything, if you promise to safeguard my family.' He chewed his lower lip and fixed his gaze on Mr Donaldson's back.

Gabriel was fighting the urge to shut his eyes. Olivia was too young to die now.

Turning slowly, Mr Donaldson walked back to the table and sat down. 'I will do what I can to keep your family safe.'

'I need your word as a gentleman.'

Mr Donaldson visibly bristled, but after pursing his lips together, he gave a curt nod. 'You have it.'

'Very well, I've gathered the information on the Regent's whereabouts from my acquaintances.'

'Tell us the names of those acquaintances.'

Manning shifted once more in his seat and he looked about the room before his gaze returned to Mr Donaldson. He took a deep breath. 'Lady Abernathy and the Duchess of Winterbourne.'

The silence in the room was deafening.

Gabriel broke out in a cold sweat and his heart twisted in pain. If only he could pretend this day had never happened. But it had—and Olivia's name was now linked to an assassination attempt on Prinny.

His right hand clenched into a tight fist. He glanced at his brother and the expression on Andrew's face told him, in no uncertain terms, that he thought Gabriel was a fool for allowing other men to conduct this interview. Now, he wished he had listened. But strangely enough it was to protect Olivia more than he worried about saving himself.

He focused his attention back to the interrogation room. It appeared some of the candles had gone out and he squinted to adjust to the lower light. Colonel Collingsworth and Mr Donaldson were staring at one another in silent communication and Manning's eyes shifted between the two men while he chewed his lip.

Finally, Mr Donaldson cleared his throat. 'What information did Lady Abernathy give you?'

Manning's right leg bounced rapidly. 'She told me of the Prince Regent's trip to Brighton on the fourth.'

'I see. And did you forward this by a note left at Hatchard's?'

'I did.'

'And the Duchess of Winterbourne, what information has she provided you with?'

Both of Manning's legs were bouncing now as he rubbed the back of his neck. 'She told me of a trip she was taking with him to visit a Mr Owen to purchase a painting by Titian, and today I heard about his plans to attend Lord and Lady Nettleford's ball.'

Both Donaldson and the Colonel turned to the wall hiding Gabriel and Andrew. If Gabriel didn't know any better, he would have thought they could see him rubbing his hands on his thighs. The smooth buckskin helped dry his sweaty palms.

Mr Donaldson leaned forward. 'And this information the Duchess of Winterbourne provided you with, what did you do with it?'

'I wrote the information down and placed it in the book at Hatchard's.'

'Did these women who provided you with information know you would be forwarding it to someone else?'

'No. No. Of course not.'

'You are certain they were not part of this?'

'Yes. I'm certain.'

'Did you ever discuss harming the Prince Regent in any way with Lady Abernathy or the Duchess of Winterbourne?'

Manning's eyes widened. 'No. Lady Abernathy is the gentlest of souls and Lady Winterbourne looks upon the Prince Regent like a father. Neither could ever consciously hurt him. And I have no desire to see him harmed. I told you I had no knowledge what was to be done with the information. I just wanted to protect my son.'

'Who takes this information you leave?'

'I do not know. I was told to place the information on page eighty-nine in the book and leave.'

'And you never remained, out of sight, to see who comes to collect it?'

'No, I just wanted to leave as quickly as possible.'

Mr Donaldson turned to Colonel Collingsworth. 'I have no further questions. Do you?'

Colonel Collingsworth shook his head.

'Very well, then. You will remain in Colonel Collingsworth's custody until we determine if you will stand trial.'

Manning squeaked. 'But I told you I had no knowledge of a plan to murder the Prince Regent.'

Mr Donaldson stood and turned towards the door. 'Then you should have no problem convincing a jury of that should that be your fate.'

Falling back in his chair, Gabriel rubbed his eyes. He could breathe again.

'You're one lucky devil,' Andrew said, standing up and stretching. 'That could have ended very differently. Do you think he was telling the truth? About Olivia?'

'I do.' He felt it in his bones. And Manning was right, Prinny was like a father to Olivia. Guilt ate away at him that he had even considered she would want to see the man dead. It was disturbing to know the man on the other side of the wall understood his wife better than he did.

Andrew opened his mouth to speak, as Mr Donaldson stormed into the room, pointing an accusing finger at Gabriel. 'Dem you. You knew she would be named.'

Gabriel stood, preferring to face Mr Donaldson at eye level. 'She had nothing to do with the attempt on Prince George's life.'

'She bloody well did! Your wife's information was used to determine where he would be the day he was shot at.'

'My wife gossiped to an artist while he was painting her portrait to pass the time. She had no notion he would take that information and give it to someone intending to harm our sovereign. You heard him.'

'And how can you be so sure? Surely you do not expect me to believe that she discussed this with you over the breakfast table? The two of you barely speak to one another.'

The state of his marriage was common knowledge. While veiled comments in the past had annoyed Gabriel, more because he considered his private life his business and no one else's, this time he battled with himself to keep his right fist from crashing into Donaldson's jaw.

Just as he was about to inform the man that he could go to hell, Andrew stepped up to his side. 'I am certain he was telling the truth. In fact, the Duchess of Winterbourne told me about her conversation with the artist,' he said, not even glancing at Gabriel.

'Why would she have told you?'

'Because I asked her.'

'You expect me to believe this?'

Andrew raised his chin and moved his hands behind his back. 'You have my word as a gentleman.'

Gabriel glanced up, expecting lighting to strike Andrew through the roof of the house.

'You have had no time to question her since he was apprehended,' Mr Donaldson said, eyeing Andrew sceptically.

'We discussed her portrait session recently over dinner. I enquired how she could sit for someone for days and not grow bored. She said their conversations helped to pass the time and she gave me examples of what they discuss.'

'She still may have been aware this information would be passed on.'

As far as Gabriel knew, Mr Donaldson had

never spoken to Olivia. He knew nothing of who she was and yet he thought nothing of questioning her character. His stomach turned as he realised he'd had the same thoughts about her less than an hour ago.

Gabriel never used his height and muscular form to intimidate men. He had never needed to. His title had been enough—until now. Now, he would use whatever means to deter Mr Donaldson from pursuing any suspicions about Olivia. 'My wife is the embodiment of all that is good. I will not have you besmirch her character. If I thought she was involved in any of this, do you honestly believe I would have you here to question that man?'

It appeared Mr Donaldson was suddenly at a loss for words.

Gabriel needed to return home and sort out his jumbled thoughts. He knew he had been right to pay attention to the facts that pointed to Olivia. However, he now began to realise she was probably the last person in London who would want to harm the King or Regent. And it hadn't escaped his notice he had been more worried for her facing the gallows than himself. He had much to consider—but there was one thing he needed to do first.

## Chapter Sixteen

Hanover Square was nearly deserted at this late hour of the evening—or rather early morning if one was to be exact. However, one building stood like a beacon with the glow of candlelight in one of the upper windows. Thankfully for Gabriel it was not the building he needed to break into.

As Andrew stood guard, Gabriel crouched before the front door. Squinting in the dim light, he pressed two metal pins into the lock and jiggled them.

'Are you certain you do not wish to have me give it a go?' Andrew asked over his shoulder.

'I almost have it.'

'Do you even recall how it's done? I cannot imagine you've had a need to do that for quite some time.'

How he wished he could go back to a time when he was not the kind of man who would pick the locks of his wife's possessions—to a time when he had no idea of the horrors of betrayal. What would his life be like now if he had never gone to his uncle for advice?

A satisfying click broke the silence. Slowly he turned the handle of the door to the building that housed Manning's studio. Hopefully the man's landlord was a heavy sleeper. The last thing he needed was to have to explain his presence in the house.

He pulled Andrew inside the darkened hallway by the sleeve. Faint streaks of moonlight from the transom over the door lit their way to the staircase. They took the steps gingerly, hoping to avoid potential squeaks. When they finally reached the third floor, both Gabriel and Andrew took a deep breath.

With all the practice he'd had recently, this time it only took Gabriel two tries to pick the lock. Moonlight flooded into the studio from the large windows, making it easy to navigate the large room.

'What exactly is it you believe we will find?' Andrew whispered.

Gabriel's gaze landed on the easel, draped with a white cloth. That was what he had been hoping to find. 'We are looking for anything that might prove he was blackmailed.'

'But we agreed he was telling the truth. Why are you questioning it now?'

'It's prudent to be certain.'

Andrew studied him carefully. 'How do you propose we divide and conquer?'

'I'll search out here. There is another room behind that screen. See what you can find.'

Gabriel waited until Andrew was in the next room before he removed the knife from his boot and uncovered the painting of Olivia. Most people would never know it was the Duchess of Winterbourne reclining on the divan—but he would. He would not leave it here unattended. Should Manning be executed or transported, who knew what would become of this painting? He needed to bring it home. He needed to protect her reputation. It was the least he could do after today.

With a resolved breath he sliced the canvas from the frame, rolled it up and secured it with a strip of black ribbon.

'What are you doing?' Andrew asked from the doorway.

'It's of no concern of yours. Did you find anything?'

'Amazingly, I did not. Have you even begun your search or have you spent all this time taking Olivia's portrait?'

'What do you know of her portrait?'

Andrew walked closer to him. 'I know she was sitting for the man. Was he able to complete it?'

Gabriel shook his head.

'Pity. I'm sure it would have made a nice addition to the gallery.'

Thank God this painting would never see the light of day in any gallery, but Andrew did not need to know that.

'Yes, a shame. Well, if you are finished in there, perhaps you can help me look out here.'

With the portrait secure, Gabriel was eager to finish searching the studio and put this day behind him.

Throughout his ride home, guilt over his suspicions about Olivia continued to plague him. She didn't deserve his suspicions and had never done anything to indicate she could not be trusted, or that she hated the monarchy. She wasn't Peter.

For over five years Gabriel had had to live with the fact that Matthew's death was all his fault. He was the one who had confided his responsibilities to his uncle. When Peter asked to accompany Matthew up north to gather intelligence on the rumblings of a plot against the Crown, he should have said no. He knew Peter was a zealous supporter of Catholic emancipation. And that year Prinny was very vocal he was not. But in his wildest dreams Gabriel never thought Peter would try to prevent them from stopping an assassination attempt over it.

He would never know if Peter had intentionally killed Matthew to stop the intelligence they uncovered from reaching Gabriel. It might have been an accident. Peter took that knowledge to his grave. What Gabriel did know was that night when his uncle stood over him with cold rain pelting them both, Peter had every intention of killing him.

After that night, Gabriel vowed he would never again be responsible for anyone else's death. He would never again share what he did or the names of those that worked for him with anyone else. But his feelings for Olivia were running deep. During Manning's interrogation it became apparent he cared more for her life than his own. He wanted to trust her. He wanted a real marriage. Perhaps there was a way to have one.

When Olivia awoke the next morning, her suspicions about Gabriel and the mysterious package in Richmond continued to plague her. Luckily she would be spending her morning in Manning's studio. He would be a welcome diversion and today she would make him hold an extended conversation with her, whether he wanted to or not.

When she knocked on his door after breakfast no one was home, which did nothing to improve her mood. At least he could have sent a note cancelling her sitting for the day.

There was no sense in returning home where

she would be tempted to enter Gabriel's study and probably get caught trying to pick the lock to his desk again. So she took Colette with her to Madame Devy's to lose herself in a morning of shopping.

When she walked out of the dressmaker's shop an hour later, she spotted Janvier standing in front of the milliner next door, deep in conversation with a willowy, dark-haired woman with fine features and a prominent brow. Olivia couldn't recall seeing the woman before, and from the simple appearance of her dress one could assume she did not move within Olivia's elevated circle.

Having no desire to interrupt their conversation or stand on the pavement on such a windy day, Olivia was about to walk towards her carriage when Janvier appeared startled to see her. She gave him a friendly smile and he whispered something in his companion's ear before he left her and approached Olivia.

'What a pleasant surprise,' he said with a tip of his hat.

'This is a surprise. I was just seeing about a dress for the theatre.'

'For the opening night of *Douglas*?'

'Perhaps.'

'Will you tell me the colour or will you keep me in suspense?'

'A bit of suspense keeps life exciting.'

He flashed her a grin. 'I agree. Well, I am certain whatever colour you have chosen, you will look lovely in it.'

It was just like Janvier to try to charm her after being seen with another woman. She held on to her bonnet as a particularly strong gust of wind blew down the street. 'I must be off before the wind takes me. Good day, Janvier.'

He tipped his hat and helped her into the carriage, where Colette was waiting to accompany her to more shops. It would take quite of bit of funds to distract her from thinking about the enigma she had married.

Hours later the man himself emerged from his study as she stood in the entrance hall, removing her bonnet. Crossing his arms over his broad chest, he leaned against the doorframe of his private sanctuary. 'You've been busy,' he remarked casually as he watched two footmen carry in boxes and wrapped packages from her carriage.

She handed her bonnet and gloves to Colette, then dismissed her with a nod. 'I realised I was in need of new slippers and gloves, and I saw a lovely fan for the theatre.'

'How many slippers does one woman need, I wonder?' he asked, with a slight smile.

'As many as she can afford.'

He nodded slowly, holding her gaze across the empty hallway. 'There is something I need to discuss with you…when you have the time.'

'I have a few things to attend to. Perhaps we can speak before your family arrives for dinner this evening?'

He tipped his head. 'I shall look forward to it. Shall we say six in my study?'

She nodded her agreement, even though having a conversation with him, knowing he was hiding something from her, was the last thing she wanted to do. What if he discovered she had been in his study and taken the cryptic note he'd tried to burn? Well, so be it! She needed answers and she was not afraid to press him to get them.

The idea of sharing his secret life with Olivia terrified Gabriel. There was no other word to describe it. But after weighing his options all morning on how he could have a real marriage with Olivia while also keeping his people safe, he knew it was the only solution.

She had sat in that carriage. She had found that box. And just yesterday he'd caught her trying to pick the lock to his desk.

He'd always known she was a smart, inquisitive woman. A person like that would not stop until they had answers. If she decided to poke into his affairs she might uncover the truth anyway—along with the identity of any number of the people who worked for him. He might be able to trust her with his involvement protecting the Crown, but he could not trust her with the identity of his operatives. The scar below his ribs was a daily reminder why. He would tell her the truth— at least the part he thought she needed to know.

At precisely six o'clock Olivia arrived at the door to his study. From the determined expression on her face, it appeared she had come with a purpose. It wouldn't surprise him if she wanted to discuss that carriage again.

'I gather from your earlier comment about the fan you purchased, you're planning on attending the theatre,' he said, closing the door behind him and leaning against it. That wasn't exactly a polite way to begin a conversation, but it was something.

She walked to the fireplace, where the ashes appeared to be more interesting than he was. 'Yes, *Douglas* will be opening, and Mrs Siddons is to return to the stage. Prinny and I were recently discussing how we've missed her performances.'

'He told me you brought marzipan. That's an interesting gift to give someone with the gout.'

'While you and I both know he suffers from terrible bouts of it, we also know he's not plagued with it now.' She finally looked at him. 'Was there a particular reason you wanted to see me? I cannot imagine it was to discuss Prinny.'

All of this had to do with Prinny.

Gabriel pushed away from the door and walked towards her. 'I have something I would like to discuss with you.'

'You said as much.'

He waited politely for Olivia to sit before taking the chair next to her. For the last hour he'd thought about what he would say—now he wished he'd considered how to begin. He spun his ring, searching for the right words.

When Olivia raised an expectant brow, he knew he needed to forge ahead. 'I believe we have spoken to each other more now than we have in the last five years. We are behaving as a family, in every sense of the word, and I was wondering if it would be possible for this reconciliation between you and I to continue, even after you are with child?'

Her eyes widened momentarily before her forehead wrinkled. He waited for her response. The awkward moment stretched between them and Gabriel began to wonder if she understood what he was asking.

'Why now?' She only said two words, but her scepticism spoke volumes.

'I told you—'

'No, not really.' She stood and took a few steps

away before spinning on her heels to face him. 'I know what you're about. I am not naïve. You believe I was trying to pick the lock to your desk. That carriage and odd box I asked you about, they have significance even though you claim to know nothing about them. You are hiding something and think that by flattering me I'll run into your arms and brush my questions aside.'

He stood so she was no longer looking down at him. 'I'm not asking for a true reconciliation to trick you. I'm asking because I have genuine affection for you and I'd like to try to start over again with you if that is possible.'

'Interesting timing.'

'Is it? We have just begun this temporary reconciliation. I've just started to realise how much I've missed you. Is that truly questionable timing? I couldn't possibly have realised I missed you, a year ago. You weren't speaking to me. You weren't giving me the opportunity to remember how much I enjoyed your company.'

Gabriel spun his ring, uncomfortable with admitting he cared for her and missed her when she had yet to tell him she felt anything close to that about him. Early in their marriage he could see she had genuine affection for him. He thought he'd sensed those feels returning. Perhaps he was wrong.

'Yes,' he continued, 'I do believe you were attempting to pick the lock to my desk and, yes, we did discuss that carriage and the box, but my wanting to be with you has nothing to do with that.'

It now appeared it was her turn to search for the right words to express herself. 'I like you, Gabriel, I do, but I do not trust you.'

The absurdity of her not trusting him when all along he had never trusted her almost made him laugh. If neither of them trusted the other they had no chance of being happy together. Prinny was her dear friend. She would never want to see him harmed. It was time she knew the truth. 'There is something I need to tell you, Olivia, but before I do, I need you to swear you will not reveal what I am about to say to anyone.'

'That's a bit dramatic, wouldn't you say?' But when he remained silent, waiting for her agreement, she must have realised his earnestness. Her eyes searched his. 'Very well, I swear.'

He gestured to the chairs beside them and they both sat down.

'Do you remember the day my father died? No, wait, it began before that. It started when I was a child.'

Confusion crossed her brow.

'My father had very strong opinions about the French Revolution. He had a deep-seated fear that what had happened in France would cross the channel and cause a revolt here. He believed strongly that King George needed protection and Prinny as well. Believing if they were safe, there would be little chance of members of the *ton* facing the same fate as the French aristocracy. You see, he worried for the safety of this family. He created a secret organisation made up of men and women whose sole purpose was to ferret out any threats against the Crown and to protect the royal house with their lives, if necessary. On the day he died, he made me promise him that I would do everything in my power to ensure King George and Prinny remained safe before I assumed his role in overseeing that select group of individuals.'

The look of confusion was still in her eyes, along with some disbelief. 'Surely you are joking.'

He shook his head. 'It is all true.'

She pointed to the portrait of his father above the mantel. 'You expect me to believe that man organised a secret society to protect the Crown? *That* man?'

'He did.'

She studied the image of his father through narrow eyes, as if she would find a clue to his father's secret dealings within the portrait. Then she turned back to him and gave him the same appraisal. 'I do not know why you find it necessary to tell me such a fantastical tale, but I do not find it amusing and it does not improve my trust in you.' She looked away and brushed out non-existent wrinkles from her lap.

'Olivia, what I am telling you is the truth. I am responsible for protecting the Crown.'

'And I am a Grand Duchess of Russia, simply raised in England as a girl,' she bit out with sarcasm.

'You yourself admitted you have suspicions about me. That is why I am telling this to you. Why did you feel it necessary to try to open a locked drawer to my desk? You know deep down what I have told you is possible.'

Her hand stilled from where she had been about to pick an invisible thread from her sleeve and she stared at the hearth. Her eyes were moving as if she was reading a message in the ashes and he could see she was considering what he said.

'You are too clever to discount what I am telling you, Olivia. You know what I am saying is possible—that it is the truth.'

She looked back at him and he could see she was struggling to believe him. 'How long have you been involved in this?'

'I took a vow to give my life for the Crown when I was at Cambridge.'

'So when we were introduced you were already working for your father?'

He nodded and saw the moment she realised what he told her was possible.

'You've been deceiving me from the moment we met!'

'We are sworn to tell no one. One of the reasons we have been successful in stopping plots against Prinny and King George is because we operate in secret. My own mother and most of my closest friends do not even know. Lyonsdale doesn't know.'

'Lyonsdale is not your wife. I am,' she spat with fire in her eyes.

'I swore an oath.'

'Then why tell me now? What has changed?'

'Everything has changed,' he replied forcefully. 'I misjudged you and did not know you well enough to trust you with something like this years ago. I see now how much you have come to care for Prinny and know you would never do anything to cause him harm. If I continued to keep this secret from you, it would pull us further apart. I do not want that.' He placed his hand over hers. They remained cold under his touch through her embroidered silk gloves. 'I do not want to go back to the way things were between us. I like waking up to you. I like being together with you and Nicholas even if at times it is at an absurdly early hour of the morning. And I like knowing that when I want to see you, I will not be turned away. I have missed your intelligence and your wit. And there is no place I would rather be than in your bed. There is no other woman I want more than you, Livy.'

She slid her hands out from under his. 'Explain the carriage I was brought home in yesterday.'

'It's used when we have a need to observe people who we suspect have plans against the Crown.'

'And the box?'

'There are times disguises are necessary.'

'Tell me about the package in Richmond.'

Bloody hell, she was even craftier than he thought! 'What do you know of Richmond?'

She reached inside her glove and withdrew a charred piece of paper. 'Tell me about the package you received in Richmond,' she repeated, holding it out to him.

'An attempt has been made on Prinny's life—'

'He is hurt? Is—'

'He's fine. I have him in Carlton House to keep him safe until we are certain we have in custody all those involved in this plot. The package this refers to is a person. It's the man who has been supplying information on Prinny's whereabouts.'

'You saw this person last night?'

'I did.'

'Well, I hope someone beat him to a bloody mess.' From the anger rolling off her, he'd wager she would volunteer if given the chance.

'You may not feel that way when I tell you his name.'

'Why should I show concern for such a person?'

He had an urge to beat Manning himself for the hurt this was sure to cause his wife. Instead he walked to the fireplace to take his anger out of the logs. As he jammed the poker into the flames, sparks flew up the chimney.

'Gabriel, do I know this man?' she asked, walking over to him.

From her expression he thought it best to place distance between Olivia and the heavy metal object in his hand, so he hung the poker back on the rack. 'Mr Manning was informing the assassin of Prinny's plans.'

She backed away from him. 'That's not amusing.'

'It was not meant to be.'

'John Manning would never do such a thing.'

Gabriel took a step closer to comfort her, but she took another step back.

'You are just saying that because you do not like me sitting for him. You will find any excuse to prevent him from painting that portrait.'

'That is not true. He was gathering information about Prinny while painting those within the royal circle. That information was given to someone who intends to kill Prinny. We have his confession.'

Her breathing became more rapid as she processed what he had told her. 'He asked me to sit

for that portrait. He said it was because only I…'
She stormed past him and grabbed the poker.
'That weasel! And to think I recommended him
to friends.'

By the time she had finished stabbing the logs,
they would be tiny bits of ash. At least she had
got over her shock and wasn't a sobbing mess. He
took a step closer just as she whirled around, waving the poker at him. He backed up just in time.

'I hope he can no longer stand this morning.'
She turned back around and jabbed the logs.
'What kind of person seeks the blood of another?'

Gabriel went to step closer and she yanked the
poker out of the fire.

He froze.

'He should be punished for this,' she said
through her teeth.

'He will be. Once we have captured whoever is
responsible for this, Manning will face trial. You
should know that he was coerced into giving away
the information. If he did not oblige, members of
his family would have been maimed.'

'He still should have found a way to get out of
his predicament.'

'Sometimes that's not always possible.'

'I don't believe that. If you think clearly, you
can always find a way.'

It was hard to imagine what it would feel like
to be sheltered from the ugliness in the world.

'Put the poker down, Olivia. You have successfully reduced the logs to ash.'

She narrowed her eyes at him and hung the poker on the rack. Dusting off her hands, she turned her head towards his desk. 'Why do you keep your desk locked? Is that where you hide your secret papers?'

He knew she would never have simply forgotten all that she suspected. Taking off his ring, he adjusted it so it formed the key to his desk. Her surprised expression brought a smile to his lips. 'Open it and you will see,' he said, handing her his ring.

She crossed the room as if she were heading to her own execution and pushed the chair away from his desk. The key stalled momentarily in the lock before giving way with a click. There was a slight hesitation before she cautiously slid her hand inside.

There were only three things Gabriel kept in that drawer. Apparently she had no interest in the pistol. She took out the stack of papers, but once she saw they were blank she returned them to the drawer. Then she removed the small box and placed it on top of the desk. She stared down at it as if it would devour her where she stood.

'Open it,' he commanded softly into her ear.

Holding her breath, she raised the lid and

picked up the lover's eye. It took a moment before she almost dropped it.

'I had Cosway paint it from your wedding portrait. The jeweller who set it brought it to me the day after Nicholas was born. I wore it for a year before I realised there was no hope for reconciliation between us. It sat there unopened for years until yesterday when I found you in my study. Now you have uncovered the secret of my locked drawer.'

She looked back at the small gold brooch in her hand. 'You wore this?'

'Every day for a year.'

'How did I not notice?'

'You barely looked at me and even if you did, you would not have seen it. I wore it under my coats. I've missed you, Livy. I hadn't realised how much until recently.'

She searched his eyes as if gauging his sincerity. Finally her lips curved into a small sad smile and she placed the pin back in the box. 'I have missed you as well.'

'I want you as my wife, in every sense of the word.'

'I want that, Gabriel, I do, but I will not take you back into my life knowing you will run to Madame LaGrange to satisfy your needs. Most women would look the other way. But I cannot.

I would rather we lived here as strangers than to have a marriage like that.'

For years Madame LaGrange would trust only him with the intelligence she had gathered. She knew the danger she was putting herself in and he could not blame her for wanting to have only one person as her contact. But what if he could convince her she could also trust Andrew? Then he would no longer have to see her and there would be no danger of Olivia believing the worst. They could begin again and put the past behind them. 'I won't. You are the only woman I need. There will never be another.'

All this time he had not been alone in missing what they had. He cradled her neck in his palm and lowered his lips to hers. What had started out as a kiss of mutual affection turned into much more. He poured out everything he couldn't say to her—didn't know how to say to her—into that kiss.

As if she needed to be as close to him as he did her, Olivia worked the buttons of his tailcoat and then his waistcoat. He picked her up and settled her lovely bottom on the surface of his desk, all without breaking the kiss.

He needed her and needed to be inside of her to reassure himself she was his. The silk of her gown glided over his hands as he skimmed his fingers up her soft, warm legs. Her breath caught within their kiss as his hands moved higher and higher.

A soft knock stilled them and Gabriel looked at the door. Olivia pushed against his shoulders, but with one hand he grabbed her about the waist and the other hand remained on her thigh.

'Yes?' he called out, sounding as if he had spent the day in a loud debate within the House of Lords.

The handle of the door turned halfway before the lock prevented it from making a full rotation. 'Your guests have arrived, sir, and are waiting in the Green Drawing Room,' was the muffled reply from Bennett.

Gabriel and Olivia looked at one another in mutual confusion, until they both recalled they were having dinner with his family. Olivia pushed harder against Gabriel and this time he let her go. Stepping away from the desk, he buttoned his waistcoat and began to tidy his clothes.

'Tell them we will be there shortly,' he called to the closed door.

'Yes, sir,' was the muffled reply.

When he turned back around, Olivia was adjusting the neckline of her gown.

'May I help you with that,' he asked with a grin.

'I believe you have done enough for now.'

'I'd like to do more.' Visions of entering her

were not going away. 'It is unseasonably warm this evening,' he said with an arch of his brow.

Her hand stilled from shaking out her skirts and she looked up at him. 'Perhaps we should venture out into the garden when our guests leave.'

It was uncanny how quickly she could follow his train of thought. 'Perhaps we should.' He took her hand in his and pressed a kiss to her skin. 'I haven't been in the walled garden in ages. Are we still in possession of that sun dial?'

The tip of her tongue ran over the dip in her upper lip. 'We are, but it won't be of much use in the dark.'

'It will be most useful when I bend you over it and take you from behind.'

Her brown eyes darkened and he knew she was picturing it just as he was. If he made it through dinner without dragging her out of the room and into the garden it would be a miracle.

Olivia was the first to look away as she flattened out her skirt. 'Do I look presentable? I don't resemble a doxy who has just had a tumble?'

He laughed and shook his head. 'I assure you my family will have no idea what we've been doing.'

Her eyes widened as she glanced at the door. 'Your family... Gabriel, we cannot keep them waiting.'

Grabbing his arm, she propelled him towards

the door. When they reached the door, he spun her around and kissed her one last time. Then she pushed him away, turned the key in the lock and before Gabriel was able to say another word, she was practically running with him down the hall to the Green Drawing Room.

Aside from their heavy breathing from running through their house, Gabriel thought they had disguised their activities rather well. That was until his mother, Andrew and Monty turned towards them from where they had been sitting near the window. His mother's eyebrows rose into her hairline, Andrew's right brow arched with a knowing look of amusement and Monty's mouth had opened so wide he resembled a fish.

Gabriel glanced at Olivia. Not a hair was out of place. So what was causing such a reaction?

Olivia dropped his hand.

It suddenly felt cold and empty. She looked at the buttons of his tailcoat with a pointed stare and he re-buttoned them properly. No one uttered a word. The awkwardness of the moment would not do. Their family should know they had reconciled and, in a short time, so would all of London.

He tugged Olivia closer and kissed her knuckles slowly. Her eyes softened at the gesture. A discreet cough came from the sofa. When they both turned their heads, his mother smiled.

'We were beginning to worry that something was amiss with Nicholas. Now I see it was nothing dire at all.'

'Nicholas is well, I assure you,' Olivia said, tugging her hand back and walking towards his family. 'He will be down after dinner and you will be able to see for yourself.'

His mother kissed his cheek. 'It is lovely to see you, Gabriel.' Her wise eyes scanned his wife's face. 'You look well, my dear. I dare say you have a bit of a rosy glow. Are you well?'

'Yes, I am. Thank you. I just had a bit of difficulty with my gown this evening and Gabriel was kind enough to wait for me.'

'He did,' his mother said, eyeing her son from his shoes to his cravat as if she were looking for a strand of Olivia's hair on his clothing.

'I thought it would be the proper thing to do. We did not anticipate it taking as long as it did.'

'I suppose that comes with age,' Andrew mumbled through a smirk.

'What was that?' their mother asked, narrowing her eyes at his brother.

'I said it must be difficult to gauge,' he replied, looking at Gabriel with laughter in his eyes.

His mother glared at Andrew and Gabriel was certain, if his brother had been sitting closer, she would have rapped his knuckles with the fan she was tapping against her thigh.

'I understand dinner is ready to be served,' Olivia said, her gaze narrowed on Andrew as well. 'Andrew, would you please escort me to the dining room?'

Bowing to Olivia, Andrew flashed her a devilish smile as if he was preparing to charm his way out of trouble. 'Of course, the honour is mine, sister dear.'

'Monty, some day Andrew will find a bride and you will not have to walk into dinner alone,' Olivia said sweetly.

'And when will that be, Andrew?' his mother prodded. 'Each day I move closer and closer to my grave.'

'You are not even sixty years of age, Mother. I believe you are far from your grave.'

'I hope she isn't bookish,' Monty interjected from the back. 'I should hate to be forced to talk about literature or some other nonsense when we are together.'

'What would you like to discuss?' Gabriel asked.

'I don't know. Olivia is easy to speak with. Perhaps, Olivia, you know someone just like you that you could introduce to Andrew.'

'There is no one else like Olivia,' replied Gabriel, turning his head and catching her eye. 'Besides, the only lady Andrew would find interesting would need to have extensive knowledge of pugilism and ale.'

'Oh, dear Lord, I think I feel faint,' his mother said.

'At least she will probably be of a hardy stock,' Olivia interjected over his mother's shoulder.

'That sounds perfect to me,' Monty said. 'Do find her soon, Andrew, or I might be married before you.'

'That suits me, brat. Why don't you find a lady and keep out of my affairs.'

'Affairs?' Olivia asked in a conspiratorial whisper. 'Are you having an affair?'

Andrew cleared his throat. 'That is not what I meant and you know it. Do not encourage them. I thought I was your favourite?'

'You are.'

'But you told me I was your favourite brother,' Monty said petulantly.

'And you are as well.'

'You cannot have two favourite brothers,' he replied.

'I am a woman. Of course I can.'

'That does not make any sense.'

'The longer you are around women, the more you will see it makes perfect sense, brat.'

They reached the smaller dining room used for intimate meals. The conversation around the table was lively and pleasant. Knowing he would spend more evenings like this made Gabriel smile.

His mother wiped her mouth delicately with her napkin. 'So, I understand Mrs Siddons will be coming back to the stage at Drury Lane. With your appreciation of the theatre I imagine you will be attending, Olivia.'

Olivia's smile brightened the room. 'Yes, I've been looking forward to tomorrow night for quite some time.'

'I know Prinny adores her performances,' his mother continued. 'Goes on about them for days. I expect he will attend.'

'We had discussed it just the other day,' Olivia said smiling, as if she was recalling a rather pleasant conversation. Then her brow creased and her expression darkened. 'However, he has been suffering terribly with the gout. I do not know if he will attend.'

Gabriel did not miss Andrew's side-glance at the mention of Prinny attending the theatre. If Olivia knew he had been planning to attend the theatre, had she discussed it with Mr Manning? Did anyone else know of Prinny's partiality for Mrs Siddons?

'I will go with you.' Gabriel knew full well his statement sounded like a command.

Everyone at the table turned to him in surprise.

He kept his eyes focused on Olivia. 'I think it is time we announce our reconciliation.'

'You do?'

'I do. I can think of no better way to do so than to arrive together to a performance a good portion of London will be attending.' He raised his brow expectantly for her agreement.

Her smile warmed him. 'I would like that.'

'Excellent. Would anyone else like to accompany us?'

Andrew began to say something when he suddenly looked down towards his leg and let out a muffled cry. Their mother, sitting next to him, smiled sweetly.

'Did you want to join us, Andrew?' Gabriel asked.

His brother shook his head, while he sunk his teeth into his lower lip.

Gabriel turned to Olivia. 'It appears it will just be you and I.'

# Chapter Seventeen

Gabriel was finishing up reviewing a speech Lyonsdale was preparing to give to the House of Lords and anticipating an exceptional evening with his wife when Bennett knocked on the door to his study. A letter had arrived. Gabriel was tempted to put it aside when he noticed the hand that had addressed it. He knew that writing. Closing his eyes, half in exasperation, half in dread, Gabriel broke the seal and read the words that were written for his eyes only.

Bile rose in his throat.

It might have been from the exotic scent of the paper, although it was more likely from the request made by Madame LaGrange to see him. As usual, her timing was impeccable. But Gabriel knew if she was contacting him, it must be urgent.

He hadn't yet determined how he was going to convince her to trust Andrew with her communications in the future. If he had, perhaps he could have sent his brother to meet her. But he could not send Andrew to her without her permission. There was no doubt in his mind, if he did, she would sever her ties with him and refuse to provide any more information. He would have to go to her.

He threw the note into the fireplace and watched it burn. Glancing at his watch, Gabriel calculated how long it would take him to reach her establishment, meet with her and return home. If he left quickly, he should be back in enough time to escort Olivia to the theatre and no one would be the wiser. Leaving word with Mr James as to his location, Gabriel instructed him to contact Andrew should he not return home in three hours.

He took his own horse, which would be faster to manoeuvre through the streets of Mayfair. In no time, he was in front of Madame LaGrange's nondescript white house on the edge of the fashionable district. Even though it was late afternoon, the entrance hall was filled with shadows from the clouds outside. He walked by the empty gaming rooms and saloons where gentlemen could relieve themselves of large amounts of cash in a rather short amount of time. At least no one was here to carry tales of his visit to her private suite of rooms.

Rapping his knuckles on her door, Gabriel was met with a muffled command to enter. The same exotic fragrance from her letter drifted through the tastefully furnished sitting room that served as her office. She was seated at her escritoire near one of the windows. Her blonde head was bent over a ledger while she scratched her pencil along the page. She was a very beautiful woman. He assumed her to be around his age.

Gabriel strode past a small grouping of chairs, till he stood a few feet from her. This was a woman who did not stop what she was doing for any man—even one with his prestigious title. Running his thumb along the smooth brim of his hat, he waited for her to finish her calculations. It did not take long before she placed her pencil down, closed the ledger and turned to him with a friendly smile.

'You look well, Winterbourne. It has been a while.' Her voice was like fine brandy, warm and velvety.

'Eight months and twenty-seven days.'

'How ridiculously precise of you,' she replied, as amusement tugged at her full lips. 'What a lovely coat. Such an exceptional fabric.' She ran her graceful fingers down his right sleeve and rubbed the superfine fabric at his cuff. 'Still fond of Mr Weston's work, I see.'

'I am, but I do not believe you invited me here to discuss my tailor.'

'No, I did not. You might find what I have to tell you more interesting. Would you care to have a seat?' she asked, gesturing to a nearby delicate chair. 'I am pleased you were able to arrive so quickly.'

He took a seat and adjusted his cuffs. 'You indicated it was urgent. I saw no reason to delay.' He didn't want to be rude, but he wished he could forgo the pleasantries and return to Olivia. Being here always brought back memories of the night Nicholas was born. How he wished he could have sent Andrew...

She leant her arm on the escritoire, her keen gaze sweeping over his face. 'There is something different about you.'

'I am the same man I was when my father introduced us.'

She didn't appear convinced, but knew enough not to pursue the subject. 'Very well, what I have to tell you concerns the Prince Regent.'

Gabriel's heart kicked up speed. Would he finally have information that could be used to track down whoever wanted Prinny dead?

'One of my girls had worked for a time as a seamstress at Drury Lane. A certain gentleman had made her acquaintance there and last night he sought her out here. When they were together in her room, he began to question her about the theatre, back entrances, closets near the boxes and the like. She mentioned it this morning during breakfast. I didn't think much of it at the time, but then later today I read in the papers that *Douglas* is opening tonight at Drury Lane and the Prince Regent is expected to attend. It might not mean anything, but I thought it might be relevant.'

She was right to bring it to his attention. The coincidence was too great. And Gabriel did not believe in coincidences. Was it possible they were planning to kill Prinny tonight in Drury Lane? Eighteen years ago, an attempt was made on King George's life in that very theatre and Gabriel's father had been one of the men to interrogate that gunman.

'Do you know this gentleman's name?'

Madame LaGrange nodded thoughtfully. 'He's a Frenchman by the name of Comte Antoine Janvier.'

Oh, hell! Were all the men in Olivia's circle traitors to the Crown?

The hair on the back of his neck rose. The Frenchman who'd spent countless hours in his wife's company, who had been in his very home, could be the man who wanted Prinny dead. Their friendship had to have been orchestrated. He must have been using his friendship with Olivia to get closer to Prinny. But why would he want him dead?

'Do you know of him, Winterbourne?'

Gabriel could only nod, still processing how close Olivia had placed herself to a dangerous man. If something had happened to her... He almost knocked his chair over as he stood.

She looked up at him and her green eyes widened. 'I was right to tell you. You believe there is a connection.'

'Yes, you were right to bring this to my attention. Janvier may just be the man I have been looking for. I cannot thank you enough.' He reached the door and spun around when she called out his name.

'Some day I may require your assistance. For a proprietress such as myself, it is reassuring to know I will be able to turn to you.'

'I would gladly assist you in any way I can. I know you continue to place yourself in great risk providing me with valuable information.'

'Betrayed men are not the most pleasant. As long as no one finds out where you acquire your information, all should be well. But, Winterbourne, you must see there is more unrest in our country than I believe you or I could stop. The streets are teeming with men and women unhappy with our government. There may come a day when what you and I do simply is not enough.'

She tilted to her head, studying him. 'I sensed when you arrived there was something on your mind. Is there something you wish to tell me?'

How was he to begin? 'While I like you and enjoy your company, I'd like you to consider using someone else as your contact.'

Her head tilted the other way and she smiled.
'You have reconciled with your wife.'

Gabriel wasn't about to discuss Olivia with her.
He chose to chew his lip instead.

She stared at him for a long time before she
gave a small nod. 'Very well, I will consider it.
Who?'

'My brother, Andrew.'

'He has been in here. I know of the man. Why
should I trust him with my life?'

'Because I trust him with mine.'

Silence stretched between them and then she
turned back to her work. 'Give me time to consider it. I will send a note with my answer in five
days.'

In five days Gabriel hoped all this would be
over and she would not have information for him
for a very long time.

During his ride back home Gabriel debated
if he should warn Olivia about Janvier. She was
hurt by Manning's betrayal. He couldn't predict
what she would do when she found out Janvier
was also involved in this plot. Perhaps it would be
best to wait until he had proof of the man's guilt.

However if his instincts were correct, Drury
Lane would not be the safest place tonight. For
her own safety, he needed to somehow convince
Olivia not to attend tonight's performance. Know-

ing how stubborn she could be, he knew it might not be easy. He would send word for Andrew and then pray that his wife would be reasonable.

It was to be their first public appearance together in over five years. Olivia strolled around her dressing room, studying the gowns draped over her wardrobe doors and every available chair. Most of the eyes in the theatre would be focused on her and Gabriel tonight as London speculated on their reconciliation. And what she wore would be on everyone's lips by morning. If she were forced to endure that much scrutiny, than at least she would look spectacular while doing it.

She paused before the jonquil silk gown spread across the chair closest to her wardrobe and cocked her head. The exceptional creation had exquisite draping and a scandalously low neckline. The silk was so fine that it glided across her skin like water. Her dressmaker had outdone herself with this creation and Olivia had worn it only once because she found it too seductive for the life of a chaste duchess. This might be the perfect choice to silently announce to London that Gabriel was sharing her bed once again. Her lips rose into a satisfied grin. Perhaps it would also entice her husband to draw the curtains of their box during the interval.

Then she recalled they wouldn't be alone tonight. She let out a groan as she remembered inviting Janvier to share her box for tonight's performance. At one time she intended to invite others to join them, but had forgotten.

Gabriel would not be happy. And if she were honest with herself, she would have preferred to spend the entire night alone with Gabriel. But it would be rude to rescind her invitation to Janvier. She would not do that to her friend. It was no secret how Gabriel felt about him. The best thing to do would be to tell Gabriel about their guest before Janvier walked into their box. She just needed to find the best way to tell him their special evening would include another man.

The loud knock startled her out of her thoughts. Colette made her way around the colourful confection of slippers that were scattered about the room, and opened the door. Past her maid's shoulder, Olivia spied her husband's powerful frame encased in blue and brown. She wasn't certain if she was excited to see him or disappointed that it wasn't Bennett with a note from Janvier saying he was unable to attend this evening. When their eyes met, she decided excited was closer to what she felt.

He entered the room with commanding strides and glanced around before he clasped his hands behind his back. Had he ever witnessed her dressing room in such a state? She was certain none of his garments had ever been treated so carelessly.

He was the very picture of masculine elegance and, surrounded by all her finery, she couldn't have felt more feminine.

'Forgive me, I hope I am not interrupting anything important,' he said, stopping in front of her. 'I was hoping to beg a moment of your time.' He reached for her hand and circled his thumb along her palm.

'Of course, would you care to sit?' she asked, signalling to Colette over his shoulder that they were to be left alone.

He eyed the various colourful silks, muslins and satins melting over every available surface and arched his brow. 'Your dressing room appears to be occupied with colourful gowns at the moment. I imagine there is a semblance of order to them that I cannot fathom, so I shall remain standing.'

'We can easily move one. There truly is no order that must be maintained.'

The idea that her gowns were placed about the room in a willy-nilly fashion seemed to both amuse and astonish him. Looking around her messy room, he shifted uncomfortably and she brought her hand to her lips to stifle a laugh.

'I came to speak with you about tonight,' he said, rocking on his heels.

So he was eager to announce to the *ton* their reconciliation as well. 'What exceptional timing you have. I've been trying to decide which gown to wear. Perhaps you could give me your opinion.'

He lowered his gaze and began to spin his ring.

'Is something troubling you?'

He shifted his stance again. 'No, not at all. All is well.'

It was apparent all was not well and his thoughts were elsewhere. The spinning of his ring hadn't stopped and his attention was focused on her celery-green silk gown that was spilling onto the floor from the chair on her right. That wasn't a good sign. If only he would unburden himself to her… The best she could do was to offer him comfort and hope he would eventually confide in her.

Stepping closer to him, she combed her fingers through his thick hair by his temple. She thought she saw a flash of regret in his eyes, but it was gone before she could be certain. Reaching up on her toes, she brushed her lips along his cheek that was slightly rough with early evening whiskers.

'You can tell me anything,' she said, hoping that would spur him on.

He pulled her body into his. 'You are all that is good,' he replied, placing his lips to her forehead. A warm puff of his breath danced across her eyelids.

The lovely gesture touched her heart, even though unease swept through her. Hoping his warmth would ease the chill that ran along her spine, she brought his palm up to her cheek and burrowed her nose in the cuff of his coat.

Her body froze at the familiar cloying scent lingering there.

Victoria's words came back to her, echoing loudly in her head. *'Men cannot remain faithful. It is not their nature. He will never be satisfied with just your bed.'*

It had been too easy. He had agreed to remain faithful too quickly. He didn't even love her. She wanted to vomit.

Dropping his hand as if she had been burned, she stared at the traitor before her.

'How could you?' she choked out. 'My God, I am so stupid.' Covering her lips with her hand, she backed up a step.

The confused expression on Gabriel's face was not helping the matter. Did he think she was so naïve that she would not find out?

'Olivia, I do not understand—'

A cold sweat spread across her skin. 'You went to see that harlot again. Even after you promised you would remain faithful! You went to Madame LaGrange!' She pushed against his marble-like chest with all her might.

'Olivia—'

'I smell her on you…on your coat! I will never forget that scent. It is the same horrid smell you stank of when you came to my bedside after Nicholas was born. How could you?' Her voice wavered and she took another step back, needing to distance herself from him. 'How could a man appear honourable one minute and so selfish the next? Can you honestly look me in the eye and tell me that you were not with her today?'

'I cannot.'

'My God! What is wrong with you? How many women do you need? Or is it just that you do not want me? I have heard about her. They say she does not take the men who come to her establishment to her bed except for you. Does she know that you were in my bed again? Or did you reassure her the same way you reassured me, that she was the only one you wanted? Do you offer her pretty sentiments to ensure that she is available when your needs arise?'

Her nails were cutting into her palms and she wouldn't have been surprised if they were bleeding. 'Do you have a lover's eye of her tucked away somewhere?'

'Olivia, stop.'

He went to grab her forearms, but she stepped back. 'Do not touch me! I cannot believe a word you say. I was a fool to think I could trust you. Rest assured, it will never happen again.'

He opened his mouth to continue, but she couldn't bear to listen to any more of his lies. And she needed to stop talking before her voice would catch and he would see just how close to tears she was.

'Get out of this room, Gabriel.'

'We need to talk about tonight—about the theatre.'

Had he even heard a word she said? A bubble of laughter escaped her lips. 'Do you honestly believe I would be seen anywhere with you now? After this, the last place on earth I care to be is surrounded by the very people who probably watched you leave her house, or should I say brothel?'

'If you would just listen to me for a moment—'

'I am done listening to you, Gabriel. We have nothing more to say to one another.' Walking towards the door, so he would not see her face, she opened it with a flourish.

'We are not finished here, Olivia.'

'Yes, Gabriel. Yes, we are.'

He hesitated before giving her a quick nod and striding out of her dressing room like a man with a purpose.

Slamming the door behind him, she collapsed to the floor, silently sobbing and wondering what it was about him that made her lose all rational behaviour and slip blindly back into wanting to trust him. Now she knew for certain, she could never trust him again. This was the last time she would allow herself to be hurt by him.

## Chapter Eighteen

Entering his study to wait for Andrew was one of the hardest things Gabriel had ever had to do. He was fighting the need to turn around and march up the stairs to settle matters with Olivia. Things were not over between them. They couldn't be.

She just needed time to calm down. When he spoke to her next, he would find a way to smooth things over between them. At the moment Prinny's life was in eminent danger. That had to be his priority. And yet, his heart felt torn to ribbons at the pain he had inadvertently caused her. She didn't deserve this.

He sucked in a deep breath and rubbed his eyes. How could he explain this to her? He wanted to tell her why he was at Madame LaGrange's, but he just couldn't. He swore to himself he would never do something like that again. It was much too risky.

He would find another way to settle this with

her tomorrow. There had to be something he could say. At least he could console himself with not having to worry that Olivia would be in danger this evening. Ignoring the burning sense of guilt, Gabriel sat at his desk to draw a sketch of Janvier and waited for Andrew.

Olivia paced her room after allowing herself a half-hour to silently sob for the last time over Gabriel. How could she have been so stupid as to believe his sweet gestures and placating words? Was he even capable of devoting himself to only one woman? Her mother and sister had been right. Men only saw their wives as a means to an heir. They would never fall in love with them. Why would they, when men in their prominent positions could afford to have any number of women for their choosing?

He had appeared so sincere that it was easy to convince herself this time things would be different—that she mattered to him more than anyone else in the world, save Nicholas. He must have been very proud of himself that he'd duped her so easily. Obviously he had never worn that lover's eye and he'd most likely placed it in his desk drawer after he caught her snooping around his study.

Olivia stormed over to the fireplace, picked up the poker and jabbed one of the unlit logs, wishing it were Gabriel's head. She wasn't certain who she was angry with more, herself or him.

She didn't even try to hold back a loud groan as she tossed the poker aside. It landed on the carpet with a thud. Vowing to herself that she would conquer her feelings for him, she brushed her wet cheeks and rang for Colette.

She had put Gabriel behind her once before. She could do it again.

Her life these past five years had been a good one. If she wasn't already with child, she would be content with Nicholas. This room was choking her. There were too many memories of their time together here. She glanced at her bed and ran her hands over her face, uncertain how she would sleep in it again. She could no longer reside in the same house with Gabriel.

Tomorrow she would call on her sister and see if she and Nicholas could stay with Victoria until she decided where they should go. It was too late in the Season to find a house in town. Perhaps she would go off to one of the estates. Time away from Town and any reminders of Gabriel would probably be for the best. If people thought it horrid that she should avoid her commitments to steal away, that was their concern, not hers.

Just as she began scanning the walls for the artwork she would take with her, she remembered her invitation to Janvier for the theatre and threw her head back. She was swearing off men for the future. None of them was worth her time.

She knew she needed to let Janvier know that she would not be attending tonight's performance and give him a token for her box. As much as she had been looking forward to it for weeks, being surrounded by those people while feeling like she was the stupidest woman alive would be more than she could manage. She had intended to invite other friends to join them. At least she only had one person she needed to make an excuse to.

Walking through the doorway to her adjacent sitting room, she made her way directly to her escritoire prepared to write him a note. She could cry off with a headache or other such ailment. Picking up her pen, she stared at the blank paper. It lay there, mocking her.

Realising what she really needed was to get out of her house, she returned the paper to the drawer and decided to take the unprecedented step and go to his house instead.

Gabriel sat across from Andrew, resting his elbows on his desk and stabbing his fingers through his hair. His attention should be on the plans they were laying out on how they were going to catch Comte Janvier. And yet, whenever he tried to focus, his thoughts continued to turn to Olivia. Guilt was slashing his gut.

'How can you be certain that a few enquiries about Drury Lane indicates Janvier plans to kill Prinny?' Andrew asked. 'Even you have to admit, the pieces of that puzzle do not seem to fit easily together.'

Gabriel blinked and rubbed his brow, bringing his brother back in focus. 'I can't tell you for certain why I think the coincidence is too great. I simply believe it is. I believe he was looking for a fast escape or a place to hide. Why else would he be interested in the floor plan of the theatre?'

Andrew sat back and cocked his head. 'Some men might be interested in ideal locations for a tryst. Hart seems to find public venues rather stimulating. You know he is not the only one. Perhaps the Comte has plans to steal away with some fine bit of muslin.'

The image of Olivia entering Janvier's coach flashed in his mind before he quickly dismissed it. 'The man obtained the information from a harlot.'

Andrew shook his head. 'And to you that means he cannot want to lift the skirts of another? Men have been known to tup more than one woman in the course of a week.'

'Not all men,' Gabriel replied more forcefully than necessary. 'When you find the right woman for you, no other can take her place.'

Andrew stared at him as if he had spoken in a foreign language. 'Are we still discussing Comte

Janvier? I have the distinct impression we have moved on and are now discussing some other annoying gentleman.'

Gabriel stood and restlessly walked around the room, trying to pull all of his attention to the business at hand. He was having no luck.

Andrew turned in his seat and watched him. 'Would you care to tell me what is wrong? It is simply a guess, mind you, but I think the conversation has turned to you and Olivia.'

'She knows I was with Madame LaGrange this afternoon and says she wants nothing more to do with me ever again.' The words were bitter on his tongue and Gabriel wished he could have said them without hearing her own voice saying them.

'And you no longer wish to live in estrangement?'

He looked into the watchful eyes of his brother, the only person he trusted completely. 'I cannot go back to living the way we had been.'

There was a hesitation before Andrew spoke. 'I wish there was some wisdom I could impart to you right now, but I am far out of my element on this one. If you want to know who you should bet on in Friday's race or which equipage will carry you the fastest I can help you with that. I can even go a round with you when you need to attempt to beat someone to a bloody mess. However, when it comes to this…' He shook his head in pity.

Gabriel closed his eyes, to shift his thoughts away from Olivia. 'I need you to trust my instincts regarding Janvier and not make me doubt the importance of my meeting with Madame La-Grange today. The Comte wants Prinny dead. I am certain of it.'

'Very well, let's spring a trap for him tonight and then you can find a way to woo Olivia back over breakfast.'

That was what he needed. His brother's levity and confidence had him outlining his plan. 'Everyone is expecting Prinny to attend the theatre this evening. However, we both know he is still confined to Carlton House. I'll disguise myself as our Prince Regent and go to the theatre in his place. You and some of the others will mingle through the crowds and look for Janvier. Once you find him, observe him closely. The moment there is any indication he intends to cause harm, you need to stop him. And I would appreciate it if you would subdue the man before he manages to fire a shot at me.'

'I took care of the last man who shot you, I will do my best to take care of this one before it comes to that.'

Their eyes held with the weight of what Andrew had done to protect him.

'Take this sketch I drew of him. Circulate it amongst our agents so they are familiar with his face and send word to me in the royal box when you catch him.'

Andrew eyed him sideways. 'You have too much to lose here if something should happen to you. I shall play the part of Prinny and place myself in harm's way.'

Gabriel leaned forward. 'I cannot ask you to do that. This is my duty. I will not put your life in danger and risk losing you. I would not be able to live with myself if I knew I was responsible for your death.'

'You are not asking me, I am willingly volunteering.'

Before Gabriel could reply, the sound of a carriage rolling up to the house drifted in through the window and he strained his neck to peer outside. When his crest came into view, the hair on the back of his neck rose.

*She wouldn't.*

Flying out of his chair, Gabriel raced to the door.

'Where are you off to? Who has arrived?'

'It's Olivia, I need to stop her from leaving for the theatre.'

'But the performance doesn't begin for another few hours.'

'It doesn't matter. Our box is next to Prinny's. She is not to be anywhere near that building tonight.'

Just as he entered the hall, a vision of solemn resolve descended the stairs, adjusting her gloves. Her cool expression was focused directly in front of her, even though Gabriel was certain she knew he was standing a few feet from the bottom of the staircase.

She went to walk past him, and he reached out, holding her forearm. The warmth of her skin, exposed over the top of her glove, burn every cell of his body. Their eyes met before she arched a condescending brow.

He didn't release her. 'Where are you going?'

'I don't see how that is any concern of yours,' she replied, calmer than he expected.

'Regardless of what you believe, your welfare does concern me.'

'Then we have very different views on what that means. Release my arm, Gabriel.'

He tightened his grip. 'Where are you going, Olivia?'

'Why should it matter? Are you worried I'm heading for an assignation?'

The thought hadn't entered his mind—that is, until Olivia had just firmly placed it there. He took a deep breath and tried to force the image from his head. She cocked her head to the side as if waiting for some response. Had she asked him a question? He was so focused on getting control over the mixed emotions running through his body, he had no idea.

She appeared to continue speaking. 'Well, regardless, soon you will not have to concern yourself with my comings and goings. Tomorrow I will be leaving here with Nicholas. I find I can no longer abide residing under the same roof as you. Living apart seems a more agreeable option.'

'Olivia, do not be foolish.'

Apparently by the look on her face that was not the correct response one said in this situation.

'Gabriel, if you do not release my arm right now I will create such a spectacle that the servants and our neighbours will be speaking about it to their grandchildren years from now,' she said calmly.

Knowing her to be a woman who did not issue idle threats, he lowered his hand.

Her gaze was direct and unwavering, and her expression held no emotion. It appeared as if she had long been resigned to the fact that this would have been the outcome of their reconciliation.

His skin grew cold and clammy. He was losing her and there was nothing he could say to her now that would mend this chasm between them—unless he told her everything.

If she knew about Madame LaGrange, knew that when he was with her all he was doing was gathering intelligence, she would understand. She would see that he had never betrayed their marriage vows—not five years ago and not now. But to do that he would have to confide in her the identity of someone who worked for him. Memories of sitting in front of the fire confiding in his Uncle Peter came flooding back, making his chest ache. He swore he would never do that again with anyone.

She turned towards the door.

'Olivia—'

'I cannot do this any more, Gabriel. I have no strength left to listen to your lies.' She accepted her cloak from a visibly uncomfortable Bennett and turned towards Gabriel with sadness and resignation in her eyes. Shaking her head, she rubbed her lips together. 'You have not been a part of my life for the last five years. I shall have no problem removing you from my remaining years. And this time, I will do so while residing somewhere else. I will send word to Mr James of which of our houses I have chosen. Of course you are free to see Nicholas whenever you wish, but I will make arrangements not to be home when you do.'

Without waiting for a reply, she nodded to Bennett and walked out the door.

Ice spread through his body. She was walking out of his life and his gut was telling him it was for good. He needed to stop her. He needed to somehow fix this. And, he needed to do it now.

Gabriel took a step towards the door and heard his brother call his name, stopping him in his tracks. Demmit! Duty demanded that he go to the theatre to apprehend the Frenchman. This was what he had vowed to do. He was fighting the need to go after his wife when his father's words echoed in his mind.

*'The responsibility is ours to protect the safety of our sovereign and our family. The personal sacrifices you will be forced to make will be a small price to pay for ensuring we will not endure what our friends in France had to. The lives of those you care for depend upon it.'*

Living his life without Olivia was not a small sacrifice. Didn't he deserve to be happy, too?

Andrew approached his side in the empty hall. 'I can manage this for you, Gabriel. Let me impersonate Prinny. You need to trust that we can fulfil our duty even when you are not here. This operation needs to work without being solely dependent on one individual.'

Pulling in an unsteady breath, Gabriel noted Andrew's commanding stance. His younger brother, who he had teased and wrestled with as a boy, had become a formidable ally. Giving up control was not in his nature, yet Gabriel was certain Andrew was prepared to handle such a monumental assignment.

'I assume this means you heard?'

Andrew nodded. 'I did not know what to say to you earlier, but I do know now. Listen to your instincts; they will not lie to you. Only you know what the right decision is for you. But regardless of what you decide to do, know that we will do all in our power to stop Janvier.'

# *Chapter Nineteen*

As the carriage rolled to a stop outside Janvier's town house, Olivia needed to make certain she was composed enough to hold a conversation with him without raising her voice—or throwing any objects within her reach.

Leaving Gabriel had been the hardest thing she had ever done, but she refused to be made a fool of by more of his lies. She might not have any control of his actions, but she could take some satisfaction knowing that she was the one to sever all contact. The anger she was feeling was directed at herself. He'd fooled her once, but this time she was to blame for stupidly trusting him. This time, the fault was all her own.

She had cried enough over the realisation that the man she loved would never love her in return. She was finally finished crying over what might have been. The course of her future was her own.

Placing her hand on her stomach, she took a

deep breath. The air was heavy with the scent of rain. Looking out the window at the grey clouds rolling in, Olivia was grateful she reached Janvier's house before the heavens opened up and ruined her slippers. The fury bubbling under her skin was certain to spring forth with the smallest inconvenience. Janvier had played no part in Gabriel's betrayal. He didn't deserve to bear even the smallest bit of the wrath she was keeping in check.

As she walked into his home, the diamond brooch that had been affixed to her cloak fell to the floor. She took a deep breath and counted to ten. The catch had come loose and she threw it in her reticule in annoyance.

The distant sound of thunder rumbled through the dimly lit entrance hall. His grey-haired butler was just about to take her card, when the sound of approaching footsteps caught her attention. When she turned, Janvier rounded the corner dressed in fashionably tailored, black eveningwear.

She forced herself to smile at the sight of her friend. If being in his company would improve her mood, even the slightest bit, then coming to see him tonight was the right decision.

Although he appeared happy to see her, there was a brief flash of apprehension in his eyes. Showing up on a man's doorstep alone would probably warrant that reaction.

'This is a pleasant surprise,' he said.

'Good evening, Janvier. Forgive me for calling, but it was imperative I see you.' Thankfully her voice did not expose her strained emotions.

'Of course, I hope you are well?' he asked with concern.

'I am, thank you.'

He turned to his butler. 'You may leave now. I will see to Her Grace.'

The man nodded before stepping around a few trunks and heading down the hall, the sound of his footsteps growing fainter and fainter.

'May I take that for you?' he asked, gesturing to her cloak.

She allowed him to slide it from her shoulders. 'It's starting to rain,' she said, looking to break the awkwardness of the situation.

'Never a pleasant thing, however it is all too common here in England. I would offer you tea, however I suspect you would prefer a glass of claret.'

She took a deep breath and forced herself to smile. 'Thank you, I would like that.' Accepting his arm, she accompanied him to a well-appointed drawing room, styled in the fashionable Grecian manner.

The clouds outside had obscured the waning sun, leaving only the light from the fireplace and a single candelabra to cast moving shadows in the room. Walking to a table near the window,

Janvier lit five additional candles. In the darkened window glass, his reflection gave away an expression of serious concern. Was it possible he was unhappy with her calling on him? She wasn't certain she could manage another rejection today.

However, when he turned to face her, his expression changed into one of welcoming interest. She shook off the foolish uneasiness and let her gaze wander from the gilt-framed landscape paintings to the marble statues resting on pedestals. If only it wasn't in poor taste to ignore him and explore his artwork.

Then she spied a rather large royal-blue Sèvres porcelain urn painted in the Empire style atop a Sèvres bisque pedestal. It was a stunning piece of craftsmanship and she wished she had time to study the intricate bucolic scene painted on it.

'That is lovely,' she commented, stepping towards it.

Janvier approached her. 'Thank you, it is a recent acquisition. Please, won't you have a seat?' he asked, gesturing to the sofa near the fire.

The gold-brocade cushions were well stuffed and she made certain to leave room next to her so that when he sat down their thighs wouldn't touch. She was being foolish. He would not try to kiss her again. She had made her feelings for him quite clear. This man was her friend. Her emotions were frayed more than she had thought to make her uneasy around Janvier.

Olivia looked into his chocolate-brown eyes that were keenly focused on her and forced herself to smile. 'I hope I have not arrived at an inconvenient time?'

'You have not. However, I must confess your arrival is a surprise. Did I misunderstand? I thought we were to meet at the theatre instead of arriving together.'

'That was our arrangement.' She rubbed her brow. 'Forgive me. It has been a trying day.'

He cocked his head to the side. 'I'm sorry to hear that. Perhaps your mood will improve tonight. I have been awaiting this evening for a long time.'

Olivia accepted the glass of claret from Janvier as he took a seat beside her. While he sipped his wine, he watched her over the rim of the crystal.

'It is an excellent vintage,' he commented, nodding towards the glass in her hand.

'I would expect no less from you.'

'Since you will not tell me what is troubling you, perhaps that wine will help return your smile.'

'Forgive me, I did not come here to dampen your evening with my mood,' she said apologetically.

'Having you in my home could never put me

in an ill mood.' His grin only enhanced his handsome face.

She wished she could have unburdened herself. Being able to voice her disappointment in herself and her husband might help her straighten out the emotions that were an enormous jumble inside her head and heart. But she would not confide her secrets to someone simply because the timing was convenient.

'The wine will help,' he said, as he leaned back.

He was right. Wine would help. Only she knew she would need the entire bottle and perhaps another one as well. She brought the glass to her lips, then remembered she would need a clear head to be firm in her resolve to move out of her London residence when she returned home, so she lowered the glass to her thigh. 'This room is lovely,' she said, changing the subject.

'So this is how it is to be. I am excellent at keeping secrets. Should you choose to confide in me, I will be willing to listen.'

'I appreciate that, Janvier, I do. However, I think it best if we do not discuss it.'

'If you have not come to confide in me, what does bring you to my door? Not that I am unhappy you are here, but you can understand why I am curious.'

'I'm sorry to say I will not be able to attend the theatre this evening.'

An unreadable expression crossed his face before he took another slow sip of wine. 'I will not lie and say I am not disappointed.'

'I am disappointed as well and I was hoping to introduce you to the Prince Regent, but circumstances are preventing me from attending.'

He sat up straight, no longer appearing the epitome of relaxed elegance. 'Has His Grace forbidden you from being seen with me?'

'No, that isn't it.'

'Then help me to understand. He does not like you spending time with me. I have seen it colour his expression when we are together.'

She shifted uncomfortably at his prodding and looked down at her glass. 'You're wrong. His Grace is not a jealous man. Of that, I can assure you.'

'You are mistaken. He is a man not accustomed to having what is his taken away.'

This discussion was pouring salt into her open wound. She needed to change the subject. She remembered seeing trunks in the entrance hall when she arrived. 'Are you leaving London?'

'I will be returning to Paris for a time to visit friends. Are you certain I cannot persuade you to change your mind about this evening?'

'I am certain, however I have no wish to deprive you of such wonderful entertainment.' Reaching into her reticule, Olivia pulled out two tokens for her box at the theatre. She held them out to Janvier. When he went to take them, she snatched her hand back.

'I have one condition. You must tell me about the performance when next we see one another.'

'Agreed.'

Clinking their glasses together, they raised them to their lips in unison. The warm spicy wine slid down her throat smoothly. There was an intensity rolling off her companion. Not for the first time since arriving here did Olivia question her decision to deliver the tokens herself.

'As you are aware,' she said, 'my box is to the left of the royal box. The hallway can become crowded with people hoping to catch sight of the royal family. It's best to arrive early, if possible, to avoid the crush.'

'The idea of becoming lost in a crowd does not distress me.'

She took another sip, this time a longer one, and she felt her body begin to soften into the gold brocade cushion. 'I hope you enjoy your evening. Although I realise it is late, please ask anyone you wish to accompany you. There is no reason you need to attend alone.'

'That is very kind of you.'

'Have you not heard? I am all that is kindness,' she said, taking an even longer drink.

He grinned in amusement. 'I see the wine is helping. Allow me to pour you some more.'

Glancing into her glass, Olivia raised her eyebrows. When had she finished all of her wine? It was exceptional and after the day she had, she was entitled to enjoy an excellent vintage. She handed him her glass and took in his well-made form as he sauntered over to the cellaret housing numerous bottles of wine.

Her time with Gabriel was over. She would never know a man's touch again—unless, she took a lover.

Janvier had impressive shoulders, which were showcased nicely by the cut of his black tailcoat. His waist and hips were slim—much slimmer than Gabriel's more muscular form. Janvier's build was long and graceful. Gabriel's form suggested strength and power.

What would it feel like to be held in the arms of a man Janvier's size?

Just as she was trying to imagine such an encounter, he looked at her from across the room.

'I would love to know what you are thinking.'

Olivia did not want to contemplate what her expression had obviously betrayed. 'I was thinking of the wine.'

Stalking towards her with two glasses in his hands, his face became almost tiger like. 'I am certain you were contemplating something delicious. I do not believe it to be the wine, though.' Stopping in front of her, he stood there with a heated gaze looking down at her. 'I know you feel this attraction between us.'

He was attractive, but Olivia hadn't felt any desire for him. From the time he'd kissed her in his carriage, to staring into his brown eyes now, her body wasn't flush with the need to press herself against him and feel him buried deep inside of her. Those were the feelings her foolish body had only for Gabriel. She peered closer at Janvier as if she could will herself into a state of arousal.

Why couldn't he make her heart race and her body quiver in her most intimate places? If he had, she might have been able to transfer some of the feelings she had for Gabriel to Janvier. She was destined to die alone with only the love of Nicholas and, God willing, her grandchildren— but without a man's love and comforting touch.

And it was all Gabriel's fault!

The clock on the mantel began to chime and Janvier turned his head to look. In that brief instance, she studied him again.

Still nothing.

He turned back to her and again caught her examining his form. She really needed to leave before she embarrassed herself further.

'You do feel this attraction. However, if we

begin exploring our shared passion now, I will miss the performance.'

Well, that was insulting. He wanted her, but not enough to give up seeing the performance of a play.

Men were toads!

This day had gone from wonderful, to horrible, to absurd in a ridiculously short period of time. She needed to leave, return to her rooms and pack her things. Tomorrow she would be at Victoria's house, where she could begin to arrange a new life for herself and Nicholas.

She picked up her reticule, looped the braided handle around her wrist and rose from the sofa. 'I shall be off.'

'Forgive me, I did not mean for you to leave immediately.' He held out her refilled glass. 'We should drink to friendship before you leave.'

She stared at the glass and imagined throwing the contents into his face. But after the day she had had, numbing herself with more wine sounded like a better notion. She accepted the glass and his watchful gaze never left her as he took a sip from his glass. Did he, too, wonder if she was planning on decorating his form with the ruby liquid?

Olivia raised her glass to her lips.

'Don't you dare drink that, Olivia,' boomed a familiar voice from the doorway.

Her hand jerked, sloshing a small amount of the red wine over the side of the glass and down the front of the skirt of her gown. Uttering an unladylike word, she placed her glass on the table.

'What in the world are you doing here?' she demanded, glaring at Gabriel.

# Chapter Twenty

Gabriel had ridden as fast as he could through the streets of Mayfair to reach Olivia. She was his world and he was not about to lose her—not this time. He needed to increase Bennett's wages for his discretion during her departure and for supplying Gabriel with the address she had given her coachman. He'd assumed she would be going to her sister's house. Victoria and Olivia had always been close and he knew in his bones she would be the one person Olivia would turn to for help. But this address had been foreign to him.

When Gabriel had arrived at the nondescript town house, he had run out of the names of people he thought might occupy the building. Never in his wildest imaginings did he think his wife would turn to Janvier. It wasn't until his knock went unanswered and he picked the lock on the front door, that he realised he was in the home of the blackguard he had been preparing to apprehend that very night—a man who Gabriel had just seen place something from a small vial into Olivia's wineglass.

After following the sound of voices, he stood outside the doorway to the drawing room and listened to their unguarded conversation. A part of him wanted to storm into the room and remove his wife from this dangerous man. But this other part of him, this sick twisted part that would be bound forever by a sense of duty, wanted to listen and see if the Frenchman revealed his plans.

It wasn't until he saw Olivia raise the glass to her lips that he knew he needed to interrupt the intimate tête-à-tête before his wife was poisoned. It was taking all of Gabriel's control not to rip the man limb from limb.

'Your Grace,' said the Frenchman, his eyes narrowed on Gabriel. 'I had not heard your knock.'

'Neither did your staff.'

'My staff is now off for the evening. I'm afraid there is no longer anyone here attending the door.'

Olivia's attention had been focused on blotting up the wine from her skirt until Janvier uttered his last statement. 'You had not told me you had given your staff the night off.'

The man smiled at Olivia and Gabriel's right hand tightened into a fist.

'You had not asked,' Janvier replied with a smug smirk.

That was all it took. Thoughts of trapping the man in his plan no longer mattered. He was going to break his legs so he wouldn't have the opportunity to go to the theatre. Gabriel advanced into the room, but stopped suddenly at the sight of Olivia picking up her glass.

'I told you not to drink that.'

'As if I have any interest in what you want.' She brought the glass closer to her lips.

He snatched it out of her hand.

'I am not tipsy and that glass will not make me the least bit inebriated. Give it back to me.'

'No.'

'No?' She stood up and crossed her arms.

'Your friend put something in your glass.'

'Don't be absurd, Janvier would never do such a thing.'

'I resent such an insinuation,' the Frenchman stated, placing his own glass down on the nearest table.

'I wasn't insinuating anything. I am stating a fact that you put something into my wife's glass. What is in here?'

'Nothing but some of my finest wine.'

Gabriel held the glass out to Janvier. 'Then why don't you have a sip?' He tilted the glass and surveyed the contents. 'There isn't much left. It would be a shame to waste it.'

Olivia let out an exasperated breath. 'I have no

notion of what you think you are trying to prove. Are you attempting to have me question everyone I associate with?' She took the glass from him and almost had it to her lips when he swatted it out of her hand. It flew across the room, landing with a crash and splattering the remainder of the wine around the fine furnishings and his wife.

He knew the look on her face. She was incredulous and he had pushed her too far. His gaze dropped to the reticule she was holding and he considered how heavy it might be.

She glared at him and it looked as if she might be trembling with rage. 'You have thoroughly and completely ruined this dress.'

He wanted to laugh at the absurdity of her statement, spoken through clenched teeth, but he needed to concentrate on Janvier. 'What did you put in it?'

'You believe I wish to kill her? I adore her. Why would I do such a thing?'

'Why indeed? But I did see you place something in her glass from a small vial.'

'I did no such thing.' But his eyes shifted. It was a gesture his very astute wife did not miss.

She stepped closer and searched Janvier's eyes. 'Did you?' she asked as if she could not believe her friend could be so evil.

His gaze darted from her to Gabriel and back again. A cold shiver ran along Gabriel's spine,

raising the hairs on his neck. There was no telling
how Janvier would react to being cornered and
Olivia was standing too close to him. Her safety
was paramount. Gabriel needed to distract him
and keep her out of harm's way.

'Is that what you planned to use tonight to kill
the Prince Regent at Drury Lane?'

He should bang his head into a wall. That was
the worst distraction in the history of Britain—
no, the world! His concern for Olivia had stopped
his brain from thinking clearly. He knew enough
not to reveal his hand too early and he had just
shown Janvier all of his cards.

Olivia was about to back away from Janvier
when the Frenchman spun her around by the
waist and pulled her back against his front. Gabriel reached behind him under his coat and
pulled out his double-barrel pistol just as Janvier removed a sharp knife from his sleeve. The
silver of the blade at Olivia's throat flashed in
the candlelight.

They were at an impasse. Olivia remained motionless. The sound of her breathing was as loud
in Gabriel's ears as if her head had been resting
on his shoulder. He needed to keep his entire concentration on Janvier to read any signs that would
indicate what this man was about to do. He knew
he had to block out Olivia entirely, or he risked
being caught again by surprise.

'Well, it appears we are both not what the world sees. How is it you are aware of plans against your monarch?'

'I have heard rumblings.'

'I see. And those rumblings brought you to my door? Convenient.'

'Coincidence. My wife is here. I came to bring her home.'

'But that will not happen. You see, your wife will be leaving with me, or she will die because of you. If you had done nothing to cause her to arrive at my doorstep, none of this would be happening. The evening would have ended very differently.'

Guilt burned throughout Gabriel's body at the truth that was boldly stated.

'That was not poison in her glass, but something to make her sleep for hours,' Janvier continued. 'It occurred to me during our visit that I could take her to France with me as insurance, shall we say. But alas, you have forced my hand.' He wiggled the blade by her throat. 'I will be leaving with your wife now, Winterbourne, and you will remain here for three hours. Should you try and stop me, I will not hesitate to kill her.'

'I will not allow you to take her. Let her go and we can resolve this like men, not like children who hide behind a woman's skirt.'

'Should I release her, you will not let me leave

here a free man. I know the penalty for what you are accusing me of and I have no intention to die now.'

Olivia tried to edge her way closer to the table with the large vase, but Janvier jerked her back. 'Do not move,' he whispered in her ear. 'I should hate to mar that pretty neck of yours.'

'You said you wanted me to go to France with you,' Olivia whispered. 'I will go willingly. There is no need for any of this.'

'Why should I believe you would do so? I thought to take you with me in the event I needed to bargain your life should my actions be discovered. And now it seems I need you more than ever. Make no mistake, I will injure you should you or your husband force my hand. And if you startle me with any sudden movements, there is no telling how much my hand will move.'

She swallowed deeply, causing Gabriel's hands to sweat as he continued to point his gun at Janvier.

'You don't even know Prinny,' she said. 'What reason could you possibly have for wanting him dead?'

'Your beloved friend has been boldly bragging about all the spoils of war he has acquired—items that rightfully belong to France and not Britain—and especially not to that fat, stupid man. He boasts how he defeated France. How he has brought down Napoleon. What is next? Will he decide to take France as well? I spit at his arrogance. We will not be subject to the rule of an idiot, forced to call ourselves British subjects. Surely you can understand how that would not be acceptable to me or any Frenchman.'

Gabriel was trying to calculate the best angle for a shot at Janvier that would pose no danger to Olivia, but he was having no luck. His heart was pounding so hard it must have been visible through his coat. There had to be a way to get Janvier to release her.

'Of course I understand.' Olivia's soothing voice broke the silence.

'How could I live with myself if I saw my family and friends harmed by British tyranny?' His gaze remained fixed on Gabriel.

'So you are doing this for your family and friends back home?' she asked softly.

'I would die for those that I hold dear,' he spat out.

'Please, do not say such a thing,' Olivia said gently. 'Surely there must be a peaceful way to settle this. Prinny is sympathetic to the Bourbons.'

In his peripheral vision Gabriel noticed Olivia slowly and carefully opening the strings of the reticule she held down in front of her. If Janvier caught her movement, he might slit her throat. A cold clamminess crept along Gabriel's skin. Why couldn't that woman do as she was told?

'For how long will his sympathies last? With your Regent eliminated, Britain will focus inward. I do not believe his brothers have the same fascination with France. We will be free of a British threat.'

Olivia took in a shallow breath. 'I understand you are doing what you must to protect your family. That is to be commended.'

Why did Gabriel feel as if the words she spoke were directed at him? Were these to be her last words to him? He swallowed hard and forced his mind to focus on getting her free from Janvier.

'That is one of the things I admire about you,' said the Frenchman. 'You are an intelligent woman.'

'I like to believe so.'

Janvier let out a cry of pain.

He dropped his arms from Olivia as the knife fell to the ground. '*Salope,*' he growled through clenched teeth while grasping his thigh.

'You said you admired me,' she sneered back, quickly darting out of his way.

Stunned at his wife's actions, it took a few seconds for Gabriel to realise he had a clear shot at Janvier. But before he was able to pull the trigger, Olivia grabbed the Sèvres vase and smashed the man over the head with enough force to cause him to collapse to the ground. The pieces of the vase scattered around him.

She surveyed his still form cautiously. 'You don't think he is dead, do you? I find I am not bloodthirsty enough to kill him.'

All the bones in Gabriel's body disintegrated.

She was alive.

She was safe.

And she was staring at him, waiting for an answer.

Stepping closer to the motionless Frenchman, Gabriel could see what she had done to impede him. There, embedded in his thigh, sparkled a brooch encrusted with diamonds. He poked his foot into the man's side. 'He is still breathing. Do you need a moment?' Gabriel certainly felt like he did. 'Perhaps you should sit down.'

She brushed her shaking hands against her skirt, cleaning off the remnants of the porcelain vase. 'Do not concern yourself with me. Tell me what we do now.'

*We?* Gabriel marvelled at her fortitude. He placed his pistol back under his coat. '*We* are not doing anything. You are going to return home and I will see that he is taken into custody.'

'You would not have been able to subdue him without me.'

That was a bit of an overstatement, but Gabriel thought it best to let her feel as she did.

The first time one captured a criminal it was heady stuff.

'You are not sending me home while you see this through,' she continued.

She was too stubborn for her own good. Kneeling down before her, Gabriel reached under her skirt and tore a strip off the bottom of her chemise.

She slapped his hand away. 'Was the destruction of this gown with the wine not sufficient enough that you felt a need to attack the rest of my wardrobe as well?'

Stepping over to Janvier, Gabriel rolled him over with his boot, brought the man's hands behind his back, and twisted the linen around his hands. 'It's prudent to ensure he will not get away should he wake up.'

Olivia crossed her arms. 'What do we do with him?'

'Ordinarily I would have Bow Street hold him. But I will not take the chance he has a sympathiser there. I know of a place to take him for now.'

'Richmond?' She didn't even wait for him to reply, as if the answer was a foregone conclusion. 'How did you know Janvier was planning on killing Prinny tonight?'

They were perilously close to a topic he had never wanted to discuss with her. 'I received intelligence that led me to believe it was what he planned.'

'So you arrived here to stop him.'

'No, I had no idea where he lived. The plan was to stop him at the theatre.'

'You expect me to believe you intended to give up capturing a man who wanted Prinny dead to come after me?'

'I did come after you. Why you decided to come here is your tale to tell and you will tell me, Olivia.'

'Janvier was to join us tonight to see Mrs Siddons. Since I would no longer be attending the performance, I came here to give him the tokens to our box.'

Prinny's assassin would have been sitting with them, mere feet from his intended target. Gabriel pushed his thumb against the bridge of his nose. 'I was going to impersonate Prinny tonight, but I needed to come after you so someone else has taken my place. There are people throughout the theatre looking for Janvier.'

'You will notify them the vile beast has been captured?'

'I will, but I doubt I will use those exact words. I will go myself to inform them once I have Janvier secure.'

Stepping closer to him, she rested her hands on her hips as if her small stature could intimidate him into agreeing to what she wanted. 'I will go with you.'

How she could try his patience. At least she was speaking to him. As he'd raced through the street of Mayfair to find her, he wasn't certain he could convince her to see him, let alone speak with him. It was time to tread carefully.

He rubbed his forehead and stared at the unconscious Comte. 'Why are you not hysterical? I believe most women, if a knife were held to their throats, would be a shaking, sobbing mess. But you appear to be unaffected.'

'I have had a horrid day! I am too angry at this moment to even consider crying!'

She'd saved herself and Prinny by smashing that piece of porcelain over Janvier's head. If she wasn't his wife, he would think of recruiting her. 'Very well, you will go with me to Richmond. I will take Homer and you will follow in your coach. In light of this evening's events and your actions you have every right to see this through to the end. However, I need your word that whomever you see me converse with, you will forget their identities by morning. Trusting people is not in my nature. I need to know I can trust you.'

'You're speaking of trust? Oh, that is almost too much to bear,' she sputtered. He waited for her to agree to his condition and she must have realised he would not be taking her anywhere until she gave him her promise. 'You have my word. Now, how do we get his unconscious form out of here without anyone seeing?'

'Help me empty one of the trunks in the entrance hall, then go fetch your coachman. We will strap him to the roof of your carriage in the trunk and take him to my safe house in Richmond. He will be held there under guard until his trial. By my estimates, he will swing in less than a week.'

Once Janvier was secure in Richmond, Gabriel needed to inform those at the theatre the Frenchman had been apprehended. Of course Olivia wasn't content to return home while he did that and with more coaxing on her part he let her accompany him. Strangely enough, the idea of sharing this with her was no longer terrifying.

They had not spoken one word to each other since they had left Richmond and as her carriage rolled to a stop in front of the theatre Gabriel glanced at his wife, who sat silently across from him staring out the window.

He rubbed the stone of his ring through his leather glove. 'Remember, you are to tell no one what you see tonight. Trusting you with this is harder for me than you realise, Olivia. I need you to promise that you will not tell even Victoria.'

'I understand and have already given you my word. Shall we go in now?'

Gabriel opened the carriage door and jumped down onto the pavement. Without pulling down the step he reached into the carriage, grabbed Olivia by the waist and lowered her to the wet ground.

Olivia discovered it wasn't easy to keep her cloak closed to hide the disastrous state of her gown when Gabriel took it upon himself to lift her out of her carriage. Thankfully the rain had stopped. However, the puddles that shone in the light from the windows proved a nuisance as they navigated their way along the pavement to the door of the theatre. Heads turned as they made their way inside.

This should have been a triumphant moment. This should have been the beginning of a new life together. Instead, their arrival together was a sham.

'This changes nothing between us,' she whispered to Gabriel, lest he need clarification of her feelings for him. 'I am here with you to see this through, not because I have any intention of resuming an amiable marriage with you.'

'The world does not need to know that at the moment. Our appearance together should be believable, so I suggest you smile as if you are genuinely happy to be on my arm.'

It would be a cold day in hell before she was

ever happy to be with him again. Pulling from her years of experience disguising her feelings for him when they were in public, Olivia flashed him a pleasant smile. It must have been believable, because he gave a slight nod of his head and grinned at her with that annoying heart-melting smile of his.

The confines of the theatre amplified the buzzing around them, as happy voices greeted friends and audible whispers carried their names across the lobby. Aside from their unprecedented arrival together, she was certain people were questioning their lack of formal evening attire fitting such an occasion. That busybody the Duchess of Skeffington even had the gall to raise her quizzing glass at them. Thankfully Olivia's cloak was long enough that it covered her entire gown.

Olivia raised her chin and glanced over at Gabriel, who was discreetly scanning the crowd.

'Would I know any of your people? It would expedite our search if we were both looking.'

'I need to find Lord Hartwick,' he whispered into her ear.

She tried to school her features at her disbelief. 'Surely you don't mean the Earl of Hartwick?'

'The one and the same.'

'But he's—'

'An immeasurable asset in protecting the Crown.'

'Truly?'

'Truly. Now tell me if you see him.'

'Perhaps we should search the ladies' retiring room. I have seen him hovering outside of it on a number of occasions.'

'Not tonight—tonight he has a job to do.'

It was not long before they spotted the earl in his formal black evening attire casually leaning against the banister leading up to the boxes. He should have been the one to garner all the attention in the theatre with his handsome face. And yet for all his looks and charm, Olivia had no desire to wrap herself around him and get lost in his reputed skills. She glanced at the man next to her and wondered for the hundredth time what it was about Gabriel that set her body on fire—correction, *had* set her body on fire. Now he would simply be the man she'd married and once lived with.

Directing her attention back to Lord Hartwick, she watched him speak to a dark-haired woman dressed in a silvery-blue gown. Although one might think he was taken with his companion, Olivia could see his attention was on the crowd of people moving around him. Then his vibrant blue-eyed gaze locked with Gabriel's. When he shifted his focus to Olivia, he raised an inquisitive brow.

After excusing himself to his companion, Hartwick strolled up to them. 'Now I will say what everyone in this room is thinking. I am surprised to see the two of you together. Care to share?' he said with tilt of his head.

'Not in the least,' Gabriel replied.

Hartwick let out a deep chuckle and looked past Olivia to continue studying the crowd.

'We have to alter our plans,' Gabriel commented, flecking a speck from his shoulder. 'Our French friend is being detained in a safe location even as we speak. Has Prinny arrived?'

Hartwick raked his gloved hand through his hair, moving a shiny black lock out of his eyes. 'He has. Looking a tad sour, if you ask me.' He attempted to suppress a grin and then took measure of Olivia.

She shifted slightly under his piercing gaze.

'This is an interesting conversation for us to have,' he continued.

Olivia pulled her shoulders back and smiled warmly as if he paid her the nicest compliment. 'Situations have been brought to my attention due to unforeseen circumstances that required it. I assure you, I am the soul of discretion, my lord.'

He nodded slowly and tossed his head to the side to shift the lock of hair that found its way back over his eye. 'You always have been, madam. Now you know two of my secrets and I know none of yours. That does not seem at all fair.'

That small bit of information had not gone unnoticed by Gabriel, who looked down at her with a questioning gaze. There was no need to inform him she'd helped the earl avoid an unfortunate encounter with an unhappy husband by pulling him into her room at a house party two years ago.

Hartwick stepped a bit closer. 'So now I suppose you wish me to inform everyone they are no longer in search of the Frenchman.'

'That would be most helpful. I still want them to be diligent. There is no harm in remaining alert for the rest of the evening,' Gabriel replied.

Two fashionable women walked slowly past them and giggled behind their fans at Hartwick's obvious attention.

Olivia's attention wandered as she let the men discuss whatever it was men discussed when they were together. She watched the people moving up the staircase on their way to the boxes when her eyes settled on a willowy, dark-haired woman with fine features and a prominent dark brow. She was dressed in black and was not completely hidden by the moving crowd. Straining her neck, Olivia moved away from the men to get a better view of the woman's face. Some distant memory tugged at her as she tried to place how she knew the woman.

The slight pressure at her right elbow made her jump and she looked over, realising Gabriel had followed her.

'What is it?' he asked, leaning down with keen interest.

'I thought I saw someone I might have known.' She tightened her cloak. 'Shall we see how Prinny is faring, or do we need to locate more of your acquaintances?'

He led her to the stairs by her elbow. 'No, I believe Prinny will be very happy to see us. Let's not keep him waiting.'

They were granted permission to enter from the guards standing outside the royal box. As she crossed the threshold the sight of 'Prinny' in the second row of the otherwise empty box gave her pause. The man wore a wig that so closely resembled Prinny's own hair, one would think it was made from strands gathered from the Regent's own head. He was in profile, but his puffy cheeks marked him as an accurate replica of her friend.

The impostor turned his head to face them and Gabriel executed a respectful bow. It took a moment for Olivia to gather herself to curtsy. He appeared surprised to see them and eyed both of them from top to bottom before standing up and walking to the back corner of the box.

'My, this is a surprise, don't you know?' came the deep voice she knew she'd heard before.

Looking into a pair of familiar hazel eyes, she recognised Andrew at once.

'You?'

'Aye, it's me. Wot, wot? You look as if you've seen a ghost, my dear.'

It was difficult to keep a straight face with Andrew using a number of Prinny's favourite sayings—sayings Andrew would never think to use.

'You appear well,' Gabriel said.

'Prinny' smiled and patted his stomach as an array of serving trays were added to the table set out with at least ten trays of delicacies against the wall. 'The selection is impressive.' He leaned in closer and lowered his voice to a whisper. 'Do you have news for me, or is this simply a social call?'

'Our Frenchman is secured in Richmond.'

'How?'

'Imagine my surprise when I realised his house was my destination this evening.'

Andrew looked at Olivia, giving her a thorough appraisal. 'That's an interesting destination in light of this evening's plans.'

'I had nothing to do with that,' she stated firmly, looking him square in the eye.

'And yet, you sought him out.'

'To give him tokens to my box. He was to join me here tonight.' Could Andrew truly be questioning her motivation? 'Are you insinuating—?'

Gabriel stepped closer to her. 'There is no insinuation. Is there?'

Andrew shifted his gaze back and forth between them. 'If you feel there is no reason to make one.'

'There is not. Olivia is responsible for his capture.'

'And how did she do that?'

She pulled her shoulders back and raised her chin. 'With a brooch and a vase.'

Andrew jerked his head back. 'Surely I misheard.'

'You did not.'

He turned to Gabriel. 'So you do have an accurate assessment of her character.'

Gabriel crossed his arms and let out a breath. 'I told you.'

'Told him what?'

'That you have a temper.'

She pressed her lips together and gave her right glove a firm tug. 'Well, in a few short hours, Gabriel, you won't have the opportunity to witness my temper.'

He placed his hands on his hips in a commanding stance. 'That is up for debate.'

She unintentionally mimicked his posture. 'No, it is not.'

'Yes, it is.'

'No, it is not.'

Andrew cleared his throat. 'Well it was lovely chatting with you. Think I'll see what the footmen have brought me before it turns cold. Don't you know? Wot? Wot?'

They stood staring at one another, silently daring the other to move. Olivia won when Gabriel pulled her by the arm out into the hall.

'We are settling this right now.'

She tugged her arm out of his grasp. 'I am not discussing anything with you in the hallway of Drury Lane.'

'Then we will adjourn to our box, but make no mistake, Duchess, we are having this discussion.'

The riotous applause and cheering from the audience broke the silence between them as he dragged her into their box. Storming to the front, he jerked the curtains closed. Apparently he wasn't considering what people would think about the curtains being drawn in their box after they had been seen together earlier.

He advanced on her so he stood less than a foot away. 'You are not leaving me.'

Even with his noble actions, she could not forgive this last betrayal—and it would be the last. She could not endure crushing hurt like this again.

'It is obvious I am not enough for you. When I send out cards with my new address it will cease the chatter about us and everyone will know we care nothing for one another.'

All of Britain might believe that, but deep down she knew she still loved him and probably always would. Physical distance was the only solution she had to save what was left of her heart.

He grabbed both her hands, and she tried to

pull away. His grasp tightened, though not painfully. 'There is no one else I need. You are more than enough for me.' He looked her in the eye. 'I have sacrificed much for what I do, but I will no longer sacrifice my marriage with you.'

'Fire! Fire!' The shout came from right outside their box.

Olivia turned towards the door and sucked in a deep exploratory breath. There was a faint scent of wood burning. They needed to leave right away.

'Andrew,' Gabriel muttered and tugged her by the hand, hauling them out into the hall.

# *Chapter Twenty-One*

Still grasping Olivia's hand, Gabriel stopped outside their box and scanned the crowd of people stampeding past them on their way to the staircase. Panicked shouts and cries echoed off the walls as people sought out friends and family. A door diagonal from them was open and men were already forming a bucket brigade and throwing water into the smoking room.

This was impossible. He didn't even know who to look for.

Andrew exited the royal box behind two guards. His knowing gaze shot to Gabriel. He nodded in agreement that this was no coincidence. They needed Andrew out of the theatre quickly before it either burnt down or he was murdered.

A damp woodsy smell filled the hall as panicked people continued to run past them, shouting for their friends and warning everyone to run for their lives. This was a diversion. Gabriel knew it. He was just about to yell to Andrew to return to the royal box, when Olivia tugged at his sleeve.

'There she is, the woman in black. She's working with Janvier.' She was pointing to a tall thin woman with dark hair, standing thirty feet from them staring at Andrew.

Before he could ask about her assumption, the woman pulled a gun from her reticule and aimed it at his brother.

In an instant he was back in the garden in Richmond years earlier. Peter was pointing a gun at him. 'I'm sorry. I can't allow you to stop their plan,' his uncle had said, looking down at him and cocking the hammer of the pistol.

Gabriel closed his eyes at the resignation on his uncle's face, preparing for the end. The bullet ripped through his torso, taking his breath with it. Then he heard Peter cock back the hammer of the second barrel. He was aiming the gun now at Gabriel's head. Then suddenly a shot rang out and his uncle fell back. Andrew had come out of nowhere and saved him, killing Peter in the process.

He could never stand by and watch Andrew die. Jumping between the barrel of the woman's pistol and Andrew, Gabriel tackled his brother to the ground—and felt the burn of a bullet bury itself in his shoulder.

* * *

The crack of gunfire tore through the commotion in the hall, and Olivia watched a number of men tackle the woman in black to the ground. After wrestling the gun out of her hand, they held her firmly to the ground.

'Murder, murder.'

'Has His Highness been shot?'

'We have her. We have the cutthroat.'

'The Duke of Winterbourne has saved His Highness.'

'Oh, my God, is he dead?'

That last shout turned her legs to jelly and she looked over at the motionless form of her husband, lying atop Andrew. A stain of dark crimson was spreading near the shoulder of his coat.

*Why wasn't he moving?*

She ran to him, dropping to her knees just as he let out an agonised groan of pain.

'See that she is secure,' she yelled to the guard closest to her. 'And do not let them take her anywhere until you hear from His Royal Highness what should be done with her.'

Gabriel lifted himself off Andrew while clutching his right shoulder and fell back against the wall. Blood oozed through his gloved fingers. The pain must have been excruciating, if his grimace was any indication. 'Bloody hell, I hate being shot,' he gritted through his teeth.

Seeing him like this was making Olivia's hands shake. He was too young to die.

Blast him for making her feel anything towards him beside anger and betrayal. Part of her wanted to cradle him in her arms and take away his pain. Another part of her wanted to rail at him for jumping in the path of a bullet and getting shot. What was the appropriate thing to say to someone at a time like this?

'You need to find a new hobby.'

A spurt of laughter sneaked out between his clenched teeth before he pressed his lips together.

Shouting continued around them as people began to ignore the extinguished fire and focus their attention on the man who'd saved 'Prince George'.

Andrew knelt next to him, concern etched across his fake brows. 'We need to get you home.'

Olivia stood near the window of her husband's bedchamber, watching his valet dig a bullet out of his right shoulder. When had her life taken such an abrupt turn? She'd insisted they should call a physician, but Gabriel assured her Hodges would do a fine job. After what felt like an hour of digging, she wasn't certain that was the case.

Thunder rumbled and a flash of lightning exploded in the room as rain pelted the windowpanes. She rubbed the goose pimples on her arms and watched Bennett hold Gabriel's shoulder down as Hodges continued to dig at the stubborn ball of lead. Gabriel's hair was sticking up in all directions and his bare chest glistened with sweat in the glow of the candlelight. Having the bullet removed must have been incredibly painful, even with the long drink of brandy he took before Hodges began his attack. Periodically he would clench his teeth, the veins in his neck straining as he pushed his head back into his pillows. His breathing was rapid and shallow, and his left hand was clenched into a tight fist, his knuckles visibly white.

At the next burst of lightning she walked slowly over to the bed. The coppery smell of blood filled the air. 'What is taking so long?'

Hodges glanced up from his work. 'The ball is lodged deep, near a bone.' He began to dig again and Gabriel's body stiffened.

She should stroke his brow. She should hold his hand. She should do something to offer him comfort. Instead she wrapped her arms around herself, unable to touch him. 'Can't we give him more brandy, or try laudanum?'

Hodges shook his head. 'His Grace abhors laudanum. Best not to stop and just have at it.'

Gabriel squeezed his eyes shut and nodded. 'Tell me…about…the woman in black.'

He needed a distraction. That she could give.

'I saw her with Janvier once outside Madame Devy's. He had appeared unhappy that I had seen them together.'

He nodded and squeezed his eyes shut again.

There was a 'clunk' followed by the sound of the lead ball rolling around in the silver bowl. In unison Gabriel, Bennett and Olivia let out an audible sigh of relief.

'It's out,' Hodges said, releasing a breath. 'I'll stitch it up and then attend to these bloody sheets.'

A large stack of sheets had been placed under Gabriel's right shoulder. It appeared Hodges had previous experience handling situations such as this. How many times had Gabriel been shot? She recalled the scar Nicholas had found on him. Were there others?

Her thoughts turned to Andrew, who had changed out of his disguise and headed to Richmond to see to the interrogation of the woman in black and Janvier. If she hadn't spotted that woman…if she had not seen her with Janvier… would Andrew still be alive?

It wasn't long before Gabriel's wound was stitched, bandaged and the crimson sheets removed from under him. Hodges had given him another large glass of brandy before leaving the room with Bennett.

Now, they were alone.

Gabriel was taking gulps of brandy as he lay with his eyes closed, propped up by a mountain of pillows. His breathing was still erratic. Finally he handed over the empty glass and looked at her with sleepy eyes. Thunder rumbled in the distance.

'Thank you for staying.'

'Is there anything I can do to ease your pain?'

He blinked with heavy lids. 'Do not leave me.'

She wasn't sure if he meant for the time being or forever. Watching him endure the painful bullet extraction and knowing he had placed his own life before Andrew's had jumbled her emotions. And she didn't like it one bit. 'I will be here should you need anything.'

In what felt like a few short moments, his breathing was deep and even. At least he could sleep.

Olivia tried to recall the last time she had been in the very masculine room, with its forest-green walls and dark furnishings. Her gaze skimmed over his large tester bed with the silk-brocade bed hangings and settled on the two wingback chairs by the fireplace. She would guard his bedside from there.

As she rested her head against the back of the chair, her eyes were drawn to a hint of beige cloth sticking out from under Gabriel's bed. Getting down on her hands and knees, she pulled out a long rolled-up piece of canvas, tied with a black ribbon. Curious what he would keep in such an unusual location, she moved closer to the fireplace and untied the ribbon. The sight of her unfinished portrait left her breathless.

Gabriel hated the portrait. He must not have wanted anyone to find it. But why hadn't he burned it? Or shot holes through it as he had done with the candles in their ballroom?

She stood with her hands on her hips over the painting that had resulted in the downfall of two men she had considered her friends. There was a low flame in the fireplace, giving Olivia a way to remove some memories of the past few weeks. The canvas burned quickly, replacing the coppery smell of blood in the room with smoke. All that was left was ash. The portrait was gone, as if all her sittings had never happened. If only she could erase her feelings for Gabriel that easily.

Thinking about him was making her head hurt along with her heart. She needed to find something to occupy herself until morning. Then she would direct Colette to pack her things and she and Nicholas would leave for Victoria's.

It was difficult for Gabriel to open his eyes to the sound of Bennett's voice and the soft patter of rain. He stretched his legs under the piles of blankets and went to turn onto his right side.

That's when the shooting pain ripped through his shoulder.

'Easy, sir,' his butler said in a soft whisper. 'Your injury is fresh.'

It was as if his mind had blocked out the events of the last few hours except for the image of Olivia at his bedside. He struggled to sit up with the aid of Bennett. 'Where is my wife?' He knew he sounded a bit panic-stricken, but at the moment he didn't care.

A terrible sense of foreboding gripped him. The pain in his heart outweighed that of his wound. He no longer believed love was purely sentimental drivel reserved for schoolboys and poets. He knew in his heart he loved Olivia. He probably always had. And she needed to know. It didn't matter the hour. He would go to Victoria's and demand to speak with her. Throwing back the covers, he swung his legs around to stand. The sudden movement made him dizzy.

'Sir, please,' Bennett begged, 'you will open your wound if you persist in moving so.'

Nothing was going to stop him from going to her. He grabbed Bennett by the arm and realised his servant was in his banyan. Bennett's astonishment at being grabbed by his employer was obvious.

'Forgive me,' Gabriel said, releasing his grip. 'Fetch Hodges, I need to get dressed.'

'But, sir, she is over there.' Bennett pointed to Olivia's huddled form, curled up in one of the chairs by the fireplace.

She was asleep—in his room—on his chair. She hadn't left him. Relief flooded his body in a rush and he was grateful he wasn't standing.

'I woke you because this letter arrived.'

Gabriel took the folded paper from Bennett, taking note of his brother's seal. 'What time is it?'

'Five o'clock. May I offer you anything? Shall we check your bandage?'

The dressing was still pristine. That was a good sign. 'No, that will be all for the night.'

His butler hesitated before leaving the room. The minute the door closed, Gabriel rubbed away tears that had been waiting to fall. She hadn't left him—yet.

He read the note from Andrew and tossed it into the fire. As the paper curled and burned away, Gabriel took a few deep breaths. It was finally over. Prinny was safe and no one had died to ensure it.

At some point during the night Olivia had changed into her nightclothes. Now she was curled up fast asleep in her dressing gown. The day had been physically and emotionally draining for both of them. Caressing her cheek gently, he took comfort in the warmth of her skin before heaviness settled around his heart.

Olivia blinked up at him through sleepy eyes. 'You should be in bed.'

A sad smile tugged his lips at the sound of her voice. 'I thought you had left,' he said.

'I told you, I would stay.'

Olivia rubbed the sleep out of her eyes and studied Gabriel. There was life back in his eyes and he was standing tall, not hunched in pain. She could leave him now. He was on the mend.

'When I awoke, and did not see you...' He took a deep, shaky breath, and lowered himself into the chair next to her. 'I thought you would want to know I received a note from Andrew. Both Janvier and his accomplice have been questioned. I'm certain they will be tried for treason and both hanged in the next few days.'

She sat up straighter at the news. 'What did they learn?'

'The woman who shot me has no wish to hang alone. She confessed to trying to kill Prinny and identified Janvier as the man who'd promised to pay for her passage home to France if she helped him with his plot. She shadowed the man who tried to kill Prinny the day we were returning from Mr Owen's and traced him to the Tower. At the Tower, she seduced a guard and convinced him to let her see the gunman. While there, unbeknownst to him, she poisoned that gunman's food. I'm certain in the coming days we will learn more.'

'Do they know anything of her?'

'She's an impoverished French aristocrat who has no love of the British Crown or the *ton*. Apparently she met Janvier at a coffee house, where they shared similar views.'

'Does this mean Prinny is safe?'

'For now,' he said on a sigh. 'However, a man in his position will always be a target.'

She walked to a table near the window and poured herself a glass of port. As she brought the glass to her lips, the warm rich smell held no appeal and she lowered it to the table.

'Will you not have some?' he asked with confusion. 'After this evening, I would think you might want the entire bottle.'

'I find I no longer have a taste for port.' She walked back to her chair and did not miss the sombre turn of his lips. 'I burned the portrait.'

His eyes widened and he followed Olivia's gaze to his bed.

'I found it while you were sleeping,' she explained. 'The canvas was visible from here. I burned it for you.'

'But I had no intention of destroying it.'

'You hated it.'

'I hated the fact that it would be seen by all

of London. I never hated the portrait. For all his faults, Manning is a talented artist.'

'What would you have done with it?'

'I don't know, but I knew I needed to take it.' He lowered his head, noticing the scrap of embroidery near her feet. 'Is that a cat?'

'No, it's not a cat,' she replied defensively. 'It's a bouquet of flowers.'

'Oh, of course.' He looked back at the tangle of string on silk. 'I see it now.'

She stared at the mess of needlework and picked it up. With barely a glance, she tossed it over her shoulder. 'I intended to stitch flowers. I think it looks more like a dog, but I suppose a cat would be accurate as well.'

'Don't leave me, Olivia.' There was a catch to his voice.

She let out a deep breath not wanting to talk with him about her decision. 'I cannot stay.'

He leaned forward. 'You can. I can fix this between us.'

'You do not want me. There is no reason for us to live together. There is nothing to fix. I will honour my word not to reveal your secrets, but we are finished. Prinny needs you and I need you to keep him safe. You will do that for me, won't you? Make sure no harm comes to him? He may be foolish at times, but he is a sweet man.'

He reached over to take her hand, but she stood and stepped away.

'I will do all in my power to ensure his safety.'

'Do not get shot again. This should be the last time.'

'I will try my best.'

She walked to the door, needing to put distance between them or she would never leave. The sad look in his eyes had tugged too strongly at her heart. Or what was left of her heart now.

'I love you.' His voice was clear and deep.

She swung back around and stared at him. For years she had wanted him to say that to her. For years she'd wanted to say it back. But now it was too late. He didn't know how to speak the truth. And she loved him too much to be able to bear to hear him say it again.

'You don't get to say that to me,' she snapped, pointing her finger at him. 'You lost that privilege years ago when you went to that harlot's bed. That isn't love. Going back to her when you promised you'd remain faithful isn't love either. My mother and sister warned me about you. They said you would never remain faithful. Imagine my surprise when they knew you better than I did!'

He hadn't moved. He was motionless in his chair, save for his heavy breathing. 'Throw something.'

'What?'

'You know you want to. Throw something at

me. Do what you must, but after you do I will have my say.'

He just didn't understand. Olivia shook her head. 'I have nothing left to give you, Gabriel. Not even my anger.'

It was as if her words had slapped him the way he reared his head back. He scrubbed his hand over his face and stood. Her husband did not want her. Couldn't he spare what was left of her heart and just let her go?

Gabriel was losing her. He could hear it in her voice and see it in her eyes. Once she walked out of his room, she would remove him from her life forever. He could not let that happen. He loved her too much to live without her.

He needed to tell her everything. His blood ran cold and his palms were sweating, but he knew there was no other way. He only prayed it wasn't too late.

'I never slept with Madame LaGrange.'

She had turned towards the door, but at his words she froze. 'Gabriel, please.'

'Hear me out. Yesterday I received a note from her, indicating that she had valuable intelligence regarding Prinny's safety. That is the only reason I went to her. She is an informant of mine. And she trusts no one else but me with the intelligence she collects.'

She turned fully to face him. 'You expect me to believe this.'

'It is the truth. Madame LaGrange provided me with the information on Janvier. That is how I knew he was behind the assassination attempt. It was an exchange of information that took place, nothing more. I never told you because I never trusted you, but I do now. I love you.' It came out as a rush, as if his soul had been waiting to say it for so long.

There was no response. Olivia just stared at him. It was gut wrenching, and he stopped breathing. It was too late. Even with his declaration she could not forgive his deception and his lack of faith in her.

He had a strong urge to rub at the stone of his ring, but his right arm was bandaged to his chest. She hadn't walked out yet. Maybe he could still reach her. 'I couldn't tell you about her years ago. We were newly married. We barely knew each other and from the time I was a small boy my father had taught me to trust no one.'

'What did you think I would do?'

'I was betrayed once by someone I held dear. That trust cost someone their life. It's not easy to trust again when your friend's life slips away in your arms because they were shot by someone you trusted.'

'Did you receive the scar Nicholas found from the person who betrayed you?'

'I did. He intended to kill me. Fortunately he did not.'

As if it were yesterday he could feel the bullet rip into his torso again and see Peter aiming the second shot at his head. Olivia would never know that his brother had murdered their uncle to save Gabriel. She would always believe that he was killed in a robbery. Andrew didn't deserve to be looked at differently.

'Trust does not come easily to me, Olivia. I am responsible for the men and women who risk their lives every day to protect the Crown. On the night Nicholas was born, Madame LaGrange sent me a letter saying she needed to speak with me. She had worked for my father before he died so I knew this was not a social request. There was a threat against the King and she recounted what she had heard. You see, men go to her establishment and, under the influence of drink and a welcoming female, they will say things they never would in the light of day. If any of those men found out that she tells their tales her life would be in danger. A man with interest in harming the Crown would think nothing of slitting the throat of a woman who provides her services or any of the girls that work there for that matter.'

'But I smelled her on you that day. You cannot deny that.'

'She has an eye for fashionable clothes and admires my taste. In her profession she is accustomed to touching men. Her perfume might have rubbed off on me when she touched my coat or played with my cravat when she takes note of a new way to tie it. Over the years she has refused to give her information to anyone but me.' He rubbed his hand on his trousers. 'Know this— from the time I have courted you, I have never been intimate with another woman.'

'I wish I could believe you.'

The fact that she was listening to him gave him hope. 'I speak the truth, Olivia. My desire for other women stopped the moment I set eyes on you. I never strayed from our marriage vows. But my people like Madame LaGrange put their trust in me to keep their identities secret. Should I have told you and she had been killed, I somehow would have found a way to blame myself and maybe even you.' He searched her gaze. 'I never meant to hurt you, Livy. I am so sorry.'

She glared at him with angry reproachful eyes and stormed across the room, stopping in front of him. Her hands were balled into fists and he braced himself.

'For years I hated you. Years! So many times I wanted to burn the letters you wrote to me. For years I wanted to sell the jewellery you had given me. And for years I wanted to remove every scrap and shred that reminded me of a time I thought you cared for me.' She looked like she was fighting the urge to kick him. 'You let me believe all those lies. You let me hate you.'

'I had no choice.'

'But I loved you…' It came out as the faintest whisper as tears rimmed her eyes.

He closed the distance between them and with his one good arm he pulled her gently to him. She rested her head lightly against his left shoulder and he held her there, never wanting to let her go.

'It has always been you, Livy. I've never wanted anyone else.'

'Say it again.'

He looked down into her watery eyes. 'There never has or ever will be another woman for me. I have wanted only you from the moment I saw you dancing with Lyonsdale and nothing and no one will ever change how I feel about you.'

She let out a small choked sob.

'Dear God, I didn't mean to make you cry. Please, Livy, don't cry.' He was pleading with her. She was the only one in the world he would lower himself to beg. Looking into her eyes, he no longer saw anger. There was something else.

'Will you stay? I couldn't bear it if you left me,' he said.

'Will you promise to always be honest with me?'

'I will. I love you, Livy, with all my heart and all that I am, I love you.'

'And I love you. I always have.'

He had been so afraid he would never convince her to stay. Leaning closer, he kissed her. It was a soft, gentle kiss because he was afraid she would disappear before his eyes. They would start over again and this time nothing would tear them apart.

## Chapter Twenty-Two

Waking up next to his wife placed Gabriel in an exceptional mood, in spite of being shot. The morning light filtered through the window of his bedchamber, casting a warm glow on Olivia's bare back. The soft, white sheet skimmed the top of her enticing backside as she slept on her stomach next to him. Her breathing was deep and steady, telling him she was sound asleep, which allowed him to look his fill.

Unable to resist, he skimmed the fingers of his left hand over her bottom. Her low groan made him chuckle.

'I pray you, I can no longer feel my legs,' Olivia mumbled into her pillow.

'I am simply touching you.'

She turned her sleepy head towards him and opened one eye. 'That was what you said last night when you somehow coaxed me to straddle you.'

'My injury prevented me from using any other

position. In addition, I do not recall you complaining at the time.'

'I was being polite.'

Gabriel laughed. 'My love, last night you were everything but polite.'

'If I could move, I would smother you with this pillow. How is your shoulder?'

Thank goodness the dressing was still intact. 'Sore, but there is no blood on the bandage. That is a good indication all is well.'

She rolled onto her side, pulling the sheet up. 'You seem pleased with yourself.'

'I have a confession. I'm more pleased with you. I had forgotten that thing you are able to do with your tongue when you—'

'Yes, yes, well, we don't need to have such details this early in the morning.'

'You're becoming flushed.'

'No, I'm not.'

'Yes, you are. Let's suppose we find out how far that lovely colour travels.'

Her bare shoulders were much too tempting and the need to taste her was too great. Gabriel kissed her soft skin, trailing his tongue in circles. Within seconds he was hard.

He needed to sink into her and remind himself she would be at his side till the end of his days. Coaxing her to straddle him yet again, he claimed her lips with a searing kiss.

Yes, waking up beside his wife had its advantages.

'Tell me that you want me inside you,' he groaned against her mouth.

The crash by the door made them jump. There in the doorway, Hodges stood frozen in place with the remains of a coffee cup at his feet.

Olivia scrambled off Gabriel and took a good portion of the blanket with her.

'Does no one bloody knock in this house?' bellowed Gabriel. 'We have a new rule. No one enters any room without knocking first!'

'I… I… I did not know. Your injury… I assumed…'

Gabriel counted to five. 'Hodges, I think it best if you left Her Grace and me alone now.'

'But I…that is to say…'

'Hodges!'

'You have callers,' his valet blurted out.

Gabriel looked over at Olivia, who was firmly wrapped in the blanket and appeared just as confused as he was. Focusing his attention back on Hodges, he noticed the man appeared to want to run out of the room but wasn't certain if he should stay or go.

'Who is here?'

With his gaze fixed on the floor, Hodges shifted in his stance. 'His Royal Highness the Prince Regent, along with Lord Hartwick. Bennett has shown them into the Gold Drawing Room and asked me to see if you were well enough to see them.'

Gabriel scrubbed his hand over his face. To-night he was locking the door to his bedchamber and no one was interrupting them until he was good and ready to unlock it—and that might not be for days.

'Very well,' he muttered. 'Inform Colette that Her Grace is in need of her assistance and let Ben-nett know he is to see our guests receive what-ever they wish. You can have a maid clean that up later. I will see you in my dressing room shortly. And, Hodges…'

'Yes, sir?'

'You did not burn yourself, did you?'

His valet finally met him in the eye with an appreciative glance. 'No, sir.'

Moments later the door was closed and the stillness of the room enveloped them.

'We need to get out of this bed,' his practical wife reminded him.

'I am aware of that,' he said, breathing in the faint scent of honeysuckle.

'And yet, you continue to lay there.'

He thought of how much he wanted to be in-side of her. 'I don't want to leave,' he said, sound-ing petulant.

'Well, I don't either. However, we have no

choice.' Her back bowed when he ran his thumb over her nipple. 'Do play fair, Gabriel.'

He sucked on that nipple, rubbing his tongue over it as he did so. When it hardened into a tight bud, he pulled his head away. At least he wouldn't be the only one physically frustrated while he sat enduring the presence of their guests.

Olivia had donned her nightrail and dressing gown, and was just helping Gabriel into his banyan when a muffled voice could be heard through the door to her room. They both stilled, listening to the sound.

'Mama, Mama, where are you?'

They both hurried to the door and as they stepped into her bedchamber, Nicholas walked out of Olivia's dressing room.

When he saw them, a broad grin lit his face, and he ran over to them. 'I've been searching for you, Mama. Did last night's thunderstorm frighten Papa again? Is that why you went to his room?'

The indignation on Gabriel's face made her laugh.

'Nicolas, for the last time, I am not afraid of thunderstorms.'

'But Mama was in your bedchamber. Don't fret, I won't tell anyone storms scare you. Did Mama make you feel better?' Before Gabriel could answer him, Nicholas tilted his head and tugged at his father's empty sleeve in a panic. 'Where is your arm?'

Gabriel opened the top of his banyan, revealing that his right arm was bent and tied to his chest. 'Last night—'

'It's true!' Nicholas's hazel eyes opened wide. 'You saved Prince George. I heard the servants whispering about it. Were you injured? They said it is in the papers. They said someone tried to shoot the Prince Regent, and you saved his life.'

'Where were you that you overheard all this at such an early hour of the morning?' Olivia asked.

'Near the kitchen. Sometimes when I go there cook will give me…porridge.' His expression brightened and he nodded. 'Yes, that's what I get…porridge, not biscuits or sweets. Just porridge.' He stepped closer to Gabriel and his voice turned faint. 'You are very brave, Papa.'

'I did what needed to be done, Nicholas, to save our Regent. Protecting the Crown is very important.'

Nicholas's face wrinkled with concern. 'Can I hug you? Will it hurt?'

'You will not hurt me.'

The sight of Nicholas clinging to Gabriel's waist with his eyes squeezed shut brought a lump to Olivia's throat.

'Please do not die, Papa. I need you,' he whispered.

'I have no intention of dying any time soon, Nicholas. You can be assured of that.'

Their son released Gabriel and stepped back, visibly relieved. 'That's why he is here, isn't it? That's why the Prince Regent came to call. He wants to thank you. I saw him ride up with his fine carriage with his splendid bits of blood from my window. I was coming here to tell Mama when I heard the servants talking in the hall.'

Olivia stepped closer to Nicholas and put her hand on his shoulder. 'Thank you. Your father and I have already been told. Once we are dressed, we will be able to find out what business he has in our home.'

Nicholas ran the tip of his shoe along the carpet. 'I suppose I will have to remain up here. Will you tell me what he wanted?'

Olivia ruffled his soft short hair. 'We will tell you every word.'

A short while later Olivia entered the breakfast room on Gabriel's arm and various smells from the food on the table assaulted her. Knowing Prinny and his vast appetite, she was certain he had been keeping her kitchen busy with his numerous requests.

'Ah, there you are,' Prinny said, looking up from cutting into what appeared to be a lobster cake from his seat at the table. His attention was on Gabriel's bandaged shoulder and arm, visible under the sleeve that was dangling empty at his side. He appeared to want to charge Gabriel, but then his gaze settled on Olivia. 'Good morning, my dear. Bennett did inform me you would both be down shortly. It's a pleasure, as always, to see you.'

She smiled at her friend and greeted him in return. Those were definitely lobster cakes and lobster was not on any of the menus for the week. She imagined there was a bit of an uproar going on downstairs this morning and bartering was being done with neighbouring kitchens. After extending a greeting to Lord Hartwick, she allowed Gabriel to hold her chair out for her. It was an intimate gesture Prinny did not miss.

'I say, we did not disturb your morning, did we?' he asked, picking up a glass of wine and arching his brow.

Gabriel caught her eye before focusing on Prinny. 'Not in the least. I expected to find you in the drawing room.'

'That was where your butler attempted to place us. I, however, had a sudden desire to be in a more personal setting.' His attention was back on his plate.

The various items laid out in platters were unbearably unappetising to Olivia and she looked away to accept her cup of chocolate from Bennett.

From across the table, Lord Hartwick reclined

back in his chair in a casually elegant pose, taking his coffee cup with him. There was no plate of food in front of him, as if he, too, found all this food repulsive so early in the morning.

'Prinny wanted to call hours ago,' he said, 'but I persuaded him to wait until at least sunrise before we ventured here.'

Gabriel studied Prinny over his coffee cup. 'Dare I ask what has brought you to my door?'

'Can't a man pay a call to a friend?' Prinny asked, surveying his plate and planning his next attack with his fork.

'You know you are always welcome.'

'I couldn't remain within Carlton House for one minute more. And all week I have had a craving for lobster cakes and your cook's beef with burgundy sauce. Though there is no time like the present. Don't you know? And low and behold, that talented cook of yours has managed to make me some for breakfast. Not up to her usual standard, mind you, however she hadn't much time to prepare. I expect the beef was what had remained from last night, but that sauce... I could bathe in it.'

That was the smell that was invading her nose, making her wish they were sitting out in the garden instead of this confining room. One of the footmen entered and placed a large wedge of cheese inches away from Olivia. She rubbed her stomach to settle it. Lord Hartwick's piercing blue-eyed gaze caught her eye. He tilted his head and his lips rose in a sympathetic smile.

Please let this be all the food Prinny had requested.

'I do not know if I should be insulted that you are here for my food and not for me,' Gabriel said, oblivious to her plight.

'I'd count myself lucky,' Lord Hartwick replied, taking a sip from his cup.

'Insolent pup. One day that unabashed bravado of yours will be placed in check. I just hope I am there to see it.' The prince turned his attention to Gabriel. 'I also wanted to express my gratitude to you for all you have done.' As if remembering that Olivia was in the room, he glanced at her and cleared his throat.

She caught Gabriel's eye across the table. It would have been wonderful if Prinny knew how she had helped catch Janvier and his accomplice. Suppressing a disappointed sigh, she managed to smile.

'Olivia is aware of the services I provide,' Gabriel said unexpectedly. 'She was also instrumental in foiling the plot against you. Her quick mind is what saved you last night on two separate occasions.'

Prinny's eyes widened and a smile spread across his face. 'Well done, my dear. I always knew there was something special about you.' His lips dropped from a smile to a serious line when he addressed Gabriel. 'You are not to place her in any danger in the future.'

'I have no intention of doing so. Last night was an unusual circumstance that I do not anticipate repeating.'

'Do I not have a say in what it is I am involved in?' she asked.

'No,' both insufferable men said in unison.

Lord Hartwick appeared to study her intently. 'I imagine it would be difficult to stop her should she decide to involve herself in the future.'

'Ply your charms elsewhere, Hart,' Gabriel said. 'And why are you here at this early hour? I would have assumed you would still be abed.'

'I found myself with nothing to occupy my time. An unusual occurrence. So, I decided to see if I could convince Prinny to have a go at a game of cards.'

'Nonsense,' Prinny said, cutting into the wedge of cheese.

The gesture stirred up the smell and Olivia held her stomach as it began to roll.

'Hart does not want to admit he was concerned for my wellbeing, but I saw it in his eyes.'

'Of course I am concerned for you. You are our Regent.'

'You think more of me than that and you know

it.' He turned his attention to Olivia. 'Since you know of the activities surrounding me recently, you should be made aware that the artist will be spared. My understanding is that he was blackmailed. He did what he did to protect his child. I know something of the feeling one has for their offspring, therefore we shall show leniency. He will be sent to live across the ocean in America. We will not have him residing here. This will also spare a trial that might bring attention to you, my dear.' He patted her hand. 'I will have none of that.'

'That is very generous of you.'

'Wot, wot, haven't you heard? I have a rather generous disposition.'

Olivia raised her cup of chocolate to her lips, hoping the smell from the contents would drown out the horrible smell of the cheese. However, when she inhaled the scent, her throat tightened up and for the first time in many years she thought she might cast up her accounts. Looking up, she caught the narrow gaze of her husband. His attention did not waver from her, even as Prinny and Lord Hartwick continued their conversation. She knew that look. He was trying to puzzle her out. Had he witnessed her queasy moment with her cup? He arched an inquisitive brow and she shook her head to reassure him that all was well.

But just as she was beginning to feel better

Prinny began to slather butter onto a lobster cake and a clammy coolness swept over Olivia's skin. If she stayed at this table much longer she was certain to make a spectacle of herself all over the floor.

She stood abruptly, startling the three men at the table. They rose to their feet and their reactions ranged from amusement, to perplexity, to concern.

'Would you excuse me for a moment?' she managed to say over the lump that had reappeared in her throat.

Prinny sat back down, eyeing his dish. 'Of course, my dear, I will be here when you return. This delicious meal will occupy me for at least another half hour.'

If one could turn green, Olivia was certain she just did. As she reached the grand staircase the rolling of her stomach had stopped and she sucked in the pure air of the entrance hall. She was so focused on inhaling deep breaths that she barely heard Gabriel's approach.

Concern was etched across his chiselled features and filled his hazel eyes. 'Tell me what is troubling you.'

The caress of his fingers along her cheek gave her comfort and she leaned into his hand. 'I find my stomach is not pleased with me this morning. All those smells mixed together were too overpowering.' She closed her eyes and took a few more deep breaths.

'I will make an excuse to our guests. You should not be forced to entertain anyone if you are not well.'

'Even if one of our guests is His Royal Highness?'

'Even then.' A gentle smile lifted his lips, and he cupped her neck with his large warm palm, seeping relief into her. 'Go to your room, call for Colette and lie down. I'm certain she can find something to ease your discomfort. I do not recall you suffering so in the past. Is this something I simply have blocked from my memory?'

She never had the urge to cast up her accounts and always enjoyed the aroma of good food—at least until this morning. Thinking back, she remembered the last time nausea overtook her.

It was when she was carrying Nicholas.

Her eyes flew to Gabriel and were met with his concerned expression.

'Tell me, Livy.'

Her legs wobbled under her and she dropped down to sit on a step of the staircase. Gabriel carefully lowered himself next to her and grabbed her hand.

'You are frightening me. Tell me.'

Excitement and fear mixed together inside of her. Only time would tell if she was correct. Taking a deep breath, she looked into the eyes of the man she loved. 'I think I know what it is that has affected me so.'

'Do I need to call for a physician?'

She shook her head and traced his wrinkled brow with her finger, smoothing out his worry lines. 'There is no need as of yet.' From the silence of the entrance hall it felt as if they were completely alone in the house. This wasn't the ideal place and time to tell him, but it was also not something she would be able to hide from him for very long, especially if the smell of food would make her ill. 'I think I am with child.'

His eyes widened, and that heart-melting smile lit up his face. 'But we haven't been trying for that long.'

'Long enough, apparently.'

He leaned over and kissed her. It was a gentle kiss—a kiss that conveyed how much he cherished her. 'You're certain?'

'As certain as I can be this early on. I only know the last time I felt this way, I was carrying Nicholas.'

He took her hand. 'It might be a girl.'

'It might. Would you be terribly disappointed if it is?'

His smile widened. 'I confess I would be rather pleased if it is. She might resemble you.'

'And we would have to continue trying to conceive a second son.'

'And there is that.'

His lips rose into that smile she remembered so
well. She would love to tell him what that smile
did to her, how it made her heart swell with hap-
piness. But they had an entire lifetime ahead of
them—a lifetime of smiles, and children, and
love.

\* \* \* \* \*

*If you enjoyed this story,
you won't want to miss
the first book in Laurie Benson's*
SECRET LIVES OF THE TON *miniseries*

*AN UNSUITABLE DUCHESS*

*And look out for the third story
AN UNEXPECTED COUNTESS
coming soon!*

# MILLS & BOON®

## HISTORICAL

**AWAKEN THE ROMANCE OF THE PAST**

## A sneak peek at next month's titles...

**In stores from 3rd November 2016:**

- **Once Upon a Regency Christmas** – Louise Allen, Sophia James & Annie Burrows
- **The Runaway Governess** – Liz Tyner
- **The Winterley Scandal** – Elizabeth Beacon
- **The Queen's Christmas Summons** – Amanda McCab
- **The Discerning Gentleman's Guide** – Virginia Heat
- **Unwrapping the Rancher's Secret** – Lauri Robinso

*Just can't wait?*
Buy our books online a month before they hit the shops!
**www.millsandboon.co.uk**

**Also available as eBooks.**

# MILLS & BOON®

## EXCLUSIVE EXCERPT

Don't miss Liz Tyner's contribution to THE GOVERNESS TALES, a series of four sweeping romances with fairy-tale endings, by Georgie Lee, Laura Martin, Liz Tyner and Janice Preston!

*Read on for a sneak preview of*
THE RUNAWAY GOVERNESS
*the third book in the enticing new Historical quartet*
**THE GOVERNESS TALES**

She would become the best songstress in all of London. She knew it. The future was hers. Now she just had to find it. She was lost beyond hope in the biggest city of the world.

Isabel tried to scrape the street refuse from her shoe without it being noticed what she was doing. She didn't know how she was going to get the muck off her dress. A stranger who wore a drooping cravat was eyeing her bosom quite openly. Only the fact that she was certain she could outrun him, even in her soiled slippers, kept her from screaming.

He tipped his hat to her and ambled into a doorway across the street.

Her dress, the only one with the entire bodice made from silk, would have to be altered now. The rip in the skirt, *Thank you, dog who didn't appreciate her trespassing in his gardens,* was not something she could mend.

How? How had she got herself into this?

She opened the satchel, pulled out the plume, and examined it. She straightened the unfortunate new crimp in it as best she could and put the splash of blue into the little slot she'd added to her bonnet. She picked up her satchel, realising she had got a bit of the street muck on it—and began again her new life.

*Begin her new life*, she repeated to herself, unmoving. She looked at the paint peeling from the exterior and watched as another man came from the doorway, waistcoat buttoned at an angle. Gripping the satchel with both hands, she locked her eyes on the wayward man.

Her stomach began a song of its own and very off-key. She couldn't turn back. She had no funds to hire a carriage. She knew no one in London but Mr Wren. And he had been so complimentary and kind to everyone at Madame Dubois's School for Young Ladies. Not just her. She could manage. She would have to. His compliments had not been idle, surely.

She held her head the way she planned to look over the audience when she first walked on stage and put one foot in front of the other, ignoring everything but the entrance in front of her.

*Don't miss*
THE RUNAWAY GOVERNESS
by Liz Tyner

Available November 2016

# Give a 12 month subscription to a friend today!

## Call Customer Services
## **0844 844 1358**\*

## or visit
## **llsandboon.co.uk/subscriptions**